D1519938

# The Four
# Queens
# of Crime

# THE FOUR
# QUEENS
# OF CRIME

## A MYSTERY

Rosanne Limoncelli

NEW YORK

This is a work of fiction. All of the names, characters, organizations, places and events portrayed in this novel are either products of the author's imagination or are used fictitiously. Any resemblance to real or actual events, locales, or persons, living or dead, is entirely coincidental.

Copyright © 2025 by Rosanne Limoncelli

All rights reserved.

Published in the United States by Crooked Lane Books, an imprint of The Quick Brown Fox & Company LLC.

Crooked Lane Books and its logo are trademarks of The Quick Brown Fox & Company LLC.

Library of Congress Catalog-in-Publication data available upon request.

ISBN (hardcover): 979-8-89242-060-0
ISBN (paperback): 979-8-89242-227-7
ISBN (ebook): 979-8-89242-061-7

Cover design by Katie Thomas

Printed in the United States.

www.crookedlanebooks.com

Crooked Lane Books
34 West 27th St., 10th Floor
New York, NY 10001

First Edition: March 2025

10 9 8 7 6 5 4 3 2 1

*To John and Valentino, who fill
my life with love, music, art,
and joy every day.*

# CHARACTER LIST

Agatha Christie—best-selling mystery writer, main characters Hercule Poirot and Miss Marple

Ngaio (*Nigh-ow*) Marsh—best-selling mystery writer, main character DCI Roderick Alleyn

Dorothy L. Sayers—best-selling mystery writer, main character Lord Peter Wimsey

Margery Allingham—best-selling mystery writer, main character Albert Campion

Lady Stella Reading—widow of British foreign secretary; founder of Women's Voluntary Service

Sir Samuel Hoare—Home Secretary

Rana Gupta—Deputy Home Secretary

Sir Henry Heathcote—Baronet and lord of Hursley House

Ambrose Heathcote—Sir Henry's brother

Lady Sarah—Fiancée of Sir Henry Heathcote

Charles Heathcote—Son of Sir Henry Heathcote

Marie Sinclair—Fiancée of Charles, daughter of a wealthy landowner in the Caribbean

Philippa Guerra—Daughter of Sir Henry Heathcote

Juan Guerra—Husband of Philippa, expatriate of Spain since the Franco regime

Kate Heathcote—Younger daughter of Sir Henry Heathcote, home from boarding school

Sofia Santucci—Kate's schoolmate
Teddy Wilson—Butler at Hursley House
Elspeth Anderson—Housekeeper at Hursley House
Bernard—Footman at Hursley House
Brigid—Housemaid at Hursley House
Mrs. Walsh—Cook at Hursley House
Detective Chief Inspector Lilian Wyles—Scotland Yard CID
Detective Chief Inspector Richard Davidson—Scotland Yard CID
Commander Dorothy Peto—Scotland Yard CID
Sergeant Olyphant—Local police
Detective Sergeant Nelson—Scotland Yard photographer
Detective Sergeant Randal—Scotland Yard fingerprint expert
Detective Constable Lee—Scotland Yard fingerprint assistant
Constable Roper—Local police

# PREFACE

The following real-life people are portrayed fictionally in this book:

Lilian Wyles (1885–1975) started her career as a sergeant in the Metropolitan Women Police in 1919 after serving as a hospital nurse during World War I. In 1922, she was promoted to inspector and was the first woman to serve as a ranking officer in the Criminal Investigation Department (CID) at Scotland Yard, specifically employed to take statements from women and children in sexual assault cases. Lilian was promoted to chief inspector (inspector first class) in 1935, expanding her role in the Criminal Investigation Department. By the time of her retirement in 1949, there were 338 women in the Metropolitan Police, with 21 of them in the CID. Her memoir is *A Woman at Scotland Yard: Reflections on the Struggles and Achievements of Thirty Years in the Metropolitan Police*.

Dorothy Peto (1886–1974) began her police career as a Female Enquiry Officer in 1920, and became the first Superintendent of Women Police at Scotland Yard in 1932. She is credited with using the Children and Young Person Act of 1933 to take ownership of cases involving child abuse, expanding the role for women police. Before she retired in 1946 she had increased the number of policewomen from fifty-five officers to more than two hundred. After her death, the Metropolitan Police published *The Memoirs of Miss Dorothy Olivia Georgiana Peto, OBE*.

Lady Stella Charnaud Isaacs (1894–1971), Marchioness of Reading, worked as the chief of staff to the Viceroy, the Earl of Reading, Britain's foreign secretary and ambassador to the United States. She became his political hostess and then his wife, devoting her life to voluntary social work. In 1938, she founded the Women's Voluntary Service.

Sir Samuel Hoare, Viscount Templewood (1880–1959), was secretary of state for India in the early 1930s, foreign secretary in 1935, and served as home secretary from 1937 to 1939.

## The Queens of Crime

During the Golden Age of Crime Fiction between the two World Wars, the top-selling mystery writers of the time—Agatha Christie, Dorothy L. Sayers, Ngaio Marsh, and Margery Allingham—were dubbed the Queens of Crime. In order of appearance in this book:

- Agatha Christie (1890–1976), the best-selling writer since Shakespeare, is best known for her Hercule Poirot and Miss Marple mystery novels.
- Dorothy L. Sayers (1893–1957), novelist and playwright, is best known for her mystery novels featuring Lord Peter Wimsey, an amateur sleuth who later married writer Harriet Vane.
- Ngaio Marsh (1895–1982) wrote thirty-two novels featuring Scotland Yard Detective Chief Inspector Roderick Alleyn, who later married painter Agatha Troy.
- Margery Allingham (1904–1966) is best known for her eighteen novels and more than twenty short stories featuring Albert Campion, an amateur sleuth and adventurer who, in the later novels, married aeronautic engineer Lady Amanda Fitton.

# PROLOGUE

Detective Chief Inspector Lilian Wyles stood behind her father as he sat in his wheelchair, facing the front window of their second floor sitting room in their home on the east side of London. She didn't want to disturb him if he was napping, but she couldn't tell if he was awake or not. Her mother was downstairs, starting the day with Cook and their housemaid Ada. It was early morning, and Lilian was dressed for her job at the Criminal Investigation Department of Scotland Yard. She had a few minutes before she had to leave and wanted to spend that time chatting with her father. He had been the most supportive of her career in the police force, despite how few women were on the job, always giving her encouragement when she most needed it. He had wanted her to be a barrister, and in fact she had begun to study the law after boarding school, but the Great War had interrupted her plans, as it did to so many people. He was extremely proud when she was promoted to the CID and when she became the first woman detective chief inspector.

Lilian's father was her true advocate and the person she felt closest to, which made it more difficult for her to watch him decline in health these last few years. There was no real diagnosis, but his body and mind seemed to be breaking down concurrently, and their cheerful talks and serious discussions were now fewer and farther between. She stepped forward and put one hand on his shoulder, feeling the thick wool of his cardigan. He reached to touch her fingers for a moment, but then let his hand drop back into his lap.

"I'm off," Lilian said, her voice soft and purposefully cheery. Her father continued to stare out the window at the blue sky that was slowly filling with clouds.

"Do good and do well," he said.

"Always, Father, always," she replied and gave his shoulder a gentle squeeze before she turned and left the room, his deep voice resonating in her ears.

# CHAPTER 1

Agatha Christie stood in a shaft of sunlight thinking about new beginnings. *"I bear a charmed life,"* she quoted King Lear to herself. *But then, things didn't turn out so well for him, did they?* She was in the foyer of Greenway House, the Devon estate she and her husband Max had recently purchased in this early spring of 1938. They had been searching for a new summer home ever since their view of the sea in Torquay had become obstructed by new buildings. One couldn't always fight progress. It was late winter when Agatha had seen that Greenway was for sale, a dream house she had admired since she was a child. They had moved in quickly, thinking it would be best to be onsite for the redecoration, and the house was still a flurry of activity.

She moved aside as burly workmen walked past carrying newly purchased furniture. There was so much to do to prepare for summer, and she couldn't possibly put her writing schedule on hold.

Her latest mystery novel, *Appointment with Death*, had just hit the bookstores on the heels of the huge success of *Death on the Nile*, and in the midst of moving and redecorating, she had been sketching out the next book that should be published in December, a murder mystery with Hercule Poirot that took place at Christmastime.

Agatha picked up the short stack of envelopes and cards that had arrived that morning in the post. She looked through them and stopped when she came upon a rich creamy envelope. She turned it over and saw it was from Lady Stella Reading, the widow of the former foreign secretary. Agatha sighed. She had been expecting this formal invitation, but in the back of her mind she had been pretending it might not actually arrive.

Agatha's friend Dorothy L. Sayers, another mystery writer, had recruited her to be one of the hosts of a fundraiser organized by Lady Stella—a gala ball to help raise money for the Women's Voluntary Service, which had been formed to help prepare Britain for the possibility of war. Herr Hitler's army had just marched into Austria, and no one knew how much farther he intended to go. Britain needed to be prepared.

Agatha wasn't fond of public appearances, but Dorothy had convinced her to be one of the hosts to help sell more tickets for such an important cause. And she trusted Dorothy, who was one of the smartest people Agatha knew. She'd had a real education, a degree from Oxford, so modern, unlike Agatha, who had been schooled mostly at home.

The plan was that the four top-selling mystery writers of the decade would act as hosts of the ball. Agatha knew she would have to put up with a noisy crowd of people, but she saw it as a chance to spend a weekend with Dorothy and to finally meet the other two—Ngaio Marsh, a New Zealander now living in London, and Margery Allingham, a decade younger than the rest of them, both writers she admired. It was a brilliant marketing ploy: *Donate to the cause and meet the Queens of Crime.* The label made Agatha laugh. Really, it sounded more like they were a crime syndicate rather than best-selling novelists.

Agatha picked up a letter opener shaped like an ancient Turkish dagger, slit open the envelope, and pulled out the invitation, beautifully hand-lettered on heavy card stock. The ball was to be at Hursley House, the country estate owned by the baronet Sir Henry Heathcote near Southampton. She didn't really know him, although she'd met him more than once.

Sir Henry was a distinguished aristocrat, a former member of Parliament, and popular for his conservative speeches on a certain sort of upstanding image of Great Britain. Not to her taste, if she were honest, but it was good of him to host the ball at Hursley House.

The four writers were invited for the whole weekend, which was convenient for her, as it would take Agatha more than four hours to drive there from Greenway. Agatha's husband Max already had a trip planned that weekend, a speaking engagement at the Society of Antiquaries, so she'd be going on her own.

She would try to think of it as a little adventure, not a chore. She shuffled through the last of the post and wondered what else she could do to procrastinate before resuming work on her most recent Hercule Poirot story. Sometimes she wondered if she was getting tired of Poirot—he certainly annoyed her more than occasionally, the old fusspot. But people seemed to like him, and surely she had a few more mysteries for him to solve before he retired.

She knew she should get to work, but she always had to force herself to get started, and with her mind distracted at the thought of appearing at the gala, at the very least tea and biscuits were called for. She made her way to the kitchen. As she moved down the corridor, she couldn't help feeling that there was something about this fundraiser that was weighing on her. It wasn't just the usual antipathy at the thought of a public appearance; there was something else, quite far back in her mind, too fuzzy for her to make out. The thought of spending the weekend at Hursley House with the baronet Sir Henry Heathcote made her uneasy, but she couldn't for the life of her pinpoint why.

# CHAPTER 2

"Here's another stack, Stella." Dorothy L. Sayers slid an opened pile of RSVPs for the gala ball across the green felt card table to her friend Lady Stella, the Marchioness of Reading, who had been dedicating her life to good works since her husband passed. Dorothy took a moment to straighten her pince-nez, smoothed a loose strand of dark hair back into its bun, and began opening the next pile.

"Your advertising experience has certainly been useful, Dorothy," Lady Stella said as she alphabetized the RSVPs into a box. The two women sat in Lady Stella's drawing room sorting the envelopes that had arrived in the last few days. Stella gathered the RSVPs and made a note of each donation in a ledger. "It was a brilliant idea to have the Queens of Crime as hosts for the ball. Look at all these cheques!"

Dorothy smiled as she watched Stella lean over the account book, her chin-length dark wavy hair, her bright eyes. Dorothy had never seen her so excited. This is exactly what her friend needed. Since Stella became a widow, Dorothy had been quite worried about her more than a few times. But seeing her so engrossed in this project, organizing and raising money for the Women's Voluntary Service, Dorothy knew that her friend was going to be fine. Stella had needed a mission, and now she had one, an important one. If they were going to have to defend their island nation from Hitler—although Dorothy still could not believe that was actually going to happen—then the women of England would need to be organized to take care of the home front.

"I'm looking forward to all this secretarial work being done and just enjoying myself at the party," Dorothy said. "I haven't been to a ball in years."

"I'm so glad all four of you consented to host. Two or three Queens of Crime would certainly not have had the same success." Stella furrowed her brow as she recorded the numbers, double-checking her arithmetic.

"Stella!" Dorothy laughed. "Anything less than four Queens wouldn't have been good enough for you?"

Stella sat up straight. "No, Dorothy, that's not what I meant! But the four Queens idea fed into your advertising brilliance." She turned over one of the invitations to admire it. The card had a colorful drawing of four playing cards, the queens of hearts, diamonds, spades, and clubs, each tiny queen face a caricature of a writer: Agatha Christie, Dorothy L. Sayers, Ngaio Marsh, and Margery Allingham.

"How could I not take advantage of the title the publishing world has given us?"

"Well deserved, I say, since you are the four top-selling writers of the decade. But how did you ever convince them all to do it?"

"Once Agatha agreed to host the gala, Ngaio and Margery jumped at the chance." Dorothy resumed slicing open the RSVPs with a silver monogrammed letter opener. "Agatha so rarely does this kind of thing, and they're both fans, actually."

Stella stopped what she was doing and looked at Dorothy. "You know, I never thought of that, writers being fans of other writers. But of course they are."

"We all are, you know," Dorothy said. "Fans of Agatha's. She is the Queen of Queens."

Dorothy continued to open envelopes and thought about the ball. It was true that she hadn't been to one in years. Her husband's health had continued to decline, time exacerbating the gassing he experienced in the Great War, and his occasional moods and drinking hadn't helped. She rarely allowed herself to wallow in self-pity, and she loved Mac, but she had to admit that marrying a man eleven years her senior whose health was so damaged had been more of a burden than she had anticipated. Still, he was an excellent cook, her ample figure in evidence, and when things were going well, there was no better friend and companion.

She stacked the last of the RSVPs and decided that she would push aside any lingering guilt about leaving Mac for a few days and allow herself to enjoy this gala ball and in fact the whole weekend. She would forget her troubles for once, and why not? She'd be with like-minded women at a first-rate celebration doing good for her country. What could be better?

# CHAPTER 3

Ngaio Marsh stood in front of her full-length dressing mirror trying on the gown she had bought for the ball, hands on her hips. She had spent a lot of time anxiously looking for the right clothes to wear. Not only did she need a proper gown for the ball, she would need outfits for three days. That was a trial for her. It was one thing to visit good friends for a weekend, where she could wear her usual gray felt trousers and striped blouses, but that sort of thing wouldn't do for this trip. This particular weekend she would be with aristocracy and, perhaps even more nerve-wracking, meeting the three writers she admired the most. She had been consulting her friends for weeks and shopping at the best stores in London.

Ngaio turned back and forth, eyeing her slim figure. She didn't often have an occasion to wear a dress, in fact she preferred slacks, and a gown, well, a gown for a ball was a horse of a completely different color. But as she scrutinized her reflection, she began to feel almost pleased with herself. The periwinkle-blue silk fell easily on her tall frame, and she walked a few steps one way, then back again, to see if the hem hung just right over the silver shoes. Yes, she was sure it was perfect.

She couldn't believe that everything had come together. Not just the clothes but the whole forthcoming adventure. To be invited to be one of the hosts, what an honor! And to be able to meet and spend time with these other authors, all so much more accomplished than she was. They had all written many more books, even Margery Allingham, who was much younger, had published nine novels and a collection of short stories. But to be fair, Ngaio had gotten rather a late start, spending years working in the theater, writing travel articles, and painting, of course. She had written her first Inspector Alleyn book only as a kind of exercise, but her mother had encouraged her to try to publish it, and last year her fifth book with the Scotland Yard detective, *Vintage Murder*, had come out and her sixth, *Artists in Crime*, had just been released.

She paused, thinking about that time her mother had visited her in London, encouraging her to publish, and what a wonderful time they had. Who knew it was going to be the last long visit? Ngaio had returned to New Zealand six years ago when her father had written that her mother was seriously ill, so was able to be with her just before she died. She still missed her terribly; no one could possibly fill that special place in her heart. And now that her father was getting on in years, she knew that it was once again time to go back home. She had always regretted taking too long to return when her mother was ill, and she wouldn't make that mistake again.

But first there was this gala ball fundraiser, something crucial she could do for England in these uncertain times before she returned home to see how she might be helpful from New Zealand. She took off the gown and carefully wrapped it in tissue paper, packing it with the other more casual clothes she had purchased for the trip to Hursley House.

She didn't know much about the baronet Sir Henry Heathcote and his family, just what she'd read in the papers. He was a widower, and his son Charles was on his way to Parliament; his older daughter Philippa was lady of the house and had a husband from Spain. And there was a younger daughter at school, but Ngaio hadn't learned much about her. She'd have the weekend to get to know them, and that would be interesting. She liked meeting new people and examining them up close. Real people always helped inform good characters in her fiction.

Maybe the weekend would inspire a new setting for a mystery that her Detective Chief Inspector Roderick Alleyn could solve. In his latest case, *Artists in Crime*, Ngaio had surprised herself by giving Alleyn a flirtation with an artist, Agatha Troy, loosely based on herself. But it seemed he was not destined to settle down, with too many conflicts between the two of them, so Ngaio had left them at odds. She was toying with them again in the new book she was working on, but she hadn't decided if they should end up together. So far the relationship didn't seem to be writing itself in that direction. But one never knew how or when characters would find their own way.

She flopped down on her bed and stared up at the ceiling. *A high-class party weekend at an aristocrat's manor house.* Sounded like her first novel, *A Man Lay Dead*. Not her strongest book, she knew, although the end was a good twist. But then she hadn't been the first to write that sort of plot; she'd just been following the classic model. In fact, each of the other three writers had published stories with similar settings. She smiled at the thought of herself as one of the four top-selling writers of this decade. And they'd all be together for the weekend. Perhaps it would provide writing inspiration for all four of them. It just might turn out to be more than a weekend for charity and fun.

She jumped up off the bed, finished packing, and checked the railway schedule. As she deliberated over which train to take in the morning, she felt a heightened sense of excitement with a tinge of apprehension. Would she fit in with this level of social class? She'd have to make the best use of her sense of humor and her anthropological curiosity. Yet, no matter what the weekend would bring, she thought, at least she'd be well dressed.

# CHAPTER 4

M argery Allingham slowed her automobile as she rounded a bend in the road. She was just entering the third hour of her drive from Tolleshunt D'Arcy, sixty miles east of the Piccadilly street where her novels' fictional protagonist, adventurer Albert Campion, kept a flat. She hadn't stopped in London, but as she drove past it, continuing farther west toward Hursley House, she felt lucky that the drive had been smooth. Heavy traffic could be such a bore. Although now her speedy journey meant she might be early, she realized, and she didn't want to be the first to arrive. *How gauche.* The ball wasn't till the evening, but they had all planned to arrive for luncheon so they could take their time getting dressed and preparing for the main event. She had been looking forward to the trip—she enjoyed parties and people and music, and the weekend promised to have the best of all three. She loved the country life in her little village, and spring was a busy time, plenty of good hard work in the fresh air, plus her writing, but these few days away would serve as a well-deserved break. She'd earned it, she told herself.

Margery parked her automobile at the edge of a field, on a straightaway near Windlesham. She stretched as she got out and then leaned against her coupé and smoked. It was a fresh cool morning and the spot where she had chosen to stop was calm and quiet. She looked over the field, above the round green trees on the other side, up to the pattern of clouds that made a mackerel sky—England at its most pastoral, she mused.

She blew out a long stream of smoke and thought about the most recent Albert Campion book she was working on. Albert was rather on a tangent, but she liked where the story was going. The more Campion stories she wrote, the more she enjoyed herself. He had started out as a rather foolhardy young man, albeit intelligent, but as he matured, she liked him more and more. In this latest book—which she was calling *The Fashion in Shrouds*—he was grappling with internal emotions, both familial and romantic, in a way that stimulated her. She couldn't wait to get back to it.

She knew there wouldn't be much time for writing this weekend, if any. She might be able to just scribble some notes. Proper pages would not be written till she got back home. But writing wasn't just about increasing the page count, it was thinking and dreaming and researching. Meeting new people this weekend would certainly feed her writer's soul. She ground out her cigarette stub under her heel and climbed back into her automobile. She was already getting hungry and she wondered what an aristocratic household like Hursley House was going to serve to crime writers for lunch.

# CHAPTER 5

The magnificent brick and marble structure of Hursley Park's manor house was lit up with spotlights to welcome the parade of Rolls-Royce and Mercedes-Benz limousines delivering the multitudes of elegant couples. They disembarked from their coaches in perfectly tailored tuxedos and fashionable gowns, excitedly greeting each other on their way inside. A banner above the door announced: "Gala Ball for the Women's Voluntary Service— Support the Home Front!" The partygoers entered the estate house as music from the dance orchestra filled the air.

Just inside the entrance in the grand main hall, the four Queens of Crime stood greeting the guests. Agatha Christie, dark blond hair curled perfectly around her face, wore a pale pink gown tailored to flatter her curves. Ngaio Marsh was next to her in periwinkle blue, her short brown hair with its usual tousled shock slightly more controlled with silver combs on each side. Dorothy L. Sayers was wearing an elegant violet gown, hair twisted up off her face in a style that accentuated her round cheeks. And Margery Allingham, her short dark hair with a straight fringe across her forehead, was wearing an unconfining but stylish moss-green gown. They stood in a row, smiling and nodding, shaking hands and kissing cheeks. At a lull in the procession, Agatha slid her glance sideways to the others.

"How long are we meant to stay here playing les concierges?"

"Do you mean, when is the soonest we can politely release ourselves from this post?" Dorothy said with a smile. They paused to greet another couple.

"You're all my favorite," gushed the middle-aged woman with silver spectacles and a triple string of pearls around her neck. "I'm so thrilled to meet you!"

"So are we," said Agatha politely. "Please enjoy the dancing, we'll be in with you soon."

"How could we all be her favorite?" Dorothy said as the couple moved toward the ballroom. "Does she understand the meaning of favorite? It's an exclusive designation."

"I'm sure she was just excited," Ngaio answered.

"She was thrilled," Agatha replied. "She said she was thrilled." The other three chuckled.

"Back to your question, Agatha," Ngaio said. "I believe Lady Stella said we should greet guests for the first hour or so—do I remember correctly?"

"She couldn't possibly have said a whole hour!" Margery broke in. "We must join in the dancing and mingling. They're expecting us to do that soon, certainly."

"Must we, Margery?" Ngaio was aware her voice was anxious. "I can't say I'm looking forward to dancing with any of the gentlemen I've seen walk through this door."

"I suppose it's quite a different situation for a single woman like you, Ngaio," Dorothy remarked. "But perhaps we three old married ladies might be looking forward to some variety in our dance partners." She smiled mischievously.

"Don't judge every book by its cover, Ngaio. Besides, it's only dancing, not matrimony," Agatha said sotto voce, just before two couples, old and young, approached them and spent a minute showering them with flattering remarks.

"Thank you so much," Dorothy said to them. "Please do enjoy the party." The guests slipped from sight.

"Personally, I am ready to dance with almost anyone." Margery glanced toward the ballroom. "Dancing is fun no matter the partner."

"I admire your courage, Margery, but when it comes to one-on-one contact, I tend to be . . . judicial," Ngaio said wryly.

"I don't blame you, Ngaio," Agatha said. "It's been almost twenty years since the Spanish flu, but my feelings regarding personal contact have remained forever altered. I'll mostly be standing on the sidelines engaging in social commentary."

"Be that as it may, we've done this long enough," Margery said. "Shall we make our way together? Or slip away one at a time?"

"I'm happy to be the last to go if you want to make your escape," Ngaio offered.

"I'll go first, if no one minds." Margery was already moving away from them as she spoke.

"Enjoy the gay and hearty!" Agatha tossed after her.

A few stragglers came in the door and smiled to them as they passed.

"Welcome, welcome." Agatha nodded. "Dorothy, you should be next. I'm sure you're dying to join the intellectual conversations being had by the aristocracy."

"More like gasping for a glass of champagne." Dorothy winked.

A small group entered and after the obligatory shaking of hands, Dorothy followed them, waving to the last two writers.

Agatha and Ngaio stood together in silence for a moment, listening to the orchestra begin a new piece.

"Ngaio, I'm happy to be last if you were just being polite." Agatha turned to her.

"That would be a rare occurrence." Ngaio chuckled. Her initial impetus was never manners before action, much to her chagrin. "No, please, Agatha, after you. I think I hear a Viennese waltz starting up."

"If you insist." Agatha nodded and disappeared down the main hall.

Ngaio stood alone for a moment, smiling to herself. She hummed along with the waltz, and when it seemed no one else was about to arrive, and she was sure no one was looking, she waltzed by herself down the main hall.

Almost two hundred people filled the ballroom, drinking champagne, gossiping in small groups, and dancing to the twenty-piece orchestra. Margery Allingham had slipped around the clusters that were standing near the dance floor, scrutinizing each gentleman she passed, sizing them up as possible dance partners. Dorothy L. Sayers had arrived at the champagne buffet and was animatedly participating in a conversation with a group of admirers. Agatha Christie had skirted round the edge of the crowd, keeping as far away from the band as possible, but she was quickly surrounded and became engaged in polite and synthetic conversation.

Ngaio appeared at the entrance of the ballroom, her eyes bright with the excitement of the crowd. She did not dive into the dancing or the gossiping but made her way to the far end of the ballroom. She was able to reach a hidden corner with a good view of the gala. Lady Stella Reading, the hostess of the evening, was chatting nearby in a small group that included Sir Henry Heathcote's fiancée Lady Sarah, the home secretary Sir Samuel Hoare, and his deputy Rana Gupta, weekend guests that Ngaio had met at the luncheon a few hours ago.

Lady Stella was glowing with excitement as she chatted with Sir Samuel, his hand resting on his plump belly, looking rather pompous, Ngaio thought. Rana Gupta seemed mildly uncomfortable but kept up a polite smile.

Then Sir Henry's son, Charles, and Charles's fiancée, Marie Sinclair, approached the group with Sir Henry's older daughter, Lady Philippa, and her husband, Juan Guerra. Ngaio felt too shy to join in the conversation, even though she had enjoyed meeting them at luncheon.

The younger sister, Kate, still a teenager, joined the group with her schoolmate Sofia. Ngaio couldn't hear them, but it seemed that the two young girls interrupted the conversation, to the displeasure of Philippa, then they ran off and danced with each other.

Ngaio looked toward the far side of the room and saw Sir Henry Heathcote and his brother Ambrose speaking with some very old-fashioned-looking aristocrats, wearing traditional tailcoats and white ties, monocles, and pocket watches all round. They looked like character actors from one of those Fred Astaire films from Hollywood. Sir Henry was animated in his speaking, and the old men were rapt. Ambrose seemed uncomfortable, and Ngaio couldn't help but wonder what they were talking about. She knew she should enter the social fray, but she preferred to watch the party guests and observe their activities as long as she could.

She moved to the champagne buffet. Charles broke away from his group, and nodded in greeting to Ngaio as he took a glass of champagne. He raised his glass to Marie, who was on the dance floor with a gray-haired man a few inches shorter than she was. Sir Henry came over to them and watched as well. Then he leaned in close to Charles, said something that Ngaio thought must've been rude, considering Charles's expression, and walked away. Ngaio pretended she hadn't noticed, turned to Charles with a cheerful smile and said, "How lovely Marie is, and what a wonderful dancer. She's actually succeeding in making that gentleman look graceful." Charles smiled back at her, grateful, Ngaio thought, for providing a distraction.

★ ★ ★

The music ebbed and flowed, and the evening moved forward. The orchestra conductor was energetic, the footmen efficiently served endless bottles of champagne, and young and old party guests danced and chatted in the ballroom and feasted in the supper room. It all seemed to be going well, Ngaio thought, as she finished dancing with a kindly gentleman and moved through the crowd. At midnight, a new band took the stand, playing music with a more modern twist as a singer took the microphone and the younger guests in the crowd danced some of the new romping dances that were popular.

The second orchestra played an especially loud and energetic tune. Ngaio broke away from the crowd and made her way up the grand staircase just outside the ballroom. Her ears felt relief as the volume faded. She soon reached the next floor and moved down the hallway toward the ladies' sitting-out lounge.

# CHAPTER 6

Agatha Christie was hiding in the upstairs room that served as a ladies' sitting room, avoiding the crowd. What had she expected? Of course it was loud music and noisy people. She might as well be attending the London season.

In spite of being all the way up the grand staircase and down a wide corridor, Agatha could hear the twenty-piece dance band. She closed her eyes to find some calm, but the vision of the gentlemen in tuxedos and ladies in their lavish gowns kept swirling through her head. Soon she'd have no choice but to return to the noise of the ballroom, with footmen pouring champagne as fast as they could pop open the bottles and the supper room lined with buffet tables full of delicacies.

Agatha settled deeper into the cushions of the gold brocade sofa, leaned back, and sighed. She let her eyes rest on the rose-patterned wallpaper. The room was a lovely respite from the long evening.

The door opened with a burst of dance music and Ngaio's tall, thin frame entered the sanctuary. She had a cigarette between her lips, and when she saw Agatha, she smiled that shy and mischievous smile of hers and closed the door behind her.

"Any matches?"

"On the side table." Agatha pointed. "They were just refilled."

"Blast, the noise!" Ngaio lit her cigarette and flopped down on a chaise longue, the long skirt of her gown fanning out. "Are you hiding out too, then?"

"Let's just call this the interval." Agatha knew their age difference was only five years, but Ngaio looked so much younger. Maybe it was her short hair and her complexion that hinted she spent time in the sun. Or because she was so thin. "Is the crowd getting to you too?"

"Oh, I don't mind the people so much, especially the bright young things, but this second dance band is playing awfully loud. I prefer the more traditional orchestra that started the party." Ngaio plucked a flake of tobacco off her tongue. "I mean, I like dance music, generally, but it used to be more forgiving, in our day. Wouldn't you say?"

"If that was just after the Great War, quite a bit has changed since then. With the state of the world today, I imagine the music is reflecting the current feeling of chaos."

"It does feel rather manic." Ngaio paused. She found herself stumbling in the conversation. Agatha Christie was the icon of all mystery writers; she'd written more than thirty books. Ngaio couldn't understand how she had ended up on the same list as this legend and felt humbled in her presence. But she must say something—the longer she waited, the ruder she would appear, and she liked Agatha, very much. And she wanted Agatha to like her. Ngaio felt her usual anxiety building as she mentally searched for a suitable topic.

"Have you known Sir Henry Heathcote long?" she asked.

"Sir Henry?" Agatha paused. She knew *of* him longer than she knew him. He had quite a reputation. His speeches on British life were popular of late and had turned him into quite a public figure. But *did* she know him? Not really. They'd certainly been in the same social circle for some time, at least since Agatha had married her second husband, Max. "If I'm honest, Ngaio, I barely know him at all. You can be in the same room with someone dozens of times for years on end and barely speak to them. Don't you find that's true?"

"Yes, I know what you mean." Ngaio was relieved to take up the topic. She rolled the ashes off the end of her cigarette into the crystal ashtray. "I've only just met him this weekend, but he seems like the kind of person who would be hard to get to know. So formal, even to his children, I noticed. He's so, I don't know, so—"

"English?" Agatha's smile was sly.

"I suppose so." Ngaio blushed but allowed herself to laugh as she ran a hand through her short hair. "Maybe it's not something I would have put into words a few years ago, but when I returned from a trip back home to New Zealand, I noticed things seemed . . . different here."

"I feel the same whenever I return from traveling." Agatha rose and smoothed the pale pink satin of her gown. "I always wonder if it's the people who've changed while I was away, or is it me? Sir Henry Heathcote never struck me as a warm and friendly person, but I agree, he does seem more, shall we say, *dignified* than usual this weekend. Perhaps he doesn't like parties."

"Perhaps he regrets letting Lady Stella talk him into using Hursley House for this gala," Ngaio offered.

"That's certainly possible." Agatha moved toward the door. "I suppose I've hidden out longer than I should. Shall we visit the buffet and have a glass of champagne?"

"Brilliant." The painter-turned-mystery-writer stubbed out her cigarette and stood. "We are obliged to mingle and give our patrons their money's worth."

"Needs must." Agatha held the door open and glanced at the brass clock on the side table. Half past midnight—still some time before they could retire gracefully to their rooms.

# CHAPTER 7

Wilson the butler was rushed off his feet making sure the caterers didn't spill wine on the Turkish rugs, break any of the crystal glasses, or steal the silver, for pity's sake. Hursley House wasn't used to parties this size, not in this century, and Wilson couldn't help wondering, for the tenth time, why his lordship had agreed to host such a circus. He turned to the housekeeper.

"Mrs. Anderson, please remind Bernard and Brigid to check the upstairs lounges and fill the cigarettes and the matches and to empty the ashtrays." Wilson's eyes were riveted on the water dripping from the ice buckets for the champagne as the waiters pulled the bottles out for pouring. "Look at those clumsy waiters."

"Bernard and Brigid just filled the cigarettes and matches, Mr. Wilson," the housekeeper said. "Everything is going so well, wouldn't you say?"

But Wilson was already moving toward the caterers to reprimand them. Things were getting more chaotic since the modern dance band took over from the orchestra, he thought. They even had a singer, mumbling something about moonrise or sunset. Why couldn't they stick with waltzes? He had been in service at Hursley House for most of his life and couldn't imagine being anywhere else. But if his lordship had a mind to change his lifestyle to include this kind of bedlam on a regular basis, Wilson just might have to start planning his retirement.

⋆ ⋆ ⋆

"This is the biggest party I've ever seen, Bernard." Brigid patted her hair, checking the bun for loose tendrils as they stood behind a column at the edge of the party.

"Mrs. Anderson says he never had no parties since his wife died, and that was long before I came to work at Hursley House. This is the biggest party this house has seen in a donkey's age, that's for sure," the footman replied. "If we're clever, we can keep out of sight but get to watch. It's better than going to the pictures."

"I just wish we could have a dance or two. This band is lovely and the singer sounds so dreamy." The housemaid's blue eyes looked wistful. Bernard felt for her—she was so young and hadn't seen much fun in her life. Watching others have fun wasn't the same as having some yourself, but it was better than nothing. He looked behind him to make sure no one could see them.

"We can sneak off to the library and I'll swing you around a few times," he suggested.

"But the master always keeps the library locked."

"I still have the keys from Mr. Wilson." Bernard pulled his hand from his pocket, jingling the keys at her. "Come on."

Brigid shook her head, her eyes wide. But Bernard grabbed her hand and pulled her through the main hall. She told herself that it would be all right to have a quick dance, even if it was in the master's library. After all, dancing was a joyful thing, so it couldn't possibly be wicked, could it?

# CHAPTER 8

Dorothy was having a brilliant time. She loved being around interesting people and was enjoying the music and the conversation and absolutely everything about the party, including (guiltily) the escape from caring for her ailing husband. At the moment, however, she found herself stuck in a tiresome conversation with Sir Samuel Hoare, the home secretary. Dorothy sipped her champagne while Sir Samuel recounted a trip to India. She was trying to be interested, really she was, but he had a rather droning voice and his story was a rambling one about trying to find the best English bar in whatever city he was going on about. Her attention kept drifting away. Across the room she saw their host, Sir Henry Heathcote, dancing with his fiancée, Lady Sarah. They seemed rather stiff, as if they were not used to the modern music being played. No surprise there.

"But you will always find cracking gin in India, no matter where you are, especially in New Delhi," Sir Samuel continued. "After all, drinking gin and tonic is the best way to avoid malaria."

Dorothy swirled the last of her champagne in her glass. For a home secretary, he should have more interesting stories, she thought. Was he being banal on purpose? Did he think she didn't have the intellect to discuss politics, or perhaps he believed it was impolite to talk about serious subjects at a party? Sir Samuel paused to sip his martini, and Dorothy turned to his deputy, Rana Gupta.

"Mr. Gupta, were you brought up in London?"

"Not exactly, Mrs. Sayers. India is my home country, but I boarded at Harrow as a young man."

"Did you enjoy it?"

"I enjoyed it very much until my last year was interrupted."

"Oh?"

"Family emergency." Rana looked down at his feet. "Couldn't be helped."

"It's difficult to have your schooling interrupted." Dorothy was about to relate a story about her time at Oxford, but Sir Samuel broke in.

"But Rana returned to be a star at Cambridge. I recruited him right out of university."

"You flatter me, Sir Samuel." For some reason the compliment didn't seem to sit well with the deputy secretary, and he went on. "My mother and I moved to England after my father died. I enjoyed university—it was a good place to take my attention away from family troubles. One must focus hard to get top marks."

"So true, Mr. Gupta, so true." Dorothy nodded. Losing his father at that age must've been hard, she thought. Her own years at university were some of the best years of her life. Her studies, her friends, her adventures in the theater, so many things that brought her to where she was today. With all the education she'd had, French, German, Latin, literature, and philosophy, she sometimes questioned her commitment to her Lord Peter Wimsey stories. There were so many other things she wanted to write. But Lord Peter had struck a chord with readers, which her publishers and her bankers appreciated, and he'd come to have a life of his own after all this time. Her own enthusiasm for Lord Peter had perked up once she added Harriet Vane in *Strong Poison*, her 1930 novel—that had been a stroke of genius and had kept her going. She did enjoy writing his stories even if sometimes she wondered why she did.

"Rana, did you ever run into Heathcote when you were living in India?" Sir Samuel asked. "After his wife passed away, he spent a good deal of time in New Delhi. Isn't that where your family is from?"

"Just outside of New Delhi, sir, we had a plantation. No, I never met Sir Henry when I was a young man, although I did hear about him." Rana Gupta cleared his throat. "I—erm—knew of him, yes."

The man seemed uncomfortable, and Dorothy felt she should change the subject. She had a flair for making people feel welcome at social functions, so she often made that her purpose when attending them. And she was one of the hosts of this gala. She opened her mouth but was saved by the approach of Charles, Sir Henry Heathcote's son, and his fiancée, Marie Sinclair.

"Hello, Charles, Marie. Are you enjoying the evening?" Dorothy put on her hostess smile. She'd met Charles on a few occasions, but this weekend was the first time she'd met Marie, who had moved to London from the Caribbean. Her friendliness was quite cheering, and her positivity magnified her beauty. Dorothy admired how her cream satin gown accentuated the glow of her skin.

"The party is simply splendid, Mrs. Sayers." Marie's dark eyes shone with excitement.

"Please call me Dorothy."

"When I tell my father I spent the evening with his favorite author, he'll be so jealous." Marie's educated accent was slightly melodic, hinting at her Caribbean roots. She turned to her fiancé. "Charles, I wish my father had been able to make the trip. He would've loved this party. And I had hoped our fathers would've had the chance to meet by now."

Charles had just taken a sip of champagne, and his face suddenly turned so red that Dorothy thought he was choking. But he cleared his throat, straightened his white bow tie, and smiled at Marie. It struck her that he didn't look much like his father, Sir Henry. Perhaps he took after his mother, but Dorothy had never met her. She knew that his mother had died when Charles was just a child.

"Yes, well, our fathers will meet soon enough, my dear."
Charles turned to Sir Samuel. "You were right, Sir Samuel, all the
right people are here tonight to help my campaign for Parliament."

"It'll barely be a contest, Charles, the place is easily yours."
The home secretary touched his own bow tie to make sure it was
straight, then downed the last of his martini.

"I do wish my father could spend a little more time introducing me around. He seems to be just ahead of me every time I move
to a new group." Charles's smile was not as confident as the home
secretary's. Dorothy suddenly felt sorry for him, but she didn't
know why.

"Sir Henry is being the consummate host of Hursley House,"
the home secretary said graciously. "He's making sure he talks to
everyone tonight."

Dorothy noticed her friend Lady Stella walking toward the
champagne buffet. As her own glass needed refilling, she excused
herself.

Dorothy passed behind Ambrose, Heathcote's younger brother.
Ambrose was not as handsome as Sir Henry, she thought, his eyes
a little closer together, his chin less square, but he had a pleasant
manner that made him attractive. He was in conversation with
Heathcote's daughter Philippa and her husband, Juan Guerra,
whom she knew was an expatriate of Spain. As the dance music
took a pause, she caught a snippet of their conversation as she
went by.

"No, we'll never go back, not while Franco is in power," Juan
was saying, his dark eyes flashing as he stroked his short beard.
"And as Hitler gets closer to these shores, Britain may very well
experience something even worse than what Spain went through.
The British government and their subjects should be paying more
attention."

"Juan, this is a party, Uncle Ambrose doesn't want to talk about
such a depressing topic." Philippa touched an earring that matched
the seed pearl trim on her silk gown, then smiled at her uncle.
"Uncle, do you know if my father and Lady Sarah have talked

about a date for their wedding? I hope they aren't going to rush. A long engagement would be best, don't you think?"

Before he could reply, Philippa's younger sister Kate and Sofia, her friend from boarding school, joined the group. The two teen-agers projected the sophistication of their class but with the added enthusiasm of youth peeking through. They both had wide eyes and heart-shaped faces. Other than their coloring, blonde and pink versus brunette and olive-skinned, they could've been sisters, Dorothy thought. Kate's blonde curls were pinned up in a twist, and Sofia's long dark wavy hair was swept to one side and plaited with a silver ribbon. Their silk gowns were the same pale color, putting Dorothy in mind of vanilla ice cream.

"I don't believe in long engagements," Kate broke into the conversation. "Father should marry Lady Sarah right away. Why not? They're not getting any younger." She and Sofia giggled.

"Really, Kate." Philippa tried to make light of her sister's comment, but her lips were tense as she turned to Ambrose. "Do you believe the impudence of these schoolgirls? If I ever spoke like that when I was their age, Father would've turned me out."

"Yes, you're so much older and wiser, Philippa." Kate made a somber face. "I'll try to be more like you. In ten years or so." She giggled again and pulled Sofia onto the dance floor where they began a well-rehearsed foxtrot to the dance music. Philippa's face turned pink.

"You were never that cheeky when you were in school, Philippa, but little sisters will be little sisters." Ambrose touched her elbow and leaned closer. "I remember how you used to tease Charles when you were her age."

"You remember everything, Uncle Ambrose. Because you were paying attention." Philippa's smile seemed to show special affection for her uncle. "It's such a happy household when you're home. That's when we feel like a real family."

"You three are my only family, dear Philippa. Don't worry about Kate and don't worry about your father's impending marriage to Lady Sarah. Everything will be fine."

"Kate will grow out of it." Juan laughed and gently touched Philippa's cheek. "It's good to have some spirit at her age."

"I don't know how she'll ever get a husband with that much spirit," Philippa groused. She looked to the dance floor, but Kate and Sofia had already been swallowed up by the crowd. Instead, she saw Margery Allingham, doing a lively dance step with a man she didn't recognize. "Who is that man with Margery Allingham?" Ambrose turned his head.

"That's Ian Colvin, the journalist."

"A journalist? What a broad range of people we have here tonight." She raised her eyebrows. As she turned away from the dancers Dorothy watched her straighten her posture as if, it seemed, to better fit her social position.

# CHAPTER 9

Margery Allingham was sometimes ill at ease in crowds of the aristocratic level, like the group that filled the gala. Both her parents were writers, and she was more used to journalists or theater people than the party guests from this social register. She loved London but was more comfortable in the quiet village life—although she did like parties and was enjoying dancing with Ian Colvin, who had recently returned from Germany.

"How long were you in Berlin?" Margery asked the journalist.

"A few weeks this last trip, but I go often." He spun her around with one hand and brought her back to face him.

"Do you enjoy it there?" Margery would rather just dance than talk, but she knew that making conversation was expected.

"I don't know if enjoy is the right word for this last visit, but I like my job and the stories are certainly getting more interesting there."

"Tell me an interesting story," Margery prompted.

Ian Colvin paused. Margery didn't know him well, but she hoped he respected her as a writer. He had complimented her on how well her books were written, but hinted he didn't think they had any sort of seriousness to them, that there were more important things happening in the world, as if she didn't know. *Wasn't she aware of the global issues surrounding them all?*

"I'll tell you what's going to be a story very soon; now that Hitler has taken Austria, and will soon take Czechoslovakia." Ian kept up the rhythm of the dance as he spoke. "An interesting story will be how fast can he take the rest of Europe."

"Not really, all of Europe!" Margery was incredulous. "That's mad."

"Yes, mad is exactly the right word for him." Ian spun her around again and brought her back in close. "When you're in Berlin you can see how much has changed since the race laws."

"The race laws?"

"One law says that Jews are a separate race from the Aryan Germans and another law conveniently states that Jews aren't citizens of Germany because they are a separate race."

"How immoral!"

"To put it mildly. And if you aren't a Nazi, you can't be sure what they might do to you. I don't think it would be prudent for me to travel there again anytime soon. They asked me a lot of questions on my last trip. I began to wonder what would happen if I gave the wrong answers."

"What were the right answers?"

"That's just the problem, I couldn't be sure. And I'm starting to feel that way wherever I am."

"Even here, at a party?"

"Especially here, at this party. Sir Henry has some interesting friends." Ian turned his head subtly to the right and she followed his gaze. Sir Henry Heathcote was in a group of other tuxedoed men, rich older men, and they seemed to be having a serious discussion. She didn't see anything odd about it—just aristocrats being aristocratic. Then Ian moved closer and lowered his voice. "Perhaps I'm getting paranoid, but I feel if I say the wrong thing to the wrong person, it'll be more than just a faux pas this evening."

Then the music ended, and he finished the dance with an elegant pose.

"Thank you for the lovely dance, Mrs. Allingham."

She nodded and he bowed. How interesting he was, she thought. He moved away, through the other dancers, looking for his next partner.

Margery couldn't picture that Berlin, such a sophisticated city, was now the political center of the Third Reich. Still, Hitler was too far away for her to worry. Wasn't he? Ian must've been making a joke—what a dark sense of humor he had.

Margery saw Lady Stella and Dorothy by the champagne buffet and moved toward them. They looked so elegant in their silk gowns, subtle enough to blend in with the rest of the elite crowd, yet each with its own unique details of embroidery or silver beading to make them stand out. Margery smoothed her own plain green gown, wishing she had taken the time to buy something new instead of going with her favorite standby. But that would've taken too much time away from her writing. Standing next to Dorothy, she reached for a glass of champagne.

"Margery, you are a wonderful dancer," Dorothy said. "I saw you with that journalist. Colvin, isn't it? Did he know your father?"

"Yes, Ian wrote some stories for the *New London Journal* when my father was the editor." Margery sipped her champagne.

"How exciting to grow up in the real world of writers," Dorothy said. "Surely that had an impact on your writing. Your prose is so admirable, and all your characters are felt so deeply."

Margery thought Dorothy was being awfully kind. Dorothy's Lord Peter Wimsey character, since her first mystery book, *Whose Body*, from the time she wrote it in 1923, had been an icon in the mystery genre. Early in her career Margery's Albert Campion had been called a parody of Lord Peter, which had never been her intent. She wondered if Dorothy had ever heard that insinuation. Regardless, for Dorothy to compliment her was gratifying.

"Dorothy, you're too kind. I could only hope that my books aspire to be a faded shadow compared to what yours accomplish."

"Nonsense," Dorothy began. "Your last book—"

"Ladies, I'm going to stop this right now." Lady Stella chuckled as she interrupted. "There will be plenty of time to talk shop when we are recovering from this event tomorrow, sitting around playing bridge or reciting Shakespeare or whatever the morning brings." The three of them laughed as Ngaio and Agatha joined them.

"What's so amusing?" Agatha asked.

"Lady Stella just saved us from a bout of excessive 'complimentation,'" said Dorothy, and they all laughed at the invented word.

At that moment, Wilson the butler came to speak to Lady Stella, consulting on what seemed to be a catering issue. The four authors refreshed their champagne glasses.

"We should make a toast," Ngaio said and raised her glass.

"What shall we drink to?" Margery asked.

"To the cause?" Dorothy suggested.

"To each other," Agatha said.

"And our continued success," Ngaio added.

"To our blessed readers, then," said Dorothy. "To readers everywhere."

"To readers everywhere," they repeated together as they lifted their glasses and drank.

Ngaio felt the bubbles in her nose and watched the dancers. Despite the moments of insecurity, she was having a wonderful time. Spending time with these three brilliant writers, attending this historic party, meeting so many interesting people, what better adventure? Soon she'd be back in New Zealand and life would be rather tame for a while. As she watched Sir Henry Heathcote dance with Lady Sarah it gave her heart a tight feeling. She hadn't been in anything near a serious relationship since she'd lost her fiancé to the Great War more than twenty years ago. But then, who had the time? She had kept busy, traveling, painting, writing, and she'd enjoyed it all. Ngaio found herself staring at Sarah's blood-red fingernail polish. She never saw the point of fingernail polish, if she were honest. She thought it a waste of time to apply, first of all, and then the maintenance was ridiculous. You couldn't do any cleaning up or gardening—or painting, for that matter—without chipping the polish.

At that moment Sarah reacted to something Heathcote said, throwing her head back, tossing her thick, wavy, blonde hair. For some reason, seeing Heathcote and Sarah dancing together made her melancholy.

As Ngaio let thoughts of the past drift through her mind, she noticed that Heathcote and Lady Sarah had stopped dancing. They stood at the perimeter of the other dancers talking to each other. It did not appear to be a happy conversation. Sarah was flushed and although she seemed to be trying to speak softly, her voice was rising.

Ngaio leaned toward the other women and tilted her head gently in the direction of the couple in conflict. The other three writers slowly turned their heads.

"Why should my mother matter?" Sarah's voice pierced through the music.

Heathcote looked as if he were going to explode. His face was as pale as Sarah's was pink, and his lips pressed tightly together.

"What other lies have you told me?" Heathcote's response was a low growl in his throat, but Ngaio could hear it, and she expected the other writers could as well.

Their host had hold of his fiancée's arm and was speaking so close to her it seemed as if he would bore his words right into her. Sarah was trying to free her arm, but it was clear she had more to say. The other guests around them were too busy dancing to notice, but all four mystery writers were focused on the couple, trying their best not to stare. They glanced at each other, as if wondering if someone should alert the couple that they were being overheard or somehow provide a distraction—Ngaio was hoping one of the more outgoing of them would move toward the couple and perhaps intervene. The intensity of the row seemed to be increasing, and just when it seemed like the argument was about to break through the rollicking music, a subtly choreographed intervention occurred without them having to do a thing.

Ambrose moved smoothly from one side of the room and Sir Samuel Hoare from the other. Sir Samuel spoke as he approached from Heathcote's side, so that Sir Henry turned his head away from Lady Sarah, just as she seemed to be getting more outraged. And as Heathcote turned toward Sir Samuel, Ambrose asked Sarah to dance, quickly taking her in his arms. She was too surprised to do anything but accept, and they swirled away to the music. Sir Samuel kept Heathcote's attention, smiling widely as if telling an amusing anecdote. Soon the two men strolled toward the bar on the other side of the room and the roar of the party swallowed them up.

The four Queens of Crime had paused with their champagne glasses aloft. It took all they had not to give each other questioning looks with raised eyebrows and open mouths. Politely pretending they hadn't just seen a near-explosion that would have detonated the gala ball, they wandered away from each other and continued to mingle with the other guests, as was their duty as hosts of the fundraiser. But they each knew they had witnessed something extraordinary, the betrothed couple losing control, as well as the two men who swooped down to disarm the situation, in rather a deus ex machina.

# CHAPTER 10

In the kitchen, close to two in the morning, the fatigued butler and the housekeeper, Teddy Wilson and Elspeth Anderson, took a short break. Soon the party would be over and they would be busy ushering the catering crew round to get things back in order so they could all retire for what little remained of the night.

"If his lordship has decided this level of entertaining is part of his new life with Lady Sarah, we'll have to hire more staff." Mrs. Anderson sipped her cup of tea. "We're not set up for all this activity, even with caterers."

"Supervising caterers is more work than serving a dinner of ten by ourselves," Mr. Wilson observed as he smoothed his short gray hair. "If Lady Sarah expects this is how things will be, I'll speak with Sir Henry about hiring on more staff, don't you worry." He patted her hand.

Mrs. Anderson looked at him gratefully, just as Bernard and Brigid entered the kitchen. They stood across the table from the butler and housekeeper. Brigid's appearance was slightly wilted but with a pink flush to her cheeks from the excitement of the evening's activities.

"Mr. Wilson," Bernard said, "the guests are starting to leave, do you want us to check through the rooms upstairs and make sure nothing's been left behind?"

"Excellent suggestion, Bernard," Wilson said. "And make sure no person is left behind either. The two of you check every room thoroughly, please. I don't want some champagne-addled son of a lord wandering down the stairs in an hour or two wondering where his ride has gone."

"Yes, Mr. Wilson," they said in unison and left to comply.

As the maid and the footman headed up the back stairs, Bernard said, "Let's start at the top and work our way down."

Brigid nodded her assent. "Must we check every room?"

"Yes, unless they're locked. Let's start at the upstairs ladies' parlor and then the gentlemen's room and the guest rooms in the west wing."

"I can't believe anyone from the party would dare to enter private rooms."

"With enough champagne in their blood, some won't know what they're doing, or care. Once I found a couple of young men in the pantry, helping themselves to cheese and sausages."

"No!"

"Yes, but that was at another house, not Hursley. Now you take this side of the hallway and I'll take the other. It'll be faster."

They made their way through each door quietly knocking first at the guest rooms, before entering, and making a quick sweep of each room. They checked that everything was in its usual place, that there were no wandering guests, sticky champagne glasses, or burning cigarettes.

Wilson watched with relief as the last of the guests drifted outside Hursley House toward their chauffeured automobiles. He slipped his watch from his vest pocket—it was just after three. He'd already sent Brigid, Bernard, and Mrs. Anderson to bed. Cook had gone to bed hours ago. He'd finish up on his own; he could sleep the extra hour in the morning while they prepared breakfast. The catering staff was packing up, quickly putting the ballroom back in order. A crew from the village would arrive the next day to give everything a good scrubbing. It would be time to retire the house for the night as soon as the caterers pulled away in their company lorries.

Sir Henry and his brother had gone into the library, and Lady Philippa and her husband had been the last to say good night to the guests. Wilson thought they were a handsome couple, so elegant. But they both seemed to drag as they mounted the stairs.

The rest of the people who would be there for the weekend, in addition to the family's guests—the four authors, plus Sir Samuel, Rana Gupta, Lady Stella—had gone off to their bedrooms upstairs as the party wound down. Wilson took a deep breath. The fragrance of the fading flowers and spilt champagne made him yawn and he covered his mouth. He watched the last of the caterers' lorries pull away outside. At least the rain had held off.

Wilson locked the front door and made his way through the great hall, stopping at the library. He tilted his head close to the door. He heard voices. Sir Henry and Ambrose must be ending the night with cigars. He knocked gently. "My lord?" When Sir Henry told him to enter, he opened the door with his key.

The baronet and Ambrose stood facing each other, Wilson noted that they were clearly tense.

"Anything else before I retire, my lord?" Wilson asked as he glanced around the room, avoiding Sir Henry's eyes.

"Yes, this cigar box is almost empty, Wilson." His employer sounded annoyed.

"My apologies, my lord. I'll get a fresh batch right away," Wilson said, as he began to back out of the room.

"Just a moment." Sir Henry took his silver cigarette case out of his jacket pocket, checked that it was empty, and handed it to Wilson. "Take this for polishing."

"Shall I bring you a new case full, sir?"

"No, just the cigars."

The house was finally quiet. When Wilson returned to the library with the cigars, he found the room empty. He filled the cigar box, took a quick look around the room, checked the lock on the French windows to the garden, picked up two empty whiskey glasses, and locked the room when he left.

Wilson felt an ache in his lower back as he walked downstairs and placed the glasses in the kitchen, then went down the hall to his bedroom. Dawn was only a few hours away, and he knew there was still much work to do.

# CHAPTER 11

Early in the morning after the gala, Mrs. Anderson told Bernard and Brigid to ready the main rooms that the weekend guests would use, the dining room and the drawing room. Sir Henry Heathcote was up early, or perhaps he hadn't been to bed at all, she thought. She had seen his bedroom door was open and went in to pick up his clothes. He wasn't in his room, his bed was untouched, and there were no soiled clothes from the night before. Perhaps he had napped an hour or two in a chair still dressed. Whatever the case, he would be waiting for his morning coffee in the library by seven, ready to take his dogs out for a walk via the French windows. The house staff knew to leave him to himself, as he liked his morning privacy.

Ngaio and Margery were the first of the guests to arrive in the dining room for breakfast, just after eight. Agatha and Dorothy were close behind them. They helped themselves to food at the sideboard as they nodded good morning to each other and to Wilson, who stood by to serve. They took seats together, and Wilson brought them a fresh pot of tea.

The majestic dining room was made cozy with its leaf-patterned wallpaper and gold velvet curtains. It had just begun to rain and the tall windows gave a saturated green light to the room. The

Queens of Crime fell into talking about the world of writing as they nibbled their scrambled eggs, kippers, and toast.

"Readers have accused me of falling in love with my leading man, of course," Dorothy said. "But that's not why I invented Harriet Vane at all. I think I just wanted Lord Peter to be happy, and what could be happier than love?"

"I could never fall in love with Poirot," Agatha contributed. "In fact, I'm getting quite tired of the old egotist. Do you think we all chose male detectives because we thought we had to for the book-buying public? I'm leaning more and more toward my Miss Jane Marple. Her village life and her point of view have been occupying my mind." Agatha buttered her toast and then heaped orange marmalade on top.

"They do get more human and take on a life of their own the more we write about them." Ngaio added. "I've been thinking, it's natural, isn't it, for them to have relationships, other than their mother and their right-hand man and so on? Something more seriously romantic?" In her new book, her DCI Roderick Alleyn was already in love with the artist Agatha Troy, but Ngaio was still deciding if Troy would fall in love with him.

"I think Albert Campion is very close to finding true love," Margery commented. "But he hasn't quite worked it out. Foolish man."

They all laughed and began to discuss the previous night's highlights, pointedly avoiding the dramatic confrontation between Sir Henry and Lady Sarah.

"My favorite thing about last night was watching people toward the end of the fete." Ngaio smiled as she pushed aside her empty plate and lit a cigarette. "People are incredibly disheveled after dancing all night."

"And drinking too much champagne." Margery rose to get more of the delicious smoked herring.

"True. Compared to how polished they looked when they arrived, it was as if they'd been caught inside a twister from Kansas." Ngaio smiled to herself and sipped her coffee. How she would've loved to paint the scene of everyone leaving the party, what a modern smash of color it must have been.

"I agree, it was like the end of *A Midsummer Night's Dream*," Agatha commented.

"An appropriate comparison," Dorothy agreed. "And it was as fun as a Shakespearian comedy."

"Good thing it was more like a Shakespearian comedy than a Shakespearian tragedy," Ngaio quipped, and the others murmured agreement.

Sir Henry Heathcote's son, Charles, looking rather pale, and his fiancée, Marie, joined the breakfast, soon followed by Ambrose, Lady Stella, Sir Samuel Hoare, and his deputy Rana Gupta.

"Ah, here comes the parade," Agatha moved over a chair to make room. "Good morning, everyone. I'm sure none of us slept enough, but not to worry, the breakfast is magnificent."

The newcomers filled cups and plates from the sideboard and sat, making polite conversation peppered with good humor. Lady Stella was exuberant in her happiness at the success of the gala.

"This is an auspicious start to the Women's Voluntary Service." Lady Stella stirred sugar into her coffee. "I want to thank you all again for joining in to help with this important work."

The four writers made polite responses.

"The world is changing quickly with this German difficulty," Agatha said. "It's almost impossible to make travel arrangements abroad. We had plans to go back to Iraq for Max's archeological dig, but I'm not sure what will happen now."

"It must be so inspiring for your books, traveling with your husband, Agatha," Margery commented. "*Murder in Mesopotamia* was absolutely brilliant. I imagine travel there might be dangerous now. It's all so staggering. But I just can't imagine that war will reach us here." Margery shook her head. "Twenty years ago in the Great War, we went through hell, pardon my language. That can't possibly happen again."

"I have to go back to New Zealand soon," Ngaio said. "My father hasn't been well, and I don't know how long I'll be gone. It's hard to leave at a time like this, with the future so uncertain." She felt guilty thinking about going home to her family, so far away from Europe, yet she also felt a kind of relief.

"Were you born in Christchurch?" Dorothy asked.

"Yes."

"So was I! Only the Christchurch near here, of course." Dorothy laughed. "By the way, I was wondering if anyone would like to accompany me to church tomorrow. St. Thomas's is lovely."

"That's over in Eastleigh, isn't it?" Lady Stella asked. "I love seeing beautiful churches."

"Churches always feel like theaters to me," Dorothy said. "Although sometimes I think we get more from a theater performance than from a church service." She smiled mischievously.

The conversation turned to churches and local architecture when Heathcote's younger daughter Kate and her friend Sofia entered. Pouring themselves coffee and tea from the sideboard, they sat near Dorothy.

"Mrs. Sayers," Kate began.

"Dorothy, please," Dorothy smiled at the young women. They reminded her so much of herself and her friends when she was in school. So eager to embrace the adventures of the world.

"Well, all right, Dorothy." Kate blushed. "Sofia and I wanted to ask you about Oxford. We'll be finishing school next year and we're hoping to continue our studies there."

"Has Father agreed to allow you to continue?" Her brother Charles broke into the conversation.

"Well, not yet." Kate gave her brother a dissembling look. "But I have a year to talk him into it. Aren't you on my side?"

"Of course, dear sister," said Charles with a tired smile. "But I also need father's help getting elected, so I won't be climbing too far out on that limb."

"Thanks so much, dear brother." Kate screwed up her face at him, and then she turned to Sofia. "One can always rely on one's family, you know." Sofia smiled at her and put a hand on Kate's.

Conversations broke out across the table, and the different clusters focused on their own discussions. The mood of the group was so positive and agreeable that even the sleepiest of them found some energy, and the volume of the chatter rose audibly, making for a cheerful cacophony.

Until a piercing scream cut through the room.

# CHAPTER 12

The breakfast guests looked at each other in confusion. Had they just heard a scream? Immediately another shriek removed any doubt. Ambrose moved quickly to the door, followed by Agatha, Dorothy, Ngaio and Margery. They rushed down the hallway as the screams continued, and then turned into loud sobs.

Mrs. Anderson stood by the open library door, Brigid in her arms, weeping. Ambrose and the others passed them and entered the library, Wilson close behind them.

It was Ambrose's brother, Sir Henry Heathcote, lying motionless on the sofa, fingers still clutching his cigar as it burned into the fabric—his eyes open, his face cherry red and rigid. Ambrose took a step back and covered his mouth.

Dorothy was closest to Ambrose, and she stared at Sir Henry. Despite all the murder stories she'd written, she'd never seen a dead body. Sir Henry's face was a horrific mask of death, wide open eyes seemingly full of fear and betrayal. She felt the room start to spin around her before everything went dark.

Agatha saw Dorothy start to slide to the floor and caught her from behind, slowing her fall. She laid her down gently and knelt next to her, holding her hand. Agatha looked at Sir Henry's face, then away, at the others staring at him. For a horrible moment, she thought this could be some outlandish, ill-conceived prank—*four mystery writers and a body in the library.* But a glance at Sir Henry's wide empty eyes told her it was very real.

Margery Allingham was backing out of the room, shaking her head. *This wasn't happening.* There wasn't a dead body lying there in front of them. She leaned on the door frame and tried to take it in. Sir Henry Heathcote was lying dead on the dark red brocade sofa. The cigar in his hand was still smoldering. She tried to catch her breath and let the writer part of her brain take over. She looked around the library, the walls lined with bookshelves, the heavy masculine furniture. A coffee tray sat on the low table near the body, the lone cup half empty. The rainy morning glow from the French windows brought in enough light to accentuate the cigar smoke that still hung in the air like a fog. A cigar box, dark wood with silver inlay, sat open on the side table. It was empty. The burnt tobacco smell turned Margery's stomach.

Ngaio Marsh watched Ambrose and Wilson start to approach Sir Henry's body.

"Don't touch anything," she blurted out. They stopped in their tracks and looked at her. "I mean, that's the usual thing, right?" Ngaio wanted to bite her tongue. This wasn't a murder mystery. This was real. The man lying dead was Ambrose's brother. This must be a great loss for him, the pain on his face giving evidence. Sir Henry Heathcote meant nothing to her, in fact she hadn't liked him at all—he had been cold and so pompous at the luncheon. And she had noticed the way he treated his family, certainly not what one would call an affectionate father. But of course his family would be devastated, his children, his fiancée. She wasn't anxious to witness what would come next. She knew what it was like to lose someone close.

Wilson was having trouble maintaining his composure, but he was a consummate professional. He turned to the housekeeper and to the housemaid, who was still weeping, and put a gentle hand on Brigid's shoulder.

"What happened?" asked Wilson.

"I just came to remove the coffee tray, like always, sir," the maid said through her tears.

"Of course, Brigid, you didn't do anything wrong." His tone was comforting.

"I knocked, like I always do, not waiting for an answer because his lordship likes me to just come in once I knock, so I used the key. And there his lordship was, on the sofa, I thought he was asleep, sir. The cigar was burning the arm of the sofa, so I was just going to move it gently, so as not to wake him, but then I—I saw his, his face and I, I—" She broke down again, and Mrs. Anderson put an arm around her.

"Bring her down to the kitchen, Mrs. Anderson." Wilson spoke softly and gently turned them toward the door. "Get her a nice cup of tea with lots of sugar." As the two women left, he looked back at the body of the man who had been his employer for more than twenty years.

Wilson took in the image of pain and shock on Sir Henry Heathcote's face, which seemed severe. *There isn't anything natural about this*, he thought. In that moment Wilson was certain that his lordship, Sir Henry Heathcote, baronet of Hursley House, had been murdered.

# CHAPTER 13

"I'll ring the doctor and he can advise us." Ambrose looked around the room for anything out of place. "Perhaps he had a stroke or a heart attack."

"Shouldn't we ring a constable, sir?" Wilson looked apologetic at the suggestion.

"Constables mean the press, Wilson, and this should be kept in the family," Ambrose said. "Let's avoid a scandal, shall we?"

Agatha was helping Dorothy into a chair. Dorothy was more embarrassed than dazed after her fainting spell. She felt like an ingénue in a Victorian romance novel.

Agatha spoke up. "I'm sure the doctor will recommend we telephone the constable, in the end, and then they'll wonder why we waited so long." She tried to sound matter of fact, as if they were discussing what color they should choose for new curtains. But she didn't feel matter of fact, she felt rather less than calm. She deliberately tried to counteract that feeling in her spoken words. "These things must follow protocol."

"Yes, of course, that is sensible," Ambrose said. "I'm just not thinking straight."

"It's quite a shock, of course." Agatha tried to sound sympathetic as her mind raced. This was a serious situation and they were all right in the middle of it. She felt the danger in not handling it correctly. But what was the correct way to handle an actual murder?

Wilson looked at Ambrose for direction. *Should he telephone?* He appeared to be torn. He was unable to leave the room where his lordship's body lay, while at the same time feeling the urgent need to report his death.

Still hanging on to the door frame at the entrance of the library, Margery could feel the tension that seemed to paralyze everyone. Wilson looking at Ambrose, who stared at the oriental carpet below his feet. Dorothy in the chair, clinging to Agatha. Ngaio stuck in the middle of the room, unable to look away from the body. Margery didn't know what to say to break the spell.

Just then Sir Samuel and Lady Stella came up next to her by the door from the hallway. No one spoke, but they didn't need to. Sir Samuel and Lady Stella saw what everyone else had seen, and stiffened in shock.

"We don't know what happened," Ambrose said. "We were just about to ring the doctor."

"And Scotland Yard, I hope." Sir Samuel's voice was gruff, as if something was caught in his throat. Lady Stella had turned her head away from the sight and gripped the door frame. She slowly regained her composure.

"Come, Sir Samuel. We'll telephone together," she said. "We need the best and the most discreet inspectors."

"Thank you, Lady Stella." Ambrose's face softened. "I am most grateful. I would hate for this to be turned into a front-page story. It must have been some sort of accident. Heathcote certainly wouldn't want this to hurt his family in any public way."

Ngaio was standing the closest to the body, her arms clutched around herself. There was no way this was an accident. The man had been poisoned, horribly so, it was clear. You didn't need to have seen death or be a writer of mystery novels to know it: she could see it on his face. And there was no way that someone with an ego the size of Sir Henry's would commit suicide. This had to be murder. She looked toward the French windows that led out to the garden, noting that they were locked, and that the rain was not letting up. She looked back at the mahogany cigar box on the side table and saw it was empty. Heathcote's cigar had finally gone out on its own, still clutched between his fingers. The acrid smell of tobacco and burnt brocade was suffocating. Ngaio resisted the urge to move to the French windows to let in some fresh air. She knew that nothing should be touched.

Dorothy stood up, still somewhat shaky, and she and Agatha moved toward the door. Dorothy wanted to get far away from the dead body. She kept her eyes averted and focused on putting one foot in front of the other, saying a silent prayer.

"Ambrose, hadn't we best leave the room and lock it up?" Agatha said gently as they passed him. "The police will want to see everything as it was." Her eyes flicked around the library, avoiding Heathcote's gargoyle-like face. Messy papers on the desk, empty cigar box, precarious pile of books on the side table, gray and white ash in the fire grate. "We shouldn't risk disturbing anything."

"Yes, right, of course," Ambrose said. "Wilson has the key."

"Yes, sir. I'll lock the door, sir."

Wilson waited a moment while everyone moved into the hall-way. They all heard the loud click as he turned the key in the lock.

"I'll take you to the telephone, Lady Stella," Wilson said. The two of them left, with Sir Samuel following.

The four crime writers stood and stared at Ambrose, and then at each other.

Suddenly Ambrose looked as if he'd just had another shock.

"I'll have to tell the others. The children. Lady Sarah." His voice faded and his eyes stared off at nothing. Margery touched his shoulder.

"We'll help, Ambrose," Margery said and took his arm. "Come on, everyone." Ngaio took his other arm, Agatha and Dorothy following behind them. Wilson met them halfway down the hallway.

"Sir Samuel and Lady Stella are making the call, my lor—" Wilson stopped himself from making that mistake. Sir Ambrose was not the new lord of the manor. Sir Henry's son Charles was now Lord Heathcote of Hursley.

"Is everyone in the dining room, Wilson?" Ambrose broke the silence.

"Everyone except Lady Philippa and Mr. Guerra. And Lady Sarah."

"Please ask them to join us in the dining room," Ambrose said. He felt breathless, his heart racing. He knew that breaking this news might be the hardest thing he'd ever done.

"Yes, sir." Yet Wilson hesitated.

"Don't tell them what's happened. I'll tell them when they come down."

Wilson nodded, his face impassive as he turned to go.

They all watched as the butler disappeared down the corridor, moving toward the grand staircase, no sound from his irreproachable stride on the thick carpet.

Ambrose began to form the words in his head, the news he had to break to his family and the guests in the dining room. Words that said one thing and meant so much more. *My brother, Sir Henry Heathcote, is dead.*

# Chapter 14

Detective Chief Inspector Lilian Wyles typed away on the report of the most recent case of indecent behavior in her caseload. As the first woman in the CID, spending years as a member of the Women Police division, and now since she had been promoted to detective chief inspector, she had long ago earned the respect of her male colleagues. It had been a rocky journey, and just when she thought she was helping make progress for the treatment of women, whether victims or perpetrators—or women police for that matter—the world would seem to backslide on her. Some people weren't even aware that there were women police, let alone women chief inspectors, but there were now more than one hundred and fifty women in uniform keeping London safe, and she was one of eight in the CID. She hadn't always been treated well by her colleagues; there had been many dark days she'd been close to resigning, but she hadn't given up.

Lilian pulled the last sheet of paper out of the typewriter and stacked it neatly on top of the pile of reports for her commander, Dorothy Peto, who was the first sworn woman superintendent the Metropolitan Police had ever had. Peto's career had grown quickly since the Children and Young Persons Act of 1933, when she pushed for women police to be more involved in taking evidence and conducting interviews with children. The plan had been extremely successful—the women police were able to better foster a sense of trust with children and young women and therefore get more solid evidence, and it made for a gentler road for those witnesses who had been abused. Peto was a wonderful commander.

Lilian smiled at the thought of the small yet passionate group of women police she worked with, as well as the policemen who supported them. The world was changing, and 1938 was a time when women could make a positive difference in the world of law enforcement. There was nothing more fulfilling than helping an abused child be able to bear witness without adding to their trauma, she thought.

Yet, whether the case was prostitution, domestic abuse, or molestation, the singular domain of the caseload was wearing on her. She was occasionally brought in on other major crimes, but the lion's share of her caseload was in the crimes against women. She'd worked her whole life in London, and she longed for more diversity. She sighed as she straightened her stack of paperwork. She knew hard work and patience always went hand in hand in life. As her father the brewer often said, the longer the fermentation, the stronger the brew. She smiled at the thought. All her experiences would serve to make her ready for whatever came next.

★ ★ ★

"Come!" Commander Peto responded to the knock on her door. She put down the file she'd been reading and sat up straighter.

"Commander?" DCI Richard Davidson stepped inside her office. In his ten years of service in the CID, he hadn't had much interaction with the head of the Women Police division. He admired Commander Peto but felt intimidated in her presence. She had a powerful reputation. Before she could look up at him, he smoothed his dark hair and straightened his suit coat over his lean form.

"Yes, DCI Davidson, what can I do for you?"

"We just got a call from the Home Office, ma'am. There's a new case. Homicide. The baronet Sir Henry Heathcote."

"Baronet?" *Homicide of titled landed gentry?* Commander Peto's eyebrows arched up high for a moment. "What do you need from my division, Davidson?"

"Apparently Lady Stella Reading is at Hursley House, the baronet's estate, where his body was found. And there are a number of, erm, notable women there, for the weekend."

"Notable women?"

"Authors, ma'am, Agatha Christie and some others. Some sort of fundraiser."

"I see."

"And Sir Samuel Hoare is also there."

"The home secretary?" Peto stood up behind her desk.

"Yes, ma'am." DCI Davidson shuffled his feet uncomfortably. "I believe it was at Lady Stella Reading's request, but we got the message through the home secretary."

The commander of the Women Police division of the London Metropolitan Police waited for him to continue. She tried to make a connection between DCI Davidson standing in her office, the home secretary, Lady Stella, and a dead baronet, but there were too many missing pieces. DCI Richard Davidson stood still, then blinked.

Peto saw he needed a little help. "And that request from Lady Stella Reading through Sir Samuel is what, DCI Davidson?"

"Oh, yes, erm, that I be sure to bring a woman detective with me. To work the case with me. Down to Hursley House, ma'am." Richard Davidson resisted the urge to stick a finger under his collar to relieve the sudden restriction he felt in his throat. "I've worked with DCI Wyles before, Commander, if she's available. If you're amenable."

"If I'm amenable?" Of course, she would be "amenable." Peto suppressed a smile, walked around her substantial oak desk, and preceded him down the hall to the office of Detective Chief Inspector Lilian Wyles.

# CHAPTER 15

Agatha noted the restlessness in the silence of the dining room as they waited for the group to be assembled. Some of them knew what had happened, and they were waiting for Ambrose to break the news to the others. But having heard a bloodcurdling scream and having to wait to be told what caused it, had put those who had not seen the body on edge. Kate and Sophia held hands and stared with worried eyes. Rana Gupta looked as if he would jump out of his skin at any moment. Charles and Marie had been speaking softly to each other, in a quiet but frenzied manner, and seemed to be disagreeing about something.

After Lady Sarah, and Philippa and her husband, Juan, entered the dining room, Ambrose shut the door and paused a moment, feeling everyone's eyes searching his face. He thought of his brother Henry, revered by so many, leader in society, famous for his love of king and country, proud father, gentleman, baronet. Ambrose looked at his hands. There would be no easy way to break the news. He looked up and caught Lady Sarah's eye and spoke the words he had rehearsed in his head. His deep voice rang out in the stillness of the room.

"My brother, Sir Henry Heathcote, is dead."

The collective gasp was audible. Sarah covered her mouth with both hands, as if to stop any sound from escaping. There was a tick of silence before Sir Henry's younger daughter Kate started to weep. Sofia put her arm around her. Charles stood.

"But how, Uncle?" Charles strode to the door, close to Ambrose. "What happened?"

"We don't know," Ambrose replied. "He was found in the library by the housemaid."

"I must go to him."

"It's not a good idea, Charles." Ambrose stopped him from opening the door, and Charles raised his eyebrows.

"Charles, please don't make a scene," Philippa begged him, her voice breathless but firm. He looked at her face, and his expression changed from shock to pity. Charles moved slowly back to the table and sank into his chair next to Marie. "This is a family matter," Philippa continued. She looked from him to the group of guests and back again.

"I am going to ring Sir Daniel, my brother's doctor. Perhaps he knows of some condition my brother had that would've led to his, erm, this situation." Ambrose paused. "And Sir Samuel has called Scotland Yard."

"Why? What do you mean?" Philippa stood. Her voice was even higher than usual, almost screechy. "Surely we don't have to bring the police into this." She looked at Sir Samuel, who did his best to look apologetic.

"Philippa, my dear, it's the best thing to do," Lady Stella pointed out. "If this was not a natural death, we need to know. We have to consider the safety of the family. Of all of us."

"Quite so," Sir Samuel said. "Sir Henry was a public figure. If this was murder—"

Several gasps interrupted him.

"Murder?" Kate cried. "How could it be murder?"

"We have to let the police do their job and confirm one way or another." Sir Samuel's voice was definitive but gentle. "If it is murder, we have to be careful."

"We're all being rather dramatic, aren't we?" Philippa sat down again and failed to look calm. "Surely it's some sort of accident."

"Sir Samuel knows best," her husband spoke up. "He's right, if your father was murdered, we must now consider our safety."

The idea that their own lives might be in danger was a thought that clearly hadn't occurred to any of them. The four writers looked at Juan and then at one another. They seemed to ask each other silently, *Is the murderer at this very table?* No one spoke for a moment, then Kate made a sudden noise that was half laugh, half sob. As everyone turned to look at her, Kate said to her brother. "Charles, you're the twelfth baronet of Hursley."

She looked as if she were about to laugh, but instead she covered her mouth and tears began flowing. Sofia put her arms around her, and Kate buried herself in Sofia's embrace.

Charles sat stiffly in his chair, his face a blank mask as he turned away from his sister. *His father was dead, and he was the twelfth baronet.* The two facts clashed in his mind as Kate's muted weeping blended with the harsh patter of rain against the windows.

# CHAPTER 16

Lilian watched the raindrops make patterns on the windshield of the automobile as DCI Richard Davidson drove (a little too fast, she thought) on the narrow country road. In her years of policing, Lilian had never been assigned directly to a murder case. Oh, she'd helped with other cases, many of them. When you work in domestic violence, prostitution, and trafficking, there would always be cases that involved violent death. But this was the first time she'd been put on a case that was singularly a murder, and one at such a high level of society. She wasn't sure what she was walking into. The commander hadn't had time to explain; they had to leave immediately. All the commander had said was that the case was politically complex.

Lilian had worked a few cases with Richard Davidson. He was hard-working and smart. Had a good education, came from a good family. Almost posh, he was. He didn't have quite the number of years of experience she had, but she liked the way his mind worked and she trusted him. They trusted each other. That was paramount. As she was the more experienced of the two, she sometimes took the lead, and he didn't seem to mind.

"Been to this part of the country often, Davidson?"

"No."

She waited a moment as they drove through rain and fog. "We came through this way for summer holidays in Southampton many times." The car went over a bump, and she felt herself lift out of her seat. She smoothed her skirt. "A few hours from Piccadilly isn't a long journey, even for my Eastender family." She gave a short laugh at her self-deprecation and looked at Richard. Nothing. *What was filling his head?* He was usually an easy companion. The air in the automobile was close.

"Did you have kippers for breakfast?" she asked, wrinkling her nose.

Davidson took his eyes off the road for a moment and gave her a look. "Yes. What of it?"

"Good for you." Lilian sighed. "I barely had time for toast." Now she had his attention. "What do you know about the case, Davidson? Commander Peto told me nothing except the baronet Sir Henry Heathcote was found dead at Hursley House."

"And we got the call from the home secretary himself."

"Is that what's got the wind up you? This isn't my first case working with a home secretary."

"What do you mean?" Richard asked.

"The Savidge case. We were best mates on that case, me and him."

"That was a few home secretaries ago."

"Well, you've met one home secretary, you've met them all." Lilian assumed an air of aplomb she didn't quite feel.

Richard gave her a doubtful sideways glance and she laughed. "Don't you worry, we'll do our best and that's all we can do."

He shook his head slowly and furrowed his brow lower. *What was bothering him?* "Okay, then. What do we know so far?" Lilian asked.

"So far? A dead baronet and a gala fundraiser the night before with some notable hosts."

Lilian caught her breath. *Gala fundraiser?* "Wait, do you mean the Queens of Crime fundraiser for the Women's Voluntary Service?"

"It seems you know more about it than I do." Richard glanced at her.

"Just that Lady Stella Reading put it together. And that the four top-selling crime writers were hosting."

"I guess that would be the thing to sell tickets." The chief inspector smiled to himself. "Who would these four top writers be?"

"Agatha Christie, Dorothy L. Sayers, Ngaio Marsh, and Margery Allingham."

"All women?"

"Yes, the best-selling crime writers of the decade. All women," Lilian replied.

"The names do sound familiar."

"Not much of a mystery reader then?" Lilian smiled.

"More of a history buff myself," Richard said. "Have you read their books?"

"Some." Lilian didn't want to admit to him that she was a fan of crime stories. One might think that police officers in the Criminal Investigation Department would want more of an escape in their reading choices, but Lilian liked the puzzle solving and the thrill-mixed-with-humor that these authors offered. They were nothing like real life, and they gave her an escape from the real crimes that filled her daily work. She didn't like romances or depressingly tragic literature. And the mysteries usually ended well, at least the good winning out over the bad, and the victim was usually someone rather unlikable. And maybe the fact that they were written by women was part of the draw, or at least, the authors seemed to know how to write for her particular sensibility.

Richard spoke again. "I don't like it. It's too much of a coincidence that four crime writers are at the scene of a murder." He slowed down to take a curve. "Very suspicious."

"More like a setup. It's a big leap to think writers could turn into murderers, even if they do write about crime for a living." Lilian was surprised at this turn in the conversation. "And there's nothing in their past to suggest they might be violent."

"I don't know about their past." He glanced at her. "But I do know that all the other guests are well respected. Sir Henry

Heathcote's son, Charles, the new baronet, is a candidate for Parliament. His fiancée is there and his two sisters, one of them married. The deceased baronet's brother is there, Ambrose Heathcote, a prominent lawyer and philanthropist. And the home secretary himself is a guest for the weekend, along with his deputy, and Lady Stella Reading, the widow of a former foreign secretary." Richard gave a nervous gulp. "How could any of those members of high society be a suspect?"

"King Richard the Third had no issue erasing the line between him and the crown."

"I'm just saying, Wyles, it's a big case. I don't need to emphasize how important it is that every step must be taken with care."

Lilian took his point. She opened her notebook and carefully took down the names of the people waiting for them at Hursley House, checking with her partner on each one. She wrote each name at the top of its own blank page, ready for interview notes.

A murdered baronet, his brother, his son the MP candidate, his two sisters, the sisters' husband and friend, the home secretary, his deputy, the former foreign secretary's widow, the four Queens of Crime. Yes, they had to tread carefully, get every detail right, make sure all the evidence was legally and carefully collected, or the press would surely have a field day, not to mention the court.

*Careful what you wish for, indeed*, Lilian thought to herself.

# CHAPTER 17

"It's too horrible." Lady Sarah's voice was just above a whisper. Agatha saw tears slide down Lady Sarah's cheeks as Ambrose poured her some brandy. The guests and family members were distributed around the dining room table in little clusters, trying not to speak about the tragedy, as they had been directed by the local constables, one of whom was posted by the door. The rest of the bobbies were securing Hursley House and grounds as they all waited for the CID detectives from London to arrive and take charge of the investigation.

Agatha was still trying to grasp the fact that less than two hours ago she had poured her first cup of tea and sat in this same spot at the corner of the dining room table farthest from the sideboard. And now they could be sitting in the room with a murderer, or a conspiracy of murderers. Was she the only one with these notions? She glanced at Ngaio, Margery, and Dorothy, lost in their own thoughts, and then down the length of the table, on the other end, at Ambrose and Sarah, who were closest to the door.

She watched Ambrose place the brandy snifter in Sarah's hand, wrapping her fingers around the cool glass to steady them. "Drink this, Sarah, it's quite a shock."

It seemed to Agatha that Sarah's shaky hands and the stark look in her eye weren't indicating sorrow but something else. The writer wished she had heard more of the argument that Sarah and her fiancé had on the dance floor the night before. She recalled the antagonism in Sir Henry's face and the anger in Sarah's. But what had it been about? Could it have led to his murder? Agatha pulled at her chin to make her mouth into a frown, and she chided herself for thinking more about the puzzle than the people affected by the baronet's death.

But details had always interested her more than people. She would rather research Mesopotamian pottery for a decade than go to a single party. That was probably why she got along so well with Max, her second husband. As an archeologist, his study of ancient civilizations meant more to him than most of the live people around him. This was parallel to how Agatha felt about her fiction. The people she wrote about often seemed more real to her than the people around her. Some people held that against her, perhaps even her own daughter, but she couldn't help who she was. She slid her eyes back toward Sarah and Ambrose. They seemed to have plenty of comfort to give to each other. That was interesting to note.

It was Marie who spoke next. "Darling, I know things are looking dark now," she said softly to her fiancé. "But Scotland Yard will sort everything out."

Charles looked at her sharply. "Sort it out or not,"—his voice was hoarse with tension—"the scandal will sort me right out of the running."

Margery Allingham heard Marie's soft voice speak a few more consoling phrases to her fiancé before she fell silent. Charles looked stunned, as expected, and didn't seem to be listening. It didn't seem to matter to him that Marie was trying to be comforting.

While Margery felt for the Heathcote family, she had no feelings whatsoever about the death of the baronet Sir Henry Heathcote. And she couldn't decide if she should feel guilty about her growing excitement at being involved in the case. Maybe it was leftover pleasure from the party and being a guest in such a majestic estate. Surely her mood was influenced by her surroundings—that must be it! She was unaccustomed to the grandeur and felt like she was in a fantasy world.

"Ahem." Margery looked at the constable standing at the door as he cleared his throat. He was looking pointedly at Marie, gently reminding them that they shouldn't be discussing anything related to the incident. But what wasn't related? Sir Henry Heathcote's death had an impact on everything Margery could think of—in fact, probably more than she could even imagine. Then she returned to the thought that the murderer might be in this very room. They must all be aware of that, probably trying to deny it in their minds. What else could they possibly talk about, the weather?

Margery felt the weight of the silence. How long would it take for the detectives from Scotland Yard to get there? And they weren't to leave the room until they came? The local constables were still searching the rooms and grounds, surely taking notes and making sure nothing was tampered with. The inhabitants and guests of Hursley House sat in the dining room, alternately listless or frightened or sad. The staff had brought fresh tea and coffee, but no one at the table refilled their cups. They were also under the watchful eye of the home secretary, which was stressful. He had made it clear that they were to wait patiently for Scotland Yard. They waited, but none of them was patient.

Margery tried to get a look at Sarah without arousing her attention. Her body was tense, her face blank. Ambrose sat next to her, nervously fiddling with a linen napkin, glancing at Sarah's face but not saying anything, then looking down at his hands. Margery looked away before he could catch her staring.

The constable cleared his throat again and straightened his uniform. Margery gave him an ironic half-smile, and her thoughts turned to the night before. She had seen Charles and Marie speaking with Heathcote a few times through the evening and had been struck by how cold Sir Henry had been to the young couple. He had looked only sternly at his son, never with pride or affection, and he hadn't looked at Marie at all, as if she didn't exist. Did he disapprove of her background? Margery knew that she came from a rich family in the Caribbean, of the highest social level. She was also quite beautiful, graceful in every way, always poised. What could he object to? Margery didn't know, but she had definitely seen the frustration and pain in Charles's face during their last conversation at the party. She hadn't heard much of what they said, but as Charles walked away, the look on his face had turned to anger.

If this were a novel that she was writing, Margery thought, someone in the room would not be who they said they were, the characters would be even more colorful, and at least one of Charles's sisters would be a scientist or engineer. But this wasn't a book, this was real life. A real person was really dead, and even if he hadn't been a very nice person, he had almost certainly been murdered, probably by someone he knew. Someone in this room. Margery felt a cold tingle of fear run up her spine.

"Scandal notwithstanding, Charles," Philippa lifted her head, turning toward her brother, "you are the twelfth baronet of Hursley and Parliament will be ready for you to follow in Father's footsteps."

Charles gave her a scalding look and then glanced at the constable, who suddenly found a flaw in the polish of one of his brass buttons.

Ngaio Marsh hoped Charles would be a different sort of baronet than Henry Heathcote had been. She didn't feel any loss at Sir Henry's death—even in their short acquaintance she had found him repellant, egotistical, and so full of himself that there was hardly any room for anyone else in his conversations. She had wondered why he had even loaned his house for the fundraiser; he didn't seem the charitable type. She assumed it was just something for him to brag about, or that he knew it would give him the appearance of someone who cared about the causes that were important to Britain as they prepared for war. He surely cared about appearances, as any skilled politician and businessman would.

As a former member of Parliament and a successful industrialist, he certainly understood the importance of public opinion. What kind of businesses did he own, anyway? Ngaio couldn't quite remember. Something to do with manufacturing?

Now, the morning after his death, Ngaio felt herself question everything. His sons and his daughters were shocked, that was clear, and she felt for them. But there was something else in her heart—an underlying feeling of danger had gripped her. Ngaio remembered something from the night before, part of a conversation Sir Henry had with Philippa and her husband, Juan. Juan was an expatriate from Spain, and Sir Henry and Juan had been discussing politics. She had only heard a few phrases. It was definitely a disagreement, but Ngaio missed the crux of it. What she noticed most was that Philippa had clutched Juan's arm, pulling at him. Juan had turned to his wife and his face changed when he saw the look on her face. Ngaio could see it too. Her eyes were wide, her face tense. She had been terrified.

Had Sir Henry threatened them? Ngaio hadn't thought much of it at the time, and it had left her mind as the activity of the party distracted her. But thinking back on it now, she wondered if it had been significant.

Ngaio glanced toward Juan and Philippa, at the far end of the table near Ambrose and Lady Sarah. Philippa looked frozen after her comment to Charles. Juan sipped his coffee, seemingly unaffected. Perhaps he'd been through much worse, Ngaio thought. Escaping the Franco regime couldn't have been a cakewalk.

Now Juan was speaking. "Philippa, my dear." It took a moment for him to get his wife's attention. "Do you want me to get you some aspirin from your room?"

"Sorry, sir," the constable broke in. "I'm not allowed to let anyone in their rooms or out of this room, at the moment, not till the detectives arrive. But I'm sure they will be here soon."

Juan looked like he was about to protest but Philippa stopped him with a look.

"I don't want any aspirin. It wouldn't help." Philippa's hands were grasped tightly together on the table. Juan reached toward them, but as he did, she put them in her lap.

There seemed to be tension between them, Ngaio thought. Ngaio was struck by the look on Philippa's face—she was afraid of something. *What did Philippa know?* In her books, Inspector Alleyn didn't jump to conclusions before he had all the facts and had checked all the alibis. But he also trusted his instincts. Ngaio couldn't help noticing that Juan's demeanor was different from everyone else in the room. He was completely calm. Perhaps too calm.

Ngaio looked around the table at the others. Closest to her right were the other three writers, then the younger daughter, Kate, with her schoolmate Sofia. At the other side of the table, Philippa and Juan were next to Ambrose and Lady Sarah, then Charles and Marie at the corner. Ngaio looked at each of their faces then looked to her left where Lady Stella, Rana Gupta, and Sir Samuel sat. They fiddled with a teacup, pushed food around a plate, and stroked a mustache, respectively.

There was sadness, shock, and even impatience in the air, but as Ngaio looked at the eyes of each member of the party, she felt sure that the universal mood of the room was more fear than anything ese.

*What were they afraid of?*

* * *

Dorothy sat closest to the younger daughter, Kate. Dorothy had seen Sir Henry express his disapproval at Kate and Sofia as they danced to the second band of the evening, which had obviously been chosen for its more modern music and for the pleasure of the younger guests. Kate and Sofia had been perfectly matched on the dance floor—Sofia was taller than Kate, and their dance routines had been skilled and practiced. They were pure joy to watch, Dorothy thought, bright young things having fun.

The two beautiful young women had danced a quick-paced, swinging sort of dance, laughing with joy, their eyes only for each other. The song ended and they hugged, catching their breath. The next tune was a slow romantic ballad, and the embrace turned into a slow dance. Kate and Sofia seemed completely lost in the music and the rhythm. Dorothy couldn't take her eyes off them. Suddenly, Sir Henry had stormed onto the dance floor and pulled them apart.

He had grabbed Kate's arm, his mouth close to her ear, saying something low and harsh. Kate's face had turned red, her fists clenched in anger. Sir Henry's hand twisted her arm as he held it tightly. Then he had marched her to the buffet, Sofia following behind them in confusion.

Remembering it now, Dorothy felt her own face flush. Being reprimanded in public by your father was not something a young person felt lightly, something she knew from firsthand experience. She had loved her own father and revered his reputation and intellect. But there had been times when his Victorian sensibility had made her heart ache. Going away to school, and the friendships she made with the other girls there, had been liberating. She looked at Kate and Sofia near her at the dining table—it was obvious they meant a lot to each other.

"*Cara mia*," Sofia was saying to Kate. "*Non ti preoccupare. Io sono qui.*"

Dorothy was fluent in Italian and knew that she had said, "My dear, don't worry. I am here." Kate was still weeping softly, on and off, Sofia stroked her hair and squeezed her hand. Dorothy wondered what exactly Kate's father had said to her as he pulled her off the dance floor. Perhaps he thought the girls were a little too close. After all, they weren't children any longer, they were young ladies, and it was a very public event. Whatever he had said, it now would linger in Kate's heart as her last interaction with her father. Unless they had had another meeting or confrontation later in the night? Tears could stem from sorrow, Dorothy thought, but also from guilt or fear.

Dorothy looked down the long table, at the delicate teacups, the uneaten breakfasts, the elegant flowers drooping in antique howls, and at all the drawn faces. They must each be feeling their own level of fear. Besides the house staff, this was the entire group that had been in the house when Sir Henry had died. By now it must have occurred to them all that they could be sharing their breakfast table with a murderer, unless one of Sir Henry's servants had decided to murder their employer.

"We're all here to help, my dear." Dorothy wanted to add her comfort for Kate in addition to Sofia's. She felt close to these two young ladies, impressed at their courage and ambition. This would be a blow to Kate's spirit, to all the family members, but she wanted to support them. "You can count on me."

Dorothy was embarrassed at having fainted over the dead body, but she didn't feel any shame about her reaction, in fact still felt rather sick to her stomach. What else should one feel when confronted with the death of another soul? She was human. She found herself struggling with many conflicted thoughts. Here she was, one of the top crime writers of the decade, having written dozens of novels about homicide over the years, and now she was confronted with a real situation.

She was realizing what a humbling experience it was to witness the aftermath of a murder. If it was murder. But what else could it be? The look on Sir Henry Heathcote's face had been horrific. He didn't have the temperament to commit suicide, and no heart attack or stroke could have resulted in such a look of terror and realization, she thought. No, Sir Henry had been fully aware of what was happening to him. Someone had poisoned him, and the baronet had nothing else to think about in his last moments except for who had killed him and why. She looked up as Ambrose spoke to Sir Samuel.

"You did tell them to be discreet, Sir Samuel, when you called Scotland Yard?"

"I assure you I did and they will be," Sir Samuel responded. "It's in the best interest of the country to be circumspect in this situation. It's not just a family matter—word of the death of a prominent public figure like Sir Henry could have a larger impact on the country, possibly even on the British economy."

Dorothy noticed that the constable shuffled uncomfortably. He couldn't possibly shush the home secretary, but he certainly didn't want to be derelict in his duties. He paced from the door by the corridor over to the window, looked out through the rain at the empty drive and the lack of arrival of CID detectives, then paced back to his original spot.

Dorothy looked at Rana Gupta, next to the home secretary. Mr. Gupta couldn't possibly be listening. His mind seemed to be racing, his eyes flicking back and forth, and the look on his face kept changing from confusion to worry to feigned indifference. Dorothy couldn't help remembering how Mr. Gupta had reacted when Sir Samuel asked him if he knew Heathcote in New Delhi. What did he say? He hadn't met him but he knew *of* him, he knew *about* him. And then he had quickly changed the subject.

Maybe it was her overly curious mind, but she felt there was something underneath that response, some history the deputy secretary had with Heathcote. It reminded her of one of the Greek plays—or was it Shakespeare? It would come to her later. Rana suddenly looked up and caught her eye. His face flushed, but then he quickly changed the look to sympathy. He nodded to her, then turned toward Sir Samuel. Rana Gupta was a fascinating person, Dorothy thought, a complex and interesting man.

Then the line she was trying to remember came to her. It was from *The Tempest*: *What is past is prologue.*

# CHAPTER 18

As DCI Davidson and DCI Wyles drove up the long private road to the impressive structure of Hursley House, Lilian tried not to let the awe she felt show on her face. The sheer marble front, the classic columns, the austere minimal plantings to each side. It was a cold and formidable structure, certainly designed to make that point to visitors. If Hursley House represented the personalities of the family members, she thought, the inside of the house might be just as chilly as the rainy day outside.

She knew about Sir Henry Heathcote, former member of Parliament, aristocrat, owner and investor in businesses, including manufacturing materials that were necessary for many essential items. And she'd heard him on the radio, making speeches about the importance of free trade and international politics. She knew he was inspiring to a lot of people, or at least that they were impressed with his wealth in the way people are when they wish they had what he had. But she had never felt that way. Like her father always said, it was easy to come from money and make more money, especially if you stepped on the necks of working folks on your way up. Hursley House was a sight to behold, but the blood, sweat, and tears it had taken to exist, and to stay so well maintained, had not been shed by Sir Henry Heathcote. Of that, she was quite sure.

DCI Davidson jumped from the automobile and moved quickly to the front door, but stopped just before he rang the bell. "Wyles, before we go in."

"Yes?"

"I trust your instincts on things, I always have."

"Thank you, Davidson. I trust yours as well."

"So don't hold back. Even though I am the lead on this case, I welcome your full collaboration."

Lilian nodded and hoped he meant what he said.

He smiled and before he could knock, the door flew open, and they both looked at the tall policeman who stood in the doorway.

"Morning, Chief Inspectors! I'm Sergeant Olyphant of the local constabulary." The man stood to one side, allowing the detectives to enter as they nodded and greeted him, introducing themselves. "The grounds are secured and searched. The library, where the baronet is still in position, has your Scotland Yard team at work, collecting evidence." The sergeant paused while they shook the rain from their overcoats. "They were told to wait and refrain from moving anything until yourselves arrived."

"And the witnesses, Sergeant?" DCI Davidson asked.

"In the dining room, sir." His eyes twinkled. "Waiting patiently, sir."

"Really?" Lilian Wyles asked.

"As patient as a flock of pigeons outside St. Paul's at teatime."

Lilian smiled. Here was someone, she thought, who knew how to handle the challenges of the job with enough humor to keep a sane balance.

"Good work, Sergeant. Much appreciated." Davidson nodded. "Take us to the library first, please. And then we'll speak to the family."

# CHAPTER 19

Agatha stood up to stretch her legs. She was used to sitting and writing for hours, but without that activity to occupy her mind, her body felt twitchy. She strolled over to the window and watched the rain make patterns on the glass; it helped to distract her from the issues at hand. Her mind wandered to her writing. She was toying with the next mystery puzzle and how she might construct it. This weekend was both annoying and inspiring. Could she, should she, use anything that might happen? It was all yet to be seen. As she peered through the rain-speckled glass, an automobile pulled up the drive, and she saw a man and a woman get out of the car.

"Ladies and gentlemen. I believe the detectives have arrived," she announced.

"It's about time," Philippa said. "How long do they expect us to sit here like prisoners?"

"Interesting choice of words, sister," Charles responded. "We're only witnesses."

"Witnesses to what?" Kate sniffed. "We weren't up early enough to witness anything."

"Ladies and gentlemen, if you please." The constable's voice was barely loud enough to be heard.

"Witness to anything that might've led up to what happened this morning," Sir Samuel explained. "Anything you might've seen, heard, touched, smelled, or tasted in the last twenty-four hours could be significant."

"I hardly see how something we tasted could have anything to do with anything." Charles seemed confused.

"Sir Samuel was being ironic, Charles, but I'd hardly expect you to comprehend that sort of nuance." Philippa stood and stalked to the window, but the detectives had already disappeared into the house.

"Really, you two," Kate almost started crying again. "Must you argue? Isn't there enough ugliness?" Sofia put her arm around Kate again and muttered in her ear.

Agatha moved next to the constable, whose face was turning a shade of crimson red that was almost identical to the color of the roses in the garden.

"All this waiting has made us tense," Agatha said. "It's understandable. Constable, would you please let the detectives know we are quite anxious to see them? Thank you so much."

The constable was more than willing to take a break from his post and exited the room without a glance behind him. As he left, Bernard the footman arrived with a fresh tray of cakes. He nodded to Agatha and placed the tray on the sideboard in front of her. Agatha turned back to the room. All eyes were on her.

"Now, who would like a pastry? They look delicious. I'm going to have two." She picked up a plate, chose her sweets, and returned to her seat.

★ ★ ★

DCI Lilian Wyles stood in the open door of the library and let the scene fill her vision. One constable stood by the French windows that led to the garden, another next to her at the library entrance. An older man and a younger woman were on either side of the room with small soft brushes, collecting fingerprints. Another woman was taking photographs of the body, and a man whom Lilian assumed was a local doctor examined the body delicately. All the activity seemed efficient, and calm. Lilian saw and appreciated the professionalism of the team immersed in the tragedy.

As she looked around at the room, she was in awe at the quantity of books. All four walls were lined with bookshelves that reached up to the high ceiling and every shelf was full. In addition to the packed bookshelves, there were stacks of books on both end tables by the sofa, on the desk at the back of the room, and on the coffee table in front of the body. She looked at the face of Sir Henry Heathcote from across the room. His frozen grimace gave her stomach a turn, and she diverted her attention to DCI Davidson. He had entered the room ahead of her and stopped near the sofa that held the body. The photographer seemed to have finished taking pictures of the baronet, and the doctor continued his examination, kneeling by the sofa. Davidson turned to see Lilian by the door and gestured for her to come closer.

"DCI Wyles, you know DS Nelson? And this is Constable Roper," he said, nodding to the photographer and the officer who guarded the door. DS Nelson moved the camera to her left hand and reached her right to shake Lilian's hand. Constable Roper nodded to them.

"Morning." Lilian nodded to Roper and Nelson. The last time she'd met DS Nelson, she had been taking photographs of the bruises on the arms and legs of two children who had been at the mercy of their father after too many whiskeys, not that that was an excuse. "Almost finished, DS Nelson?"

"Almost." DS Nelson adjusted the camera apparatus. "I'll get the outside photos when I'm done here and then leave for the lab. I'll have everything developed and printed by tonight." She spoke quietly and then moved toward the French windows that led out to the garden and took a few more photographs. Lilian's eyes fell on the face of Sir Henry Heathcote again. The grotesque expression on his face seemed to confirm that it had been a horrible way to go.

The doctor stood to face them and cleared his throat. "Nasty business." He was a soft-spoken gray-haired man, almost a foot shorter than the lead detective he stood next to, and looked to be more than twenty years older, his pale blue eyes full of sympathy. Lilian guessed he hadn't racked up many murders on his list of duties as local physician. "Dr. Daniel Edwards, Southampton. I won't shake hands, possibly a strong poison involved and I've been examining the body. Please exercise caution."

"We will, thank you," Richard said. "What can you tell us, Dr. Edwards?"

"Rigor mortis is just beginning to set in, dead about four hours or so. I believe the poison took effect instantly, most likely introduced from the cigar. I would guess cyanide." Dr. Edwards spoke factually, but his drooping eyes and the deep fatigue on his face showed the impact that the examination had on him.

"Four hours or so." Richard looked at his wristwatch. "That would be between seven forty-five and eight fifteen?" The doctor nodded. Davidson turned to Lilian with a look of significance. "Anything else, doctor?"

"Not at the moment. Not till after the post mortem." He picked up his kit bag. "Will you be wanting me to arrange the autopsy?"

"That won't be necessary," Richard said. "We'll transport the body to the morgue at Scotland Yard for further examination."

Dr. Edwards looked relieved and gave a brief nod before he turned to leave, then paused by the door and looked back. "Chief Inspectors, you should know that Sir Henry was my regular patient. He was in excellent health. There's absolutely no reason to believe that this was a natural death. I'll send you a formal statement." His last look to them was serious, heavy with the weight of his words. He left the library.

"Not that I had any doubt, but good to know we didn't waste a trip." Richard gave Lilian a wry look.

"Done with this room, sir," DS Nelson said, as she packed up her camera equipment.

Richard stepped to the center of the room. "Can I have everyone join us for a moment?" They all stopped what they were doing and moved toward them.

"Who was first on the scene? DS Randall?" Richard spoke to the fingerprint expert.

"DS Nelson and I arrived together with DC Lee here. Constable Roper had secured the room." Lee and Roper nodded as DS Randall continued. "Doors had been locked when they found him. The butler, Mr. Wilson, let us in. We spoke briefly to the home secretary." The officer shuffled uncomfortably. "He assured us nothing had been touched."

"Were the French windows out to the garden also locked?" Lilian asked.

"Yes, ma'am, no sign that anything had been fiddled with."

"Anything jump out at you that we should know about up front?" Richard's eyes flicked to the body and back again. Everyone was quiet for a moment.

"Nothing comes to mind, sir," DS Randall replied.

The young DC Lee stepped closer to her mentor with a constrained look on her face.

"Speak up, DC Lee, what is it?"

"Not so much something that was here, but something that wasn't." She spoke quietly but confidently. "There was no mud by the garden doors, but the carpet showed some damp footprints leading in up to the sofa where the body, erm, Sir Henry, is lying."

"And what do you make of that?" Lilian asked her.

"It started raining here at seven forty, ma'am, the local constable told me." The young detective constable's accent gave away her east London upbringing. "So if Sir Henry came in from the garden about that time, his feet would've been damp, but if he came in much later, he'd have surely have tracked in some mud. Bein' out in the rain and all, as it were."

"Thank you, DC Lee. Excellent observation." Lilian smiled at her. That matched the approximate time of death. This is what they needed. Every tiny detail that would eventually add up to make the whole picture, leading them to the proper conclusion, with enough evidence to convict the perpetrator.

Just then the door creaked open and the constable who had been posted in the dining room peeked in.

"Pardon me, detectives, but can I have a word?" The man's tone was respectful but indicated it was imperative. The detectives followed him out the door into the corridor.

"The family and their guests are getting quite anxious," the constable reported. "They seem to be at a breaking point. Do you have a moment to speak with them?"

"Yes, of course, Constable," Richard calmed him. "We were just about to do so. Will you lead us there?"

The constable, wasting no time answering, turned on his heel and took off down the corridor. Lilian and Richard hurried off behind him.

"No time like the present," Lilian murmured.

# CHAPTER 20

"As you both so delicately pointed out, my dear sisters," Charles was saying. "I am now the twelfth baronet of Hursley House. This house. So, if you would all please calm down and be seated, you can be well assured that I am in complete control of the situation."

"Complete control?" Philippa rolled her eyes. "What could you possibly mean?"

"He means you should be quiet, Philippa." Kate's sorrow was pushed aside by her annoyance. "Charles is the head of the family now."

Agatha wiped invisible cake crumbs from her mouth with a linen napkin and watched the reactions of the others seated at the table. The scene declined into chaos, with family members snipping and snapping at each other, until Ambrose broke in.

"Please, let's all of us take a moment and find our patience." Ambrose was obviously at the end of his own patience but doing his best to pretend otherwise. Agatha was sure none of them realized they had burst the seams of their socially acceptable norm—that they had been so emotionally inflamed that they were letting their true feelings out in front of outsiders. But these things happened, she knew.

The constable returned, opening the doors wide and stepping to the side as the detectives entered. Richard spoke to the group.

"Ladies and gentlemen, my sincere apologies that you've had to wait. Your patience is gratefully appreciated. I am Detective Chief Inspector Richard Davidson and this is Detective Chief Inspector Lilian Wyles. Please be seated."

Davidson's respectful yet firm demeanor reminded them to regain control of themselves. He went on. "If you don't mind, we have some questions for you."

Many of the faces around the table, especially those of Sir Henry's family, showed that perhaps they did mind. But they waited for DCI Richard Davidson to continue.

Lilian looked around the dining room. She recognized the home secretary, of course, and Lady Stella Reading. Lady Sarah, the bereaved fiancée, and the family members were easy, especially since Lilian had heard the end of the conversation as they approached the dining room—and she could recognize their spouses with them and Kate's school friend with her. At the far end of the table was Agatha Christie, instantly recognizable, as was Dorothy L. Sayers. Next to them were Ngaio Marsh and Margery Allingham. The Indian gentleman next to Sir Samuel must be his deputy, Rana Gupta.

"Constable," Richard turned to the still flustered man in uniform. "Let the house staff know we'll be coming through to see them soon. But please ask Mr. Wilson to meet us here in the dining room."

The constable nodded and left quickly. Lilian took out her notebook, ready to make notes.

# CHAPTER 21

The housekeeper, Mrs. Anderson, couldn't sit still in the kitchen. "Mr. Wilson, do you think sandwiches and salads are enough for the luncheon today? Or should we also have some nice hot soup, with the weather so damp?" She flitted from one end of the table to the other. Flipping through her notebooks of recipes and supply inventories one moment, then stacking them to one side and pouring herself more tea the next, but not stopping to take a sip as she moved toward the door to the hallway, listening for any approaching feet, then back to the table again.

Mrs. Walsh, the cook, kept out of her way as best she could as she prepared a cold lunch buffet.

"Sit down, Mrs. Anderson, please." Mr. Wilson was trying to sound calming, but impatience bubbled up in his voice. "Everyone, please, let me have your attention."

Mrs. Anderson settled into her chair at the end of the table. She'd never met a Scotland Yard detective before and wondered what they would be like. Clever and witty, like they were in books, or would they be dull, or even mean? She hoped for clever and witty.

Brigid sat next to Bernard, who was in his usual chair. Brigid reckoned he was glad to rest his feet between running up and down the stairs, refilling the tea, coffee, pastries, and fruit in the dining room. She would rather keep busy herself, but Mr. Wilson had kept her close, waiting for the detectives. She had never spoken to police detectives before, and all the way from Scotland Yard! She was equally thrilled and nervous in anticipation.

Mrs. Walsh kept working, even after Mr. Wilson spoke, her curly ginger hair spilling out from her kerchief, her expression daring anyone to stop her. She could listen and work at the same time, couldn't she?

"The detectives requested that I return to the dining room while they speak with the family and guests, but asked me to tell you that they will visit us here to ask some questions." Mr. Wilson continued, "I need you to please remember that this is a respectable house and that you are expected to be honest and respectful in your interview with the Scotland Yard detectives. That means no gossiping, no indiscretions, no falsehoods. Scandals can start with the smallest mention of something that might seem like an innocent observation, but easily becomes misconstrued, and would've been better left unsaid."

Brigid's head was spinning, so much had happened in the last twenty-four hours, and she tried to sort out what might count as gossip or what might count as an indiscretion. She must tell the truth, of course, but should they include everything they did and everything they saw? What if something they did or saw was indiscreet, should they keep it to themselves, even if it was part of the truth? She shot a panicked look at Bernard. He smiled at her mischievously. He didn't seem concerned.

"Mr. Wilson," Bernard said displaying a serious face to the butler. "None of us would do anything that would hurt the family. Discretion is the foundation of service."

"Well said, Bernard," Mr. Wilson smiled and nodded. "Well said." Then he headed upstairs to the dining room.

# CHAPTER 22

When the detectives had walked into the dining room Ngaio felt as if the wind had got knocked out of her. The lead detective was the spitting image of her fiancé from twenty years past. The thick dark hair, deep-set eyes and long lashes, the strong jaw. She felt like she was seeing a ghost. She could barely hear the detectives introduce themselves, but she caught that his name was Richard—that was different; her fiancée's name had been Edward.

"We apologize for keeping you waiting," DCI Davidson was saying. Ngaio let herself breathe again. With his posh London accent he seemed less of a twin than at first sight. This detective was around the same age her Edward would've been, but Edward had been from her own home town in New Zealand and spoke as such. It must've been a trick of the light when he entered the room, an optical illusion. Although, now that she identified the difference, she also realized that he was close to the image in her head of her fictional detective, Roderick Alleyn. Could she have subliminally taken some memory of her fiancé and aged him slightly to be her detective? But then, tall-dark-and-handsome was tall-dark-and-handsome. She was amused at the thought.

She looked at the other writers to see if anyone had caught her reaction to the man, but they all seemed absorbed in their own thoughts. There it was again, that feeling that she didn't belong. If only this murder hadn't happened, they might've had a lovely weekend and she might've been able to make friends with these people she admired so much. *How could that happen now?*

"If you don't mind," Richard Davidson continued. "We will be interviewing each of you individually in a few moments, but for now if you could take us through your movements from late last night, as you each retired for the night, and early this morning, all together so we can begin to understand the time line. We would be much obliged."

They all looked at him, then around the room at each other. Lilian knew she had been brought on the case to be helpful in questioning the women, but Richard didn't seem to notice that the people sitting around the table had no idea who should go first. She jumped in.

"Mr. Wilson, would you get us started?" She smiled warmly at him. "I would imagine you would've waited until the house was quiet before you turned in?"

"Yes, ma'am. The house emptied out and the catering staff took care of their final responsibilities and left by about half three in the morning. I had sent the rest of the staff to bed, and I went to check and see if I was needed. The baronet and Sir Ambrose were in the library."

Lilian looked at the people at the table; she read anxiety, boredom, and fear in their faces.

"Might I ask"—Lilian paused respectfully—"was anyone else still up and about after three in the morning last night?" Blank faces looked at her, then at each other, and each head began to shake no.

"Please continue, Mr. Wilson. You checked to see if you were needed," she reminded him.

The butler cleared his throat. "Yes, the baronet and Sir Ambrose were in the library, and Sir Henry asked me to fill the cigars. I went to the downstairs pantry to get a new box and when I returned, the library was empty. I filled the cigar box, picked up a few empty whiskey glasses, and locked the door on my way out."

"When you say a few whiskey glasses, Mr. Wilson, how many would that be?" Lilian asked.

Wilson paused. He seemed slightly flummoxed, possibly concerned with the potential weight of the question. "Two glasses, ma'am."

"Thank you, Mr. Wilson." She made a note in her book. "And you say you filled the cigar box?"

"Yes, ma'am."

"How many cigars would that be?"

"Twenty, ma'am." Wilson looked surprised at this question.

"And when you say you locked up the library," Lilian continued, "did you also check the French windows?"

"Yes, ma'am. I made sure they were locked."

"You're quite sure?" Richard asked. "That's the kind of thing that you might automatically do each night, but are you sure you did so last night?"

"Yes, sir, I am quite sure, because I had to straighten the small rug in front of the French windows. It had a corner folded over and I almost tripped on it."

"Right. Thank you, Wilson. And then?"

"I brought the glasses to the kitchen and I went to bed."

"Did you see or hear anyone on your way to the kitchen or afterward?" Lilian asked, her pencil poised over her notebook.

"No, ma'am. Not a peep."

Lilian restrained a smile as she wrote down his words. *Not a peep.*

Richard turned to the group sitting at the dining room table. "Let's continue in as much of a consecutive order as we can, working backward. Sir Ambrose, you were with your brother in the library when Wilson came in?"

"Yes, detective," Ambrose said. "We were having our last whiskey and discussing the success of the party. Henry and I had smoked the last cigars in the box."

"And did you see Mr. Wilson return with the fresh cigars?"

"No, I went straight up to bed after Wilson left us."

"And your brother?" Richard asked.

"I left him in the library. But if Wilson says the library was empty when he returned, Henry must've gone up to bed after I did."

"You didn't see him?" Lilian asked.

"No," Ambrose said. "I went straight to my rooms."

"Did you see anyone on your way?"

"No, wait." Ambrose looked down the dining room table, where his niece Kate was glowering at him. "As I came down the hallway, Kate was in the corridor."

"What time was that, Sir Ambrose?" Lilian asked.

"It couldn't have been much later than half three." Ambrose scrunched his forehead and looked thoughtful. Over dramatically, Lilian thought. But she knew that people could be so nervous when being questioned by the police.

"Miss Heathcote, do you recall seeing Sir Ambrose?" Richard asked.

"Yes, now that I come to think of it." Kate smiled guilelessly. "I was in bed, but I had such a headache and I couldn't sleep. So I borrowed some aspirin from Sofia and was returning to my room. Too much champagne." She gave a self-conscious giggle, then suddenly wrung her hands and her eyes moistened. Lilian felt for her. She was the youngest, not yet an adult, and had now lost both parents.

"Thank you, Miss Heathcote, or shall we call you Lady Katherine?" Lilian asked.

"Miss Kate is fine."

"Did you notice the time, Miss Kate?"

"No, I didn't notice."

"Thank you." Lilian looked to Ambrose. If he hadn't noticed the baronet come up the stairs behind him, how long could that have taken? She turned to the butler. "Mr. Wilson, where are the cigars kept?"

"Locked up in the downstairs butler's pantry, the lower ground floor, ma'am."

"And how long would it take you to go below stairs, walk to the butler's pantry, use your keys to get the cigars, and I assume you locked up again, and then return to the library?"

"Maybe six or seven minutes, ma'am?"

"Did you do anything else or stop for any reason?"

"No, ma'am. I was rather ready to get to my own bed."

"Of course." Lilian made notes. "So, you didn't see the baronet go to his own room?"

"No, I did not."

"Did anyone see the baronet go to his room?" Lilian looked at their blank faces. No response. She thought this over—Sir Henry still had his tuxedo trousers on when they found his body, and his dress shirt, but his jacket and tie were not found in the library. It was possible he hadn't gone to bed at all. But where had he partially undressed and why? "Or notice where he might have left his jacket and tie?" Still no answer.

"And this morning, who was up and about first?" Richard asked.

Wilson cleared his throat. "The whole staff, sir. Mrs. Anderson the housekeeper, Cook, Brigid, and Bernard were all up, preparing for the breakfast. I was up soon after."

"Brigid and Bernard are?"

"The housemaid and the footman, sir."

"Yes, of course." Richard checked his notes. "We'll see the staff when we're finished here."

"Of course, sir. I've let them know." Wilson paused. "Sir Henry was always up early, sir. He'd have his morning coffee in the library, then go through the French windows to take the dogs for their morning walk."

"Even on the night after a party?" Richard asked. "When he was up past three?"

"Yes, sir, without fail. Sir Henry always had his morning coffee at seven o'clock. He took the dogs out for thirty or forty minutes, then returned to have his first cigar of the day."

"So, it was important that cigars were there for him for his morning ritual," Lilian said.

"Yes, that's right, ma'am." Wilson smiled at her, apparently appreciating that she understood his commitment to ritual and service.

"And did you bring him his coffee as well?"

"No, that would be Brigid."

Lilian glanced at Richard. It was beginning to seem that the house staff might be more important to this narrative than the guests that sat in front of them. Not just as witnesses but as possible suspects who had opportunity.

Richard turned to the people at the table. "Did anyone see Sir Henry this morning? Before he was found, of course."

The room was silent.

"Let's go around the table, shall we?" Lilian prompted. "Sir Ambrose, we've already heard from you. Lady Sarah, would you please tell us what time you left the party and went to your room?"

Lady Sarah sat up straighter, dabbed at the corner of her eyes, and then put her graceful hands, holding her lace handkerchief, in her lap.

"It must've been sometime between half one and two o'clock. Sir Henry and I had our last dance and I wasn't feeling myself. A touch of headache." She grimaced. "I said good night to Henry and slipped upstairs."

"And did you see anyone?" Lilian asked.

"You mean did anyone see me?" Lady Sarah replied.

"You could put it that way." Lilian kept up her professional smile. Lady Sarah would be aware that the purpose of these questions was to identify or weed out suspects.

"I suppose someone on the house or catering staff might've seen me," Lady Sarah continued. "I did have to walk by the cloakroom to go up the stairs. There wasn't a mad rush to leave at that time so they weren't very busy. Someone might remember seeing me." Lady Sarah looked at Lilian clear-eyed, as if to say, *but you have no reason to doubt me.*

"Thank you, Lady Sarah." Lilian turned to Philippa, who spoke before she could be asked a question.

"My husband and I stayed till most of the guests were leaving, of course. We stood by the door saying good night to the guests until almost three. Isn't that right, Juan?"

"Yes, my memory is the same." His lilting accent was refined. Lilian wondered what his family background had been before he left Spain—certainly landed gentry.

Philippa continued. "I believe, aside from my father and Uncle Ambrose, we were the last of the house guests to go to bed. I felt it was our duty to make ourselves available to the party guests until they had all gone home." Philippa looked at her brother and sister. There was some uncomfortable rustling of the people at the table, and Kate looked like thunder.

"Of course, sister, you are the most responsible adult." Kate's voice was sharp. Lilian saw Sofia put her hand on one of Kate's. "I'm just a child, which is why Father sent me to bed before two o'clock. I would've happily stayed and said good night to our guests."

"Or stayed to drink more champagne," Philippa commented. "Perhaps Father thought you'd had enough."

For a moment, no one in the room took a breath.

Richard broke the silence. "Miss Kate and Miss Sofia, you both went upstairs just before two o'clock?" They nodded. Lilian saw something in their eyes. Rebellion? Had they gone upstairs when they were told, but then what?

Charles spoke up. "My fiancée and I saw my younger sister and Sofia to their rooms at about two o'clock. I saw Marie to her room at that time also."

"Yes," said Marie, nodding. "We went upstairs with the girls. Then I went directly to my room. I was quite ready for bed."

"Did you return to the party then, Sir Charles?" Richard asked.

"Yes, I came down intending to post myself in the main hall to say good night to the guests, but my father asked to speak to me. We stepped into the library." Charles looked uncomfortable.

"And how long would you say you were in there with your father?"

Charles didn't answer right away. He looked at Ambrose, then at his fiancée, then out the window.

"It's hard to say, Chief Inspector. It felt like a short conversation, but at that hour my conception of time may have been off."

"Any guess?"

"Perhaps twenty minutes. Then I left him in the library and went straight upstairs. Fatigue had taken its toll." Charles looked as tired as he sounded. "And no, I didn't see anyone on the way back to my room."

"And the conversation with your father," Richard asked. "What did you talk about?"

"It was a personal matter."

"Could it have been a subject that connected to his death?"

"No," Charles said flatly.

Lilian noticed that Charles was wringing his linen napkin.

Marie spoke up. "But I heard you go in, darling." She turned to the detective. "My room is right next to my fiancée's. I was still awake."

"Do you remember what time that was?" Lilian asked.

"Yes, I looked at the clock on my night table. It was ten minutes before three o'clock." She took Charles's hand, squeezed it, let go, and then put her own hands back in her lap.

DCI Davidson looked at Sir Samuel, who was seated next to Charles and Marie. He'd never spoken to the home secretary and was debating how to open the questioning—but Sir Samuel spoke without waiting to be asked a question.

"By two thirty most of the guests had gone home, and Lady Stella and I felt we could retire." The home secretary looked directly at DCI Davidson as he spoke.

"Thank you, sir, so it was two thirty when you went upstairs?"

"Or very nearly, wouldn't you say so, Stella?" Sir Samuel turned to Lady Stella.

"Oh, yes, we started up the stairs right about two thirty." Lady Stella Reading smiled politely.

DCI Davidson gave a little bow of his head and turned to Rana Gupta, the deputy home secretary.

"Detectives, if I may, what is the point of outlining our movements of the night before if Sir Henry was killed this morning?" Gupta's voice revealed his impatience. "He was murdered this morning, was he not?"

Philippa let out a soft gasp, and Kate began weeping again. Lilian looked up from her note-taking and wondered at the level of sensitivity this man had. *Didn't he care that the family was dealing with this sudden grief?*

"Mr. Gupta, we appreciate that this is an anxious and somewhat frustrating day." Richard kept his patience and his voice was calm. "However, it is important that Detective Chief Inspector Wyles and I get a clear picture of the evening leading up to the devastating death of this family's father."

Lilian watched Richard's eyebrows lift as he spoke. The phrase "devastating death" was a nice touch. Lilian waited for the outcome. A moment passed while Rana collected himself. He seemed chastened.

"And the time that you mounted the stairs to retire, Mr. Gupta?"

"It was, I guess—it was about—" Rana had lost his bluster. "It was before three, in fact, I saw Sir Charles ahead of me on the stairs, so, ten or fifteen minutes before three."

In the pause before Richard spoke next, Lilian felt everyone at the table subtly adjust their position. The moment of offense had passed.

"Thank you, everyone, we're making great progress and are very grateful for your time. We seem to just have the four esteemed writers left." Richard turned his eyes on them and indicated to Lilian that she should take over the questioning.

# CHAPTER 23

Lilian felt her heart flutter and then admonished herself. They are just people. They are not any different than anyone else in the room. There is no reason to be star struck.

"Mrs. Christie, would you tell us your movements at the end of the evening?" she asked.

Agatha spoke as soon as Lilian's words were out, smiling apologetically. "I'm afraid you are forcing me to reveal my ill-mannered weakness for slipping away from parties without formal good nights. I went upstairs at about half one without any fanfare."

"So, no one saw you?" Lilian asked.

"That is correct." Agatha responded. "I saw no one on my way to my room."

Lilian didn't want Agatha Christie to think she thought she was a suspect. The thought appalled her. But she had to treat them all equally.

"Actually," Ngaio spoke up. "I went up soon after Agatha, and I happened to see her go into her room just as I reached the top of the stairs."

"And what time was that, if you don't mind, Miss Marsh?" Detective Chief Inspector Davidson asked.

Ngaio didn't answer right away. Richard's eyes were locked on hers, and she couldn't seem to find her voice. In waiting for her reply, he almost stared her out of countenance. Lilian watched as Ngaio's face turned pink and wondered at her reaction.

"About half one, as Agatha said." Ngaio's voice came out strained. She cleared her throat. "I'm an early riser. I'm never one to be the last guest at a party." She smiled shyly and looked down at her teacup.

"Thank you." Richard made a note.

"That brings us to you, Mrs. Allingham," Lilian said.

Margery sat up straight, stubbed out her cigarette, and smiled at the woman detective chief inspector.

Lilian thought she seemed happy, almost eager, to answer their questions, unlike the others who were clearly uncomfortable in front of each other. She knew they would get more from them in the individual interviews, but it was useful to see how they reacted to each other as they talked through the time line.

"It seems I was up the latest," Margery said. "I was talking with Ian Colvin, the journalist, right until he left. We were sitting in the winter garden and smoking too many cigarettes." She pushed the ashtray in front of her farther away. "The footman came in and asked us if we needed anything, and we realized that was his polite way of telling us the party was over." She smiled at the thought. Then she cleared her throat. "We had completely forgotten the time. I accompanied Ian to the cloakroom, then he walked me to the bottom of the stairs and I watched him exit through the main hall." She had been looking directly at Detective Lilian Wyles the entire time she had spoken.

"And did you notice the time, Mrs. Allingham?" Lilian asked.

"Yes, I heard the clock strike three as I started up the stairs, Detective Chief Inspector Wyles." Margery seemed to take pleasure in saying the name and title out loud.

"Did you notice anyone on your way up to your room?" Lilian stopped writing.

"No." Margery blinked. "I mean, I could see some activity in the main hall. People were leaving, staff cleaning up. But I was alone on the stair."

"I see, thank you, Mrs. Allingham." Lilian closed her notebook and looked at Dorothy.

"Mrs. Sayers. I think you're the last on the list," she said. "What do you remember about the end of the evening?"

"I was saying good night to some guests at about two fifteen and then I went up to my room. Is that what you wanted to know?" Dorothy raised her eyebrows. Lilian got the feeling she had more to say.

"For now, Mrs. Sayers," Richard said. "Thanks to all of you for your patience. We'll speak with the house staff first and then call each of you in for a private interview." He turned to leave, then turned back. "And please, don't discuss the case."

He looked at the constable still posted at the door, nodded, and reached for the door.

"Just a moment, detective." Philippa stood, stretching to her full height. "Must we stay in this room? I'd like to go to my room and freshen up."

Richard turned to her, with his most charming smile.

"Apologies, Lady Philippa, but we are still busy being terribly intrusive coppers and searching the entirety of Hursley House, including all the private rooms."

"You—what?" Philippa's voice wasn't loud, but it was sharper than it had been at any other point that day.

"Can't be helped," Richard said cheerfully. "This is a murder investigation. We'll let you know as soon as your rooms are free. Wilson, will you take us below?" With that he followed Wilson out of the room, Lilian right behind them. The last thing she wanted was to carry on any more conversation after that moment.

# CHAPTER 24

The detectives followed Wilson below stairs and down the corridor toward the kitchen. Lilian spoke first. "That went well."

"I thought so." Richard smiled.

Lilian decided not to tell him she was being flip. But she did appreciate that he spoke the language of this upper-class family. He could play the detective from a good school, and she would be the weathered London copper. It would allow her to make the occasional more direct, even indecorous remarks, keeping them off balance, while he played the posh part. The idea of a woman police detective was probably new to them, but she was used to that.

They reached the kitchen. Mrs. Anderson, Brigid, and Bernard stood as they entered, while Mrs. Walsh was sorting out platters of cold meats and salads for lunch. She stopped for a moment to wipe her hands on her apron when the detectives came in.

"Please, stay seated," Richard said. After they were introduced, he asked, "Mrs. Anderson, would it be too much trouble if we all sat and had a cup of tea? I think we're still damp from the rain."

"Of course, sir." Mrs. Anderson couldn't have been more pleased. "Sit down and make yourselves at home." She smiled as she bustled about getting extra teacups and pouring a fresh pot from the kettle that had been kept warming on the stove. Lilian appreciated her pleasant attitude—she must run a cheerful house.

"Please, won't you all sit while we talk? No need to be so formal." Richard looked at Wilson, who nodded and took his usual chair at the head of the table. Mrs. Walsh was the last to sit, heaving a sigh as if nothing could possibly be more important than her lunch preparations.

"Thank you, Mrs. Anderson." Lilian sipped her tea. Mrs. Anderson sat next to her, and Lilian noticed how she wrapped both slender hands around her teacup and, in spite of being introduced as Mrs. Anderson, wore no wedding ring. The house staff all looked nervous but ready to talk. Certainly, the anticipation must've been exhausting.

"Miss Brigid," Richard began. "Would you start by telling us everything that you remember since you woke up this morning?"

Brigid looked at Mr. Wilson, who nodded his encouragement.

"I woke at five thirty, as usual, sir," she began. "Came downstairs before six, put on the kettle. Mrs. Walsh came down at the same time, then Mrs. Anderson, Mr. Wilson, and lastly, Bernard."

Bernard had a puckish smile on his face. Lilian guessed he was the type of footman who was better at camaraderie than hard work.

"And you prepared a tray of coffee for Sir Henry?"

"Yes, that's right, I was just about to say so. We had a bit of breakfast first, as usual."

Lilian noticed that Brigid was rather flustered. Richard was doing his best to calm her, but he didn't realize it was his posh authority that made her nervous.

"Of course, Brigid," Lilian encouraged her. "Did the baronet take milk or sugar with his coffee?"

"Oh, no, ma'am, never." Brigid turned to her conspiratorially. "Black and strong, he liked it. Right, Mrs. Walsh?" Brigid said to the cook.

"Strong as I could make it." Cook tucked her red curls into her kerchief and eyed her unfinished luncheon platters.

"And you prepared the tray and brought it upstairs." Lilian prompted.

"I prepared the tray, but first I got the key from Mr. Wilson."

"The key?" Lilian asked.

"The key to the library. It's always locked." Brigid was more comfortable now, the story rolling off her tongue. "I looked for Mr. Wilson in his office, but he wasn't there, and I was getting worried because I didn't want the coffee to get cold, his lordship likes his coffee very hot, like, and I was going to run upstairs to see if Mr. Wilson was in the upstairs pantry and that's when I saw him coming down and I asked him for the key."

"And how many keys are there to the library, Mr. Wilson?" Richard broke in.

"Just two, sir," Wilson said. "Sir Henry kept one on his person and I have the other one."

"Is there any particular reason that the library is so secure?" Richard asked. No one answered for a moment.

Wilson spoke carefully. "I suppose it's because it's where his lordship kept all his important papers, sir."

Lilian found this odd. "Is any other room kept so well guarded?" she asked.

"Well, no, ma'am," Wilson admitted. "Now that you mention it. The wine cellar has three keys, and there are four rings of keys for the rooms for rest of the house. One for myself, Mrs. Anderson has the other, one hangs in the pantry, and his lordship kept a ring in the library."

Lilian watched Richard get lost in thought for a moment. She knew that he, like herself, was wondering who could've gotten into the library after Wilson filled the cigar box and before Sir Henry Heathcote had his morning cigar. What happened to the cigars that Wilson had brought to the library at the end of the night? Someone had taken them all and left one poisoned cigar in the box. Richard looked at her, as if he was reading her thoughts.

"Brigid, did you notice the cigar box when you brought in the coffee tray?" Lilian asked.

"Just that it was where it always was."

"You didn't see if it was full or empty?"

"No, ma'am. It was closed."

"And was Sir Henry smoking?"

"Oh, no, ma'am." Brigid sounded shocked at the idea. "His lordship always had his coffee first and then took out his dogs. He didn't have his first cigar of the day until he returned."

"And he would exit and return to the library through the French windows from the garden?"

"Yes, ma'am."

Richard turned to Wilson. "Was there a separate key to the French windows?"

"Yes, sir. His lordship was the only one with that key. Although he might've had an extra copy in the library," Wilson explained.

"Brigid, once you brought in the tray, did you lock the door behind you?" Lilian asked.

"Oh, yes, ma'am, always. His lordship was very particular on that account."

"Then you returned to the kitchen at approximately what time?"

"I suppose it was ten after seven."

"And what did you do then?"

"I returned the key to Mr. Wilson and we all had work to do." Brigid looked around at the rest of the staff as she said this. "Getting the breakfast finished, onto the trays, bringing it all upstairs so the guests could have what they needed."

"You all worked together, bringing everything up?" Richard looked impatient. Lilian knew he wanted to get to the individual interviews.

"And I brought a tray for Lady Philippa, of course, to her room."

"I see. Anything unusual?" Richard asked.

"Sir?" Brigid looked embarrassed.

"I mean, did you see anything out of the ordinary?"

Brigid looked at Wilson, whose face was completely blank, then at Bernard, who lifted one eyebrow.

"No, sir, I just knocked and brought in the tray and left it for her," Brigid continued.

"And what time was that?"

"Eight o'clock sharp. That's always when she takes her break-fast tray." Brigid said this as if it should have been obvious.

"Thank you, Miss Brigid." Richard had gotten as far as he could. He looked at Lilian. They both knew they'd have more success with the staff in private interviews. Getting them each alone was the only way to get any helpful information. This had just been a start, to see if there was any reaction to each other's answers—or lack of answers. "And just one last question for you all. Did anyone see Sir Henry between the time Brigid dropped off his coffee tray and when his body was found?"

There were mutterings of no, and heads were shaken.

"Not even out in the garden with the dogs?"

"No, sir," Mrs. Anderson answered. "We can't see the east garden from the lower ground floor. Sir Henry always went that way to pick up the dogs at the shed by the garage and then he'd usually leave them there when he was done."

"Of course, Mrs. Anderson," Lilian said. "That's quite logical and very helpful. That's all we're asking for, the details of the household as you know them. We're at quite the disadvantage here, being so new on the scene." She smiled at Mrs. Anderson apprecia-tively. Witnesses never understood how important the little things that they knew were to an investigation.

"We'll let you get back to preparing the luncheon." Richard stood. "But we'll call each of you separately later this afternoon, after we speak to the guests."

"Separately?" Brigid looked confused. "But we've already told you what we know."

"Just a formality," Lilian explained. "We'll need a separate statement from each of you, we'll write down what you've said, and then you'll read it and sign it to show we got it all correct. Does that sound all right?"

Brigid nodded soberly, but she seemed upset at the thought of it. Lilian wondered if she was the anxious type or if there was something she'd held back, something she might be afraid to say in front of the higher-ranking staff.

"All right, then." Lilian smiled and stood. Richard needed practice with regular people, she thought. He did just fine with the posh set, who had an idea of what to expect, but didn't realize how disruptive and peculiar police investigations were to the working class. Her experience had taught her how to be straightforward with them and to put them at ease in tense situations.

She and Richard were a good partnership for this case, with their different backgrounds. But she'd have to be ready to step in with the house staff.

# CHAPTER 25

In the dining room, Dorothy opened her book and tried to appear as if she couldn't hear the family while a considered lack of restraint was breaking out.

"Was it really necessary to embarrass me in front of Scotland Yard?" Kate was saying to her sister, her voice rough from crying. "You both made me look like a child."

"When you act like a child, you'll be treated like a child." Philippa said this matter-of-factly, as if it was something she said to her sister on a daily basis.

Charles's face was turning red. "My dear sisters, let's remember we have honored guests. Please exhibit some decorum."

"Yes, *my lord*," Kate said, in a tone dripping with sarcasm, and then began weeping into Sofia's shoulder.

Sofia hugged Kate. "I don't understand this family. This is a very sad time. A very sad time. This is not a time for fighting. It is a time for comforting." Sofia's Italian accent made her declaration sound like a poem, Dorothy thought.

She felt for these girls. This was likely the worst thing that had ever happened to them, and it was happening in a public forum. She wanted to help, but she didn't know how.

Dorothy cleared her throat discreetly. "I wish we could give you some privacy," she said. "We have no choice but to wait here together until the police take care of their business. If there is anything we can do to make things easier for you, just say the word."

Of course there was no way to make things better. Their father was dead, dead after a night when he had treated all three of them horribly. He had ignored Charles's requests to help with his campaign, worried Philippa by political arguments with her husband, humiliated Kate by pulling her off the dance floor. Every member of the family must have felt some guilt, even if they'd had nothing to do with his death. They'd surely all had unkind thoughts about him in the last twenty-four hours. She knew she'd done so.

Philippa spoke up. "Mrs. Sayers, you are so kind—we appreciate your words more than you know. Unfortunately, there is nothing any of us can do, save wish the clock to go faster. And none of us can make it do that."

"No, we can't," Ambrose said softly. "It's understandable that we are feeling angry and frustrated, but let's try to be civil with each other. And, as the police have told us more than once, let's keep the talking to a minimum." Ambrose looked at the home secretary, who nodded.

Sir Samuel slowly stood. "I'll go and see if I can move things along, shall I?" he said and left the dining room.

# CHAPTER 26

I n the morning room allotted to question the guests, Lilian waited for Richard Davidson to take his seat—there were two mahogany chairs with upholstered seats facing a matching love seat. Richard took one of the chairs and she took the other. DC Lee sat at a writing table near the window to take notes. Constable Roper was posted outside the door, and the rest of the constables, both local and from London, were searching the house and grounds.

Just as Lilian was about to ask Richard how he wanted to begin, the door opened. Constable Roper looked apologetic as he let the home secretary into the room.

"Chief Inspectors," Sir Samuel said as he entered.

They both stood.

"In the interest of saving time, I volunteer to be your first interview." Sir Samuel sat on the love seat in front of them.

Saving *his* time, Lilian thought. But then, the home secretary's time *was* rather more important than the others.

"Thank you, sir," Richard sat and opened his notebook. "Much appreciate you coming through first." Richard glanced at Lilian. She reckoned he didn't much appreciate it at all, but the home secretary was the home secretary.

"Sir, please tell us about last night."

"Don't have much to tell, lovely party, very festive, everyone having a good time."

"Including Sir Henry?"

"Yes, as far as I saw." Sir Samuel smoothed his moustaches.

"Were there any unusual circumstances, anything out of the ordinary?" Richard sounded casual, professional, and patient, not at all as if he were speaking to the man who was the boss of their boss, the commissioner, at the head of Scotland Yard.

"I can't say I noticed anything, no."

This is going to be a short interview, Lilian thought, pencil poised over her notebook. She glanced to her right. DC Lee also had her pencil ready, eyes averted.

"You see, sir," Richard continued. "We are trying to work out any sort of motive for the murder of Sir Henry. Did he have any enemies? Do you have any idea who might've wanted him dead?"

"It's completely beyond my imagination, Davidson." The man practically harrumphed. "Sir Henry was an upstanding public figure, an admirable father, an impressive businessman."

"I see, yet someone did murder him, Sir Samuel." Richard closed his notebook, as if suggesting that anything said next would be off the record. He leaned forward and spoke softly, almost conspiratorially. "Did he say anything to you, sir, anything at all? Was he worried about anything, did he seem anxious or upset?"

"No, not anxious. He was excited about the party, of course." Sir Samuel seemed to relax. "There hadn't been a party such as this at Hursley House since before his wife died, more than a decade ago. He wanted it to go well. Perhaps he was a touch on edge. But not worried, just . . ."

Richard looked at him expectantly. Sir Samuel adjusted his position in his chair.

"He wasn't an easygoing chap at the best of times. Rather a perfectionist. And when he felt important things were at stake, he could be—"

"Irritable?" Richard offered.

"I suppose that word is as good as any."

"So he was irritable last night. At any particular point in the evening or in general?"

"In general, I would say, although as the evening wore on, he became more so."

"He was having a good time, but was more irritable as the evening progressed?"

Sir Samuel nodded.

"If I may ask, sir," Lilian broke in. "You said Sir Henry could be edgy when he felt that important things were at stake. What important things were at stake last night?"

"The success of the party, I would imagine." Sir Samuel cleared his throat. "All of high society in attendance, and so forth."

Lilian thought that if the baronet really cared about the success of the party, he would've tried harder not to seem so irritable in public. But what did she know about high society parties? She wrote in her notebook. *What was at stake?*

She continued. "And this morning, sir, did you see him or notice anything when you came down to breakfast?"

"No, I was the last of the guests to arrive in the dining room. I wanted to make sure I was packed and ready to go right after breakfast. I should be back in London already, in fact—" Sir Samuel stood abruptly, glancing at his pocket watch. "It's time for me to go."

It was difficult for Lilian to hold back a look of surprise. But Sir Samuel was a busy man. And the country was dealing with dire political situations at the moment: Germany on the march, British citizens in peril, so many things to prepare in the eventuality of war. The home secretary couldn't be expected to hang around a country estate until a minor murder was solved, aristocrat or not. And there was obviously nothing he could contribute as a witness.

They walked him to the door and thanked him. *This is frustrating*, Lilian thought.

"Who would you like to see next, Chief Inspectors?" Constable Roper asked from the door. His face was placid, expectant. Lilian felt grateful for his calm support.

"What do you think, Davidson, shall we start with the twelfth baronet?" she asked.

Richard paused. "Considering top down as a strategy, we should actually speak with the brother first. Sir Ambrose."

"Agreed." Lilian looked at the constable and he nodded as he left.

# CHAPTER 27

Agatha thought that it was clever of Sir Samuel to volunteer to be the first interview. No one would stop the home secretary; he could do as he pleased. She looked around at everyone who remained at the table. They had all been so agitated earlier, and that made her wonder: *If you killed someone out of anger, would you still be angry after the subject was dead?* Every one of these people seemed so angry, except the writers and Lady Stella. Did that make the five of them more suspect or less suspect?

But the family members and even Rana Gupta were all exhibiting ill temper. Perhaps it was boredom that made them more irritable, or the feeling of all being trapped in that room together. But how would the murderer act? Certainly, she'd written many different reactions from the murderers in her novels and short stories in scenarios like this. Calm or angry. Nervous or oblivious. But this was real life. *If only she could be in the room while the police questioned each of them.* The police would never allow it, of course. She would have to make do with observing them as they waited.

Ngaio never felt bored. People in every situation fascinated her, and this was no exception. She had taken out her sketchbook and was sketching Rana Gupta. She was trying to be subtle, not looking straight at him unless he was looking away. He had a lovely profile, excellent bone structure. Yet his complexion was slightly gray, and he was fidgeting quite a lot. Surely, if you had nothing to think about but the murder, it would spin you into deeper distress. She was thankful for her sketchbook and pencils.

And what of Detective Chief Inspector Richard Davidson? He was a most interesting subject. She'd love to draw him, not that she'd get the chance. He wouldn't possibly sit for her during a murder investigation—she smiled to herself at that thought. When her fictional detective had met the artist Agatha Troy, in her last book, *Artists in Crime*, Troy had made a sketch of Inspector Alleyn. But they had met on holiday on an ocean liner, not during a murder investigation.

Ngaio turned a page and began sketching DCI Davidson from memory. It wasn't just that this man reminded her of Edward, her long-ago fiancé—there was something else. She liked the way he was so serious about the job, yet she felt an underlying a sense of humor in his professional attitude. He must enjoy being a detective in spite of the grisliness. She could understand that. Perhaps working out puzzles was something they had in common, although as a writer you did them backward. First you had to invent the murder, and then build in all the right clues, working your way from the end to the beginning, adding some red herrings, of course. And it had to make sense to the reader without giving the answer away too easily—although surprising them a bit was all right. But you couldn't just plop a new character in at the end and announce he was the murderer. Heaven forbid! Ngaio penciled a wry smile into her sketch of DCI Davidson that mirrored her own.

Margery was trying to write in her notebook but couldn't help listening. The family and Stella were speaking in low tones, but she could still hear what they said.

"Philippa, my dear," Lady Stella broke the silence. "And my dear Charles. Perhaps looking ahead to the future would keep your mind off the moment. Think about how you'll want to proceed."

"What do you mean?" Charles asked.

"You'll need to make a statement to the press before anything leaks out, for one." Stella folded her hands on the table. "And you'll need to contact your lawyers for the estate, make preparations for the funeral for the family, a memorial for the public. Your father was a highly regarded figure. There are many things that will need doing."

"Yes," Philippa said softly. "So many things to do." It did not sound as if this was going to help her keep her mind off the moment.

"Don't worry, Philippa," Ambrose broke in. "Everything will be taken care of in due time. There's no need to rush." Ambrose turned to Lady Stella. "I've always taken care of all of Henry's legal affairs. His papers are certainly in order."

"Thank you, Uncle Ambrose," Charles said, nodding. "That's very comforting. We'll need to go over everything together. As for a funeral and memorial, there is time for that, but thank you for mentioning it, Lady Stella. It might be a good thing to focus our thoughts on how we want to publicly express our respect for our father."

Margery thought that was an unusual way to phrase it. "Publicly express our respect." *Was that another way of saying, avoid telling the truth?* She had been making notes in her leather pocket notebook and she wrote the words down. *Publicly express our respect.* She could hear her main character, Albert Campion, saying those words in his high voice. Come to think of it, this whole scenario was ripe for a novel. But there were four authors in the room, and certainly they must all be thinking the same thing.

Margery had never been one for using accounts of real crimes in her fiction—she preferred inventing her crimes. But this scenario could go so many ways, there would be no reason to stick to the facts. She could change all the names, keep what she liked, make embellishments where needed, just as she always did when she wrote. Isn't that how they all worked? But the four of them couldn't all borrow the same bits and pieces; perhaps they'd need to discuss who would use what. She smiled inwardly at the thought—it might be interesting to see what each of them would write based on this experience. She started to chew the end of her pencil, then wrote in her notebook: *List the possible motives.*

What motive would she choose if she were writing this as a novel?

Dorothy smoothed her linen napkin on the table in front of her, then looked at her empty teacup. She certainly didn't want any more tea; her stomach was a roiling mess. Wilson had popped in to tell them that luncheon would be served soon, but she couldn't imagine eating. Sir Henry's face kept wavering in front of her, with his horrible mask of death. She closed her eyes and tried to put it into a literary perspective. It was certainly something that would fit into almost any of the Shakespearean tragedies. King Duncan's face would've been similar after Macbeth stabbed him; Polonius as well, after Hamlet ran him though with his sword, mistaking him for his uncle. Or perhaps more appropriate, Romeo after he drinks poison when he believes Juliet is dead. Yes, poison. The poison that must've been on Sir Henry's cigar. The poison specifically meant for Sir Henry. Probably cyanide. That would've taken Sir Henry quickly. What went through his mind in that quick last minute of his life? Did he know who killed him? She opened her eyes.

She felt a little guilty—after all, it was much worse for the family. She slid her glance around the table. Kate and Sofia had each other for comfort. Charles had Marie; Philippa had Juan. Her eyes lingered on Ambrose. His forearms rested on the table; his head hung low. Dorothy wondered what he was thinking. He had been comforting Sarah earlier and had calmed his nieces and nephew with his sympathetic yet common sense manner, but now he was lost in thought. Dorothy thought he looked rather pathetic, and no one was trying to comfort him. She felt helpless—being able to do something useful might make her feel better, but she couldn't think what she could possibly do. Just then, Constable Roper entered the door and they all looked up.

He nodded at Ambrose, who rose slowly. It was his turn. They left the room together.

# CHAPTER 28

In the morning room, Ambrose sat, but his body was animated. Reaching in his breast pocket for a cigarette, crossing his legs, tapping his cigarette on his silver case before lighting it, flicking his lighter, then drumming it on his knee instead of putting it away.

"Thank you for your patience," Richard began. "We know this must be terribly concerning for everyone, and we'll do our best to wrap everything up as quickly as possible."

"That's much appreciated, DCI Davidson."

"Could you start by telling us about your brother's demeanor at the party?"

Ambrose shifted, tapped his cigarette on the crystal ashtray on the side table next to him, and cleared his throat. "It was a very special night. Many of his admirers, his supporters, people that revered him, were in attendance. I know that the selling point was the Queens of Crime, but really my brother was popular enough to bring in most of the donations."

"I see, and his mood?"

"His mood?" Ambrose looked surprised. "Festive. Ebullient. When he was meeting with the public, he was the model noble-man. Everyone looked up to him and he was conscious of that position. He was very aware of his public persona and how impor-tant that was to people. A lot of people. To England. He represented success, the positive picture of an Englishman—he gave people hope."

"Did he seem worried or upset about anything?"

"Quite the contrary." Ambrose set his mouth.

"No issues came up?"

"He'd had a good deal of champagne by the end of the night." Ambrose furrowed his brow. "He might've seemed moody, champagne would do that to him sometimes. But I doubt anyone else would've noticed. Other than family."

"At the end of the evening—that is, early in the morning when the two of you had cigars in the library—was this moodiness apparent?" Richard was artfully using Ambrose's words, Lilian noted. "Did he say anything out of the ordinary?"

"No, I wouldn't say so. Perhaps he was irritable due to fatigue by then, but nothing unforgivable." Ambrose looked straight at Richard. "Nothing that would call for murder, certainly not."

"Right." Richard looked back at him. "What did you talk about at that late hour?"

"I hardly remember, probably the quality of the cigars, the caliber of the guests, love of family. So many things seemed to be at a cusp, his impending marriage to Sarah, Charles's election coming up soon and his engagement to Marie, Kate making plans for university, Philippa and Juan—" Ambrose stopped.

"Philippa and Juan?" Richard prodded.

"Nothing important. Just the reshuffling of position and arrangements that might happen after Henry's marriage to Sarah." Ambrose repositioned himself in the chair. "His daughter Philippa and her husband, Juan, live here, as do I when I'm not traveling, and Charles, and Kate when she's not at school, of course. Philippa has been the lady of the house, but things were going to change. It was inevitable." Ambrose brushed invisible ashes off his knee and folded his hands together.

Richard said, as if an afterthought. "When Wilson came in and was told to fill the cigars, did you stay till he got back?"

"No, I left just after Wilson went to fetch the cigars, as I said." Now Ambrose sounded testy, Lilian thought.

"And did you notice anything out of the ordinary?" Richard went on, his tone casual. "Such as, perhaps that the French windows were open. Or Sir Henry left his keys lying around, or someone else was seen nearby—anything that would help us understand how the fresh cigars that Wilson had just brought to the library were nowhere to be found the next morning when your brother was found dead."

Ambrose stared blankly at Richard, his eyes suddenly moist. "No, none of those things."

Richard's face grew more serious. "I'm sorry to have to ask this, Sir Ambrose, but do you have any opinion on how or why someone would've murdered your brother?"

"No opinion whatsoever." Ambrose regained his composure. "My brother was beloved by all his countrymen, close to his family, a pillar of respect and prosperity." This sounded, Lilian thought, almost like a prepared speech.

"Yet he was murdered, sir," Richard said, "and died a horrible death at the hand of someone. Someone who emptied the newly refreshed cigar box and left him the one poisoned cigar for the morning. Someone who must've known of his morning ritual."

"There are always people who are jealous, I suppose." Ambrose adjusted his suit jacket and looked from Richard to Lilian. "Perhaps someone waited in the garden after the party and came in the French windows."

"Can you tell me, please," Lilian spoke up. "Was Sir Henry still wearing his jacket and tie when you left him?"

"I believe he had untied his tie, but it was still around his neck." Ambrose looked off as if to prod his memory. "And he definitely still had on his jacket."

"Thank you."

"The only possibility," Ambrose continued, "was that someone came in from the garden, after Wilson left, after I went upstairs, after Henry left the library. There's no one here who wanted him dead."

"Yes, thank you, one more question, if you don't mind." Richard looked down at his notes as he spoke. "As his legal advisor, perhaps you could tell us who would benefit most from his estate."

Ambrose looked extremely uncomfortable. "His most recent will was very even-handed to all his children. Of course, Charles inherits the title and the estate, but his daughters are well taken care of."

"And yourself?" Lilian asked.

"I will receive an equal part from the family holdings, but money is of little consequence to me. Nothing is more important than family."

Lilian heard the passion and dedication in his voice, and she believed he meant what he said.

# CHAPTER 29

Brigid and Bernard had just finished carrying the last of the full luncheon trays up to the dining room. Wilson directed them to display the salads, cold meats, bread, and tureens of soup on the sideboard. They gathered the last of the breakfast dishes and cups on trays and made their way downstairs. Wilson had stayed in the dining room to make sure everyone had what they needed. Halfway down the stairs, Brigid stopped and looked at Bernard. He bumped into her with his tray, and she almost tumbled down the stairs.

"What are you playing at, Brigie?" Bernard asked.

"What are you going to tell the detectives?" Brigid's eyes were large and anxious.

"What do you mean?"

"I mean, what exactly are you going to tell them?"

"The answers to anything they ask."

"And nothing more."

"Nothing more." Bernard shuffled his tray of dishes to one hip and moved a hand to her shoulder. "Don't worry, Brigie. We didn't do nothing wrong and we didn't really see anything worth telling."

"Right." Brigid smiled weakly. "You're right. No need to worry."

*Then why did she feel so worried?* Brigid continued down the stairs, her tray feeling even heavier than before.

# CHAPTER 30

Wilson took a moment to arrange the luncheon platters and to check that the proper serving utensils were available. Margery had helped herself to one too many delicious cakes not long ago, but she thought it might be impolite to ignore the luncheon when they had gone to all the trouble of making it.

"Please pardon the informal buffet, but Cook thought it might be more comfortable for you to make your own choices," Wilson said. "Of course, I'm happy to serve if anyone wishes."

There was a general muttering of *No, thank you*, and Wilson stood by the sideboard ready to serve if needed. His face displayed its usual professional demeanor, but the strain and fatigue certainly showed through.

Margery looked at Ngaio and they rose together. When they stood in front of the display of platters, Ngaio spoke in a low tone to Margery, making enough clinking noise with the plates and cutlery to cover the conversation.

"What are you thinking, Margery?" Ngaio muttered. And then a little louder: "This ham looks lovely!" She put some on her plate.

"Charles must benefit the most, in the inheritance department," Margery said in a low tone. "But that fight with Sarah last night won't leave my mind."

"A crime of passion," Ngaio nodded. "No inheritance for Sarah, however."

"If money isn't the motive, it could very well be one of the servants," Margery looked over the selection in the bread basket. "How long could you be subservient to someone so nasty without going to pieces?"

Ngaio glanced at the constable, but he was pacing at the back of the room. "If that's the motive, it could be any one of his children." She nodded assuredly and turned from the buffet; Margery followed and resisted taking a bite of a bun as they moved back to their seats. She wished she could be alone with just the other three writers so they could speak freely. Being stuck with the family was maddening.

Bernard came in, spoke to Wilson for a moment, and then took his place as Wilson left the dining room. Bernard stood at the end of the buffet, his roguish smile out of place among all the gloomy faces in the room.

Some of the others rose to fill their plates with food, and then Charles was summoned for his interview. He touched Marie's arm before following Constable Roper from the dining room. As Margery watched him go, she thought he looked a decade older than the day before. No matter how unsatisfying a father Sir Henry may have been, she found it hard to picture Charles as a murderer. But then again, she thought, she was beginning to realize it was quite difficult to guess who was a murderer in real life.

# CHAPTER 31

Sir Charles, the twelfth baronet, came into the morning room and nodded to the detectives. He began speaking before he sat down.

"How can I help, detectives?" Charles asked. His suit fit him well and was of the best quality wool; his shirt was pure white and starched, his cufflinks heavy gold. But his dark hair had a cowlick that made him look younger than his twenty-six years, Lilian thought.

"Perhaps you can start by telling us anything that happened during the evening that seemed unusual or out of the ordinary." Richard smiled amiably, as if they were having a discussion about the latest cricket match.

"For one, we hadn't had a party like this at Hursley House since I was a child."

"Of course. But I meant, did anything strike you as odd, was your father worried about anything, did he seem as if anything was troubling him?"

"No, not at all. He was enjoying the event. He had many friends and business associates who attended. He was quite busy." Charles sat up ramrod straight as he spoke. "So busy, in fact, I barely spoke to him all evening—he was in high demand. I had wanted him to introduce me to a few particular dignitaries, to speak about my campaign, but it never happened."

"Any particular associates he spent the most time with?" Davidson asked.

"No one comes to mind." Charles tried to relax in the chair, but his body wouldn't cooperate. "It all seems so trifling now." Lilian found herself feeling real pity for him.

She spoke up. "Earlier, Sir Charles, it was mentioned that your father sent your younger sister to bed at a certain point in the evening. Would you tell us about that?"

"It was nothing. Kate had a little too much champagne. Father didn't want her to embarrass herself. I really don't know what else I can tell you." He paused, straightened his cuffs, and stood.

"Perhaps if you think of anything else, you'll let us know," Richard said as he stood.

As he left Richard looked at Lilian.

"We'll get nothing out of the family," she said with a small grimace. "That's plain to see."

Richard sighed. "We have to be careful not to upset them."

"I suppose the aristocracy is more sensitive than the usual Londoner." Lilian glanced at PC Lee, who nodded.

# CHAPTER 32

Agatha toyed with the food on her plate at the dining room table. She didn't mind quiet, in fact usually preferred it. But the tension in the room was deafening. They had given up on conversation— what would be the use of chatting politely when all they could think about was the murder? Sir Samuel hadn't returned; she supposed he had given himself leave to go back to London. Ambrose and Charles had come back from their interviews, and Philippa was taking her turn. Ambrose was doing his best to pretend he was eating, but Agatha could see that the food was only being moved around his plate. He occasionally gave Sarah an encouraging look.

Charles was doing a bit better with his lunch plate, but young men had that type of constitution, didn't they? They could always eat, she mused. Agatha's glance lingered on Marie. Charles's fiancée was a gorgeous woman and, from what Agatha had observed, a kind and intelligent person. She would be Lady Marie soon, after they were wed. Agatha wondered if that meant something to her. She came to England from the Caribbean to marry Charles, and now she was in a world she couldn't possibly have imagined.

But then, marriage is never what you expect. Agatha's first husband went off to war soon after they were married. Perhaps they had rushed the decision, they hadn't known each other well enough, but the blush of young love is stronger than reason. That was all water under the bridge now. Her second husband, Max, was a much better match for her. Life works its way round as it should. She looked at the other people in the dining room, glad that no one could read her mind. What strange thoughts bubble up when you're trapped in a room with near strangers! Agatha looked at Dorothy, who was making notes in her book. *What could she be scribbling?*

Dorothy looked up from her notes as if someone had called her name. But everyone was silent. She had broken from being lost in thought as if she'd returned from another room. It was like that when she was writing. She was distracting herself by taking down anything she could think of that wasn't about murder. Shakespeare quotes, bible passages, epic poetry she had memorized in school, anything to keep the image of Sir Henry's death mask out of her mind. She glanced around the room at the faces of the family and friends of Sir Henry, one of whom might be the murderer. Her stomach lurched at the thought. *Except us*, she thought, and looked at the other three writers. If only they could discuss the case, talking it through out loud would certainly make her feel better. It would release the invasive thoughts that kept running around in her head. She glanced up at the constable and was surprised to see he was looking right at her. They both averted their eyes.

*If we can't talk, perhaps we can write*, she thought.

She carefully tore a page from her notebook and wrote at the top. *Questions and Possibilities*. Then, leaving space between each line, she wrote: *What did Sir Henry and Lady Sarah fight about? Why did Sir Henry send Kate and Sofia to bed before the party was over? What happened to the cigars? Why didn't Sir Henry have on his jacket and tie when they found him?*

Dorothy looked to make sure the constable wasn't watching and slipped the piece of paper to Agatha. Agatha put down her fork and pulled the paper into her lap to read it. She looked at Dorothy and nodded, then slid the paper between her plate and a napkin, out of view of the constable, and started writing, her graceful script filling in some of her own questions and possibilities.

# CHAPTER 33

The door to the morning room opened and Philippa entered. Lilian stood and watched Philippa pause in the frame of the door, the light from the hallway surrounding her with a glow. Then she moved forward, her dark green dress rustling softly, her hair perfectly pinned up in a chignon.

"I am so sorry we have to keep you all so long and bother you with our questions," Richard said, his tone low, as he walked her to the love seat and waited for her to sit down.

"It's quite understandable, Chief Inspector," Philippa said. "But I do appreciate your apology. This is not exactly what I expected to be doing this Saturday morning. Not mourning my father nor speaking to Scotland Yard." She sat and plucked a lace handkerchief from her sleeve.

Richard paused a moment and looked at Lilian, who asked. "Last night, did your father seem worried or upset about anything?"

"I wouldn't use either of those words to describe his mood, but he wasn't in an especially festive mood, that is certain."

"How do you mean?" Lilian asked.

"He was prickly." She dabbed at her nose with the lace handkerchief. "My father and my husband often sparred over politics; it was their sport, you might say. But last night Father was downright rude and things became heated. They rarely agreed, but for some reason Father suddenly seemed to take it all rather personally."

"Take what personally?" Lilian spoke gently.

"Juan is an expatriate from Spain. He escaped when Franco was declared head of state. Juan is decidedly anti-fascist."

"And your father was not?"

Philippa paused. Lilian saw the look on her face change, as if she had suddenly reined in her emotions.

"It's just that my father was decidedly anti-communist." Philippa shifted her position. "It was a difference of opinion between them. That's all. Nothing dramatic."

"Did they argue last night?" Lilian asked casually.

"Certainly not. I wouldn't call it an argument. Simply a discussion. And as I said, my father was in an irritable mood. They've had many political discussions in the past, with no dramatic conclusions." Her tone said she was finished talking about the subject.

"Thank you, Lady Philippa," Richard said politely. "Did you notice anything unusual about the evening, anyone else in conflict with your father?"

"In conflict? No, I didn't notice anyone in conflict with my father. He was a gentleman. Public conflict was not something he engaged in." She tucked her lace handkerchief into her sleeve. "Are you finished with me, Chief Inspector?" She directed her question at Richard, pointedly ignoring Lilian. Despite all of Lilian's experience interviewing women, and the fact that she usually got better results than the men detectives, it was clear that Lady Philippa was from a different world.

"One last question, if you don't mind." Richard used his best smile. "You were at the door, saying good night to guests with your husband, and it seems during that time your father retired to the library. Did you see him with anyone? Did he say good night to you, or did you go upstairs without seeing your father?"

Philippa paused. Her eyes were suddenly shiny. "My father was very busy at the end of the evening speaking to so many people, and Juan and I did our best to be good hosts. I didn't notice when my father left—there were so many people to talk to and suddenly they were all gone and so was my father and my uncle. Wilson was with the caterers. Juan and I just went upstairs, exhausted. If I had known it would be my last chance to speak with my father, I would've searched him out to say good night." Her voice cracked. "Are you quite finished with me?"

Richard stood and nodded. "Thank you, Lady Philippa. We are so sorry to bother you with so many questions at this time."

Philippa rose, smoothed the skirt of her silk dress and walked out with the carriage of a royal. Lilian watched her go, not sure what to think of her performance.

"I told you," Lilian said to Richard. "The family is going to be of no help."

"She did admit there was an argument with Juan."

"In a way," Lilian said, and made a note in her book.

Roper entered and reported that the team had finished searching all the rooms. "And we locked the bedroom of the deceased and posted a guard, sir, as requested, so you can search it yourselves."

"Right. We'll take a look," said Richard. "Anything interesting in the other rooms?"

"No, sir, they wrote up their findings, but they said nothing in particular stood out in any of the bedrooms. However, they did find the baronet's jacket and tie in the sitting room, across the hall from the library. That was the room they used as a cloakroom for the party."

*The missing jacket and tie.* Lilian looked at Richard.

"Thank you, Roper. Please lock off that sitting room as well and tell the guests they are free to leave the dining room and use their rooms now as they wish, but not to leave the house. It may give them some calm. Oh, and bring Miss Kate next."

Roper gave a short nod and left.

"Jacket and tie found in the sitting room," Lilian murmured. "The room that was being used as a cloakroom. Why would he go there after Ambrose went to bed and Wilson went to get cigars?"

"Perhaps he didn't want to bother to go upstairs to his room since he was going to have his coffee and his walk with the dogs in just a few hours," DC Lee spoke up.

"Could be," Richard said. "Or perhaps there was another reason."

Lilian was trying to think of one when Roper returned.

"The four writer ladies said they'd wait in the dining room, Chief Inspectors." Roper announced. Lilian hid her smile at Roper's term *writer ladies*. "And, erm—"

Roper opened the door wider to reveal both Kate and Sofia.

# CHAPTER 34

The family had been released, and the four writers had decided to stay in the dining room and wait for their interview. It was a relief that it was only the four of them left. The very air in the room felt buoyant after the family and the constable had departed.

Margery was the most excited. Her straight dark hair, cut blunt just below her chin with a determined fringe across her forehead, gave her face an earnest look. She jumped right into the discussion. "Neither Charles nor Philippa seemed especially sad," she pointed out.

"Would you, with a father like that?" Ngaio replied. "It doesn't necessarily mean they murdered him."

"I'm not sure we should be talking this way." Dorothy seemed concerned. "Are we allowed to talk about it now?"

"As opposed to writing notes?" Agatha asked. "Since when are you the rule follower, Dorothy?"

"It's not about following rules," Dorothy pushed her teacup away. "I'm just thinking how this is a real murder, not something made up in one of our books. It feels . . . dangerous."

"Dangerous?" Agatha's eyebrows rose. "To whom? To us?"

"What if there is a murderer in this house? Would we be putting our lives in danger by getting involved?" Dorothy looked at the other three women.

"You mean he might start picking us off one by one?" Agatha was thinking more about how that might work in a novel then the actual possibility.

"That's somewhat dramatic, Dorothy," Ngaio said. "This isn't fiction."

"But if it were"—Margery jumped in excitedly—"whom would you write it to be?"

"Agatha would choose the least likely suspect, of course," Ngaio said. Agatha lifted her teacup to her with a smile and a nod. "And Dorothy's murderer would have been driven mad with revenge."

"Am I that predictable?" Dorothy harrumphed.

"Never predictable, no! Not in guessing the suspect," Margery exclaimed. "What better reasons for murder than madness and revenge?"

"And me, Marge?" Ngaio was intrigued. "What allegory follows my books?"

"Your murderers tend to get something more practical out of their crimes, like money or position, or they might be fueled by jealousy."

"I see, so my themes tend to be fairly humdrum." Ngaio made a face.

"Not at all! I would use the word logical," Margery said. "And as for myself—"

But Agatha broke in. "No, please, Marge, allow me. I would say there is a general theme of egomania with your murderers. But you hide them well until the end."

"I'll accept that." Margery smiled. "I think we all write about what we would like to see done in reality."

"I suppose we try to fix the world in our fantasies," Ngaio agreed.

"So, back to my question," Margery continued. "Whom would you write this murderer to be?"

"This isn't a fantasy," Dorothy said sharply. "I'm only suggesting we exercise caution, that's all. And maybe if we take it seriously, we can actually be useful."

# CHAPTER 35

"Ah, ladies, thank you," Richard said. "Just Miss Kate Heathcote for the moment."

The two young women clutched hands.

"I'll wait right outside for you," Sofia said, with her soft accented cadence. Kate's eyes were grateful. Roper closed the door behind Kate.

"Please sit here," Lilian pointed to the love seat across from her.

Kate perched on the edge of the cushion and looked expectant. "I don't want you to think we usually argue like that, my siblings and I." Her eyes were still puffy from crying, but Lilian thought she seemed much calmer. "We're all rather on edge, understandably. Charles is under a lot of pressure, and Philippa, she's always felt the burden as lady of Hursley House."

Kate seemed sincere, but Lilian detected an undertone of sarcasm or perhaps jealousy.

"Your father relied on her for that?" Lilian asked.

"Yes, although lately I thought the weight of it was transferring to Sarah. But then—" She stopped and looked around the room, as if she had forgotten what she was going to say.

"But then?" Lilian prompted.

"That's all over now, isn't it?" Kate looked at her blankly. "Sarah didn't actually become part of the family, did she?"

Lilian waited a moment before continuing. "Are you close to Lady Sarah?"

"We're not close, but I like her just fine. Philippa never really warmed up to her. Not that she was against the marriage." Kate straightened the cuff of the three-quarter sleeve of her cream blouse. "But when the amount of your inheritance is subject to change because of your father's impending marriage . . ." She chose not to finish the thought.

"Wasn't your inheritance subject to change as well?" Lilian asked.

"Unlike my sister, I will have a career." Kate's mouth was in a straight line. "Not that I judge Philippa for the life she chose. She just isn't very modern."

"I see." Lilian wrote a few notes. She wondered what kind of career Kate had planned, but that wasn't relevant.

Richard cleared his throat, and Kate looked at him as if she had forgotten he was there.

"Miss Kate, did your father seem under any unusual strain or worry last night?" Richard asked.

Kate smoothed her dark coffee-colored skirt. "Strain or worry?" She seemed to be carefully considering her answer. "Not at all."

Lilian wondered for the hundredth time how much easier her job would be if she could read minds.

"Yet he sent you to bed early," Richard pointed out.

"My father was strict." Kate shifted in her seat. "But he was a good father." Her face began to crinkle, but no tears flowed. "He was a good balance to Uncle Ambrose. Between the two of them, we had an excellent upbringing."

"How is your Uncle Ambrose different from your father?" Richard asked.

"To put it simply, Uncle Ambrose isn't the strict type." Kate tilted her head to one side. "They were both protective. Just in different ways."

"I understand. So, last night, your father didn't seem particularly distressed or perturbed about anything?"

Kate looked at them both for a moment. They waited.

"There was a row between him and Sarah just before I was sent to bed." Kate shrugged. "Perhaps that's why he was so severe with me. She put him in a bad mood."

"What was the disagreement about?" Richard asked.

"I have no idea."

At that, Kate shut down. Whether she thought she'd said too much or had decided that she was finished cooperating, Lilian wasn't sure. After some useless careful prodding, they let her go.

Sofia was waiting at the door so Richard brought her in for her interview. She took a few moments to get comfortable, shifting her position one way, then the other. She was wearing a loose tan skirt and cream blouse with a wine-colored silk scarf tied around her throat that Lilian thought was quite flattering. She was tall and wore her dark hair in a long braid that she held in front of her, fiddling with the end of it.

"I don't know if I have anything to tell you that can help." Sofia's English was perfect, her Italian accent coming out only in the most subtle way. "It is my first visit at Kate's family home."

"How long have you known Miss Kate?" Lilian asked.

"We met at school, last year, but we became closer friends in the last few months." She smiled shyly.

"Is it a nice school?" Lilian smiled.

"Oh, yes." Sofia's eyes lit up. "We have the loveliest teachers, and all the girls get on so well."

"And had Miss Kate told you much about her family?"

"Yes, we tell each other everything." She was obviously proud of this.

"Since this is your first time visiting, did anything surprise you?"

"I don't know what you mean." Sofia's left eyebrow arched.

"I mean, did everyone seem as you expected them to be?" Lilian didn't know if this sideways questioning was better or worse than the direct approach.

"I suppose they were." Sofia paused. "Perhaps they all seemed bigger than life to me, if you know what I mean."

"Yes, I think I do." Lilian thought Sofia's family must be quite different from Kate's. "Tell us about when Sir Henry sent you both to bed. How would you describe his mood?"

Sofia pulled at the end of her braid, her long fingernails combing through the thick fringe. "I don't like to speak ill of the dead," she said softly. "But I felt he was quite rude. To break us up in the middle of our dancing. Send us to bed like children." Her dark eyes flashed as she looked up at them.

Richard spoke up. "Did this surprise you? That is, had he acted differently before? Perhaps more polite?"

"Polite, yes. Warm, not at all. But I understood he was not a warm person."

"Mis Kate told you that?" Lilian asked.

"In things she told me, I understood him as he was." Sofia fiddled with the silk scarf at her throat. "It did not surprise me. And as I saw him that evening, we were not the only ones who experienced his rudeness."

*Ah, at last someone was talking.* Lilian was careful not to seem eager as she continued, "Who else did you see him be rude to?"

"Lady Sarah got the force of his mood as well."

At Lilian's questioning look, Sofia continued. "Sir Henry seemed to have a disagreement with Lady Sarah, yes."

"Did you hear what it was about?"

"No, we were dancing, they were dancing, and the music was loud." Sofia scrunched her face. "Perhaps something to do with her mother? I thought I heard something like that."

"Her mother? Lady Sarah's mother wasn't here last night, was she?" Lilian asked.

"Oh, no, no, no. I don't believe so." She shook her head. "I just thought I heard Sir Henry say something about her mother."

Lilian and Richard looked at each other for a moment. This was a piece of the puzzle that didn't fit.

"Thank you, Miss Sofia." Richard stood. "You've been extremely patient with us. Much appreciated."

Sofia jumped up off the seat and took her leave, and Richard told Roper to bring Marie Sinclair in to see them.

"I'm getting a clearer picture of the baronet," Richard said to Lilian. "Was he really the popular and beloved public figure that we know from the newspapers and radio?"

"Doesn't seem to be. Let's back up a moment." Lilian looked through her notes. "According to everyone's time line, they were all in bed before Wilson filled the cigar box. Yet this morning, Sir Henry only had one choice of cigar, the poisoned one."

"So sometime after three forty in the morning when Wilson filled the cigar box and before six o'clock when the staff woke to start breakfast"—Richard looked at his notes—"or at least before seven forty when Sir Henry returned from running the dogs, someone emptied the cigar box and left one poisoned cigar."

Lilian nodded. "Someone who had access to the key." She glanced at her list. "Wilson and Sir Henry had the only keys. What does Wilson do with the keys when he's off duty?"

"We'll ask," said Richard. "Were Sir Henry's keys found on the body?"

"In his pocket. No discernible fingerprints according to DS Randal."

"Pardon me, detectives?" DC Lee spoke up. "Do we know if Sir Henry was right-handed or left-handed?"

"No, why do you ask?" Richard replied.

"I was wondering because the baronet's keys were in his left trouser pocket."

The two detectives looked at each other.

"Well done, DC Lee," Lilian said approvingly. "If he was right-handed, that would seem odd."

"Someone might've taken them and put them back in the wrong pocket," DC Lee agreed.

"The way he was lying on the sofa, the left trouser pocket would've been the easier one to slip the keys into," Lilian added. "Or he might've just slipped them in that pocket himself, if his other hand was busy."

They each thought their own thoughts for a moment.

Constable Roper peeked in the door. "Miss Marie Sinclair," he announced.

# CHAPTER 36

Agatha was standing by the window in the dining room, arms akimbo, face flushed. Ngaio was guarding the door, and Margery had placed three dining room chairs together to act as the sofa. Dorothy remained at the table, a reluctant audience.

"Now, he would have his coffee," said Agatha, gesturing. "Ngaio, you be Brigid and bring in the tray."

"Yes, I'd knock first, then he'd answer, and I'd open the door with the key." Ngaio mimed this action and carried an invisible tray to the "sofa."

"Margery, you be Sir Henry."

Margery fell into character easily and sipped the invisible coffee. "Then I go to the French windows and open them." She walked toward the windows.

"With a key—the French windows were also locked," Agatha reminded them.

"Yes, I open it with a key, then out I go and lock it behind me." Margery mimed the actions.

"Does he lock it behind him?" Ngaio asked.

"I would imagine so," Agatha answered. "Why be so careful to keep it locked and then leave it unlocked for the dog run?"

"That has to be the case, then," said Ngaio. "But I can't help thinking that he surely had little or no sleep, and how precise could he have been thinking or acting?"

"It's a good point," replied Agatha. "Just another one of the contributing factors on the list. Perhaps he was still under the influence of champagne and whiskey? Whatever the case, he routinely kept the library locked, so we should start with that assumption."

Margery turned from the window as if she was just entering.

"Then I return from taking out the dogs, close and lock the door behind me, sit on the sofa and open the cigar box." Margery walked to the three chairs that were substituting for a sofa and sat. She mimed opening the cigar box.

"And then you say, 'That barmy butler, I told him to fill this box, but there's only one cigar in it!'" Agatha did an excellent impression of Sir Henry. The other writers couldn't keep from laughing.

"Be that as it may," Dorothy commented. "He smoked that last cigar, or started to, and it did him to death." They all went silent.

Margery reclined across the chairs on her side, feet at one end, her head propped up on one elbow.

"One thing for sure, both doors were locked when Brigid found him," Ngaio said. "So someone either got hold of Wilson's keys, or they took them off Sir Henry and put them back before he would notice."

"Or after he would notice," Agatha said.

"You mean after he was already dead?"

"It's possible." Agatha explained, "After everyone went to bed, Wilson filled the cigar box, then he went to his room. Someone slipped into Wilson's room when he was sleeping, or took the keys from Sir Henry before he returned to the library for his coffee and dog run."

"In either case, they would also have to return the keys without anyone noticing," Margery mused.

"And have gotten rid of the cigars they removed," Ngaio said. "Maybe we should be looking for the cigars."

"And the poison," Agatha mentioned. "Wherever they got the poison from, there should be some evidence of it somewhere. If the police haven't found the cigars, or evidence of poison, perhaps they need help looking."

The four women looked at one another.

After a moment Dorothy spoke. "Perhaps we can have some conversations that could result in interesting information. One never knows what one might unearth in a casual chat."

The others nodded. "You're right," Agatha said. "Of course we wouldn't interfere with the investigation. But we couldn't be faulted for finding something important that would help the case."

Murmurs of agreement and more nods. They all stood and replaced the three chairs that had stood in for the sofa.

"So whatever we find," Margery said, "whomever finds whatever, we'll share the information amongst ourselves, and with the detectives, agreed?"

They all nodded.

"And if we help solve the case—"

"*When* we help solve the case," Agatha said.

"When it's all said and done," Margery continued, "we can decide what bits and pieces we can each use in our novels."

"What do you mean?" Ngaio asked.

"I mean, we can't all use all the details of this murder. We'd have to decide who gets to use what, otherwise our books will have too many clues or characters or motives in common."

That stopped them. From their expressions, it was clear that the others hadn't been thinking about this.

"Margery is right," Agatha said. "If we are inspired in our writing by any part of this real murder, we may have to divide up the particulars so our next efforts don't appear to be copying each other."

They stood in a cluster by the door, each looking at the other writers, thinking this through.

"It's not something we need to decide in the moment," Margery added. "It's just been rolling around in my head and it popped out."

"Yes, that's something to talk about later," Ngaio said. "Let's not get ahead of ourselves. We have to solve the case first."

"Perhaps if we write it all down," Dorothy said. "It will begin to make some sense."

They all sat back at the table, making notes, discussing new ideas, and staring off into the distance.

# CHAPTER 37

Marie, Charles's fiancée, took her seat in the interview room, her large brown eyes looking at two chief inspectors expectantly. Lilian thought she had never seen such striking eyelashes. Marie's dark hair was pulled back with combs so that a cascade of tiny curls fell down the back of her yellow dress, which was dotted with tiny white flowers. Richard welcomed her politely and asked her to confirm her final movements the night before.

"Charles and I took Kate and Sofia upstairs. Kate wasn't happy about it, but she wasn't going to disobey the baronet."

"Do you mind describing how it came about that Kate was sent to bed?" Lilian asked.

"I'm not sure I can help with that," Marie said. "I missed what happened—all I know is it was something on the dance floor."

"And did you hear Sir Henry send her to bed?"

"No, but I was quite tired, so I was happy to go along with the girls when Charles waved me over."

"But the girls weren't happy about going to bed?"

Marie smiled. "They wanted to keep dancing. On the way up they talked about dancing in the upper hall, but Charles put a stop to that. He said he was putting them in their rooms, and they'd better not come out and risk Sir Henry finding them."

"And that was enough to convince them?"

Marie paused and thought about her next sentence carefully. "You see, Kate was in deliberation with her father about allowing her to go to Oxford after next year, and she knew that anything she did to displease her father would put that in jeopardy."

"Sir Henry was against her continuing her studies?" Lilian asked.

"He wasn't one to support women of their social ranking going to university." Marie was choosing her words carefully.

"Is Charles against it?"

Marie looked surprised, as if it had just occurred to her that her fiancé would now have this particular power over his sister. "I don't think he's against it, no. That's how Charles and I met, at university. He thinks Kate is very intelligent, if a bit impulsive. Why shouldn't she go to Oxford?"

No one answered her question, since she seemed to be asking it of herself. Richard continued. "And before you went to your room for the night, did you notice anything about Sir Henry, or his activities, anyone he spoke to, that seemed contentious?"

"Contentious? Well—just that Sir Henry and Lady Sarah seemed to have some sort of disagreement when they were dancing. But Ambrose cut in and danced away with Lady Sarah."

"And was Sir Henry left on the dance floor?"

"I believe Sir Samuel came up to him, making a joke or something because they were both laughing soon after."

"Do you know what the argument with Lady Sarah was about?"

"I wasn't close enough to hear anything, but I'm sure it was more a disagreement than an argument."

"And did anything else stick out in the evening as contentious with Sir Henry?"

"Not contentious, no."

"Something else then?"

"Something a little odd, I suppose. Later in the evening Sir Samuel asked me to dance. He seemed irritated, and I asked him if he preferred to dance another time. But he apologized and said no, he was fine, it was just that Sir Henry had introduced him to some brutes. I must've looked surprised, because then he laughed and then called them posh ruffians and changed the subject."

"Do you know their names?" Lilian wrote down *posh ruffians.*

"He didn't say who they were and then it was just a little while later that Charles was taking Kate and Sofia out of the ballroom and Charles caught my eye. I was glad to go with them. I'm not one for staying late at parties."

Lilian looked at this young woman, beautiful, refined, yet seeming much more down to earth than either Heathcote sister. And much more so than Charles. Lilian hoped Marie would influence Charles, and not the other way around.

"And did Charles say anything about his father?"

"About his father? No, he was very busy meeting people and talking about his campaign. That was one reason I didn't feel bad about going to bed. Charles was practically working all night."

They concluded the interview and Richard walked Marie Sinclair to the door.

"That's two accounts of the row between Henry and Sarah," he said to Lilian.

"I'm very interested to hear Lady Sarah's version."

"Let's have her next, then, shall we, Roper?" Richard looked to the constable, who left to fetch her.

# CHAPTER 38

Mrs. Anderson and Mr. Wilson sat at the servants table in the kitchen. Their teacups were empty, but neither of them moved to clear them or refill them. Mr. Wilson was tapping his fingers on the table, and Mrs. Anderson was deep in thought.

"Don't worry, Elspeth." Mr. Wilson touched her arm gently.

Elspeth Anderson looked at his kind face. She was a good twenty years younger than the white-haired butler, and she usually appreciated his fatherly support. But at the moment she felt his comment was impractical and perhaps somewhat patronizing.

"Which things shouldn't I worry about, Mr. Wilson?" She slowly stood. "Taking care of our guests as they are uncomfortably detained? Serving an extra battalion of constables and detectives? Wondering about who might've poisoned our master? And not in the very least, if and/or when England may be under siege by the Nazis?"

She shook her head as she swept up their teacups and took them to the sideboard. *Men and their condescension. Ridiculous.* She had too much to do to indulge herself in worry. There was a house full of people to take care of!

# CHAPTER 39

Constable Roper opened the door wide for Lady Sarah. She came in rather timidly. Lilian felt sorry for her—she looked blanched, lost, and exhausted. More like a victim than a perpetrator.

Lilian began. "Thank you for speaking with us, Lady Sarah. Our deepest condolences on the loss of your fiancé."

"Thank you." Her voice was not much more than a whisper.

"I'm sure you are still in shock over what has happened," Lilian said. "It's not easy to take in the death of a loved one."

"I can't understand who would want to do this." She turned her large blue eyes to Lilian. "Or *why*, why someone would do this?" She shivered a little and clutched an embroidered handkerchief.

"That's what we're going to find out, Lady Sarah. We hope you can help us."

"I'll try. I just can't think straight. I can't help thinking that we're all in danger somehow."

Lilian and Richard looked at each other.

"Why do you say that?" Lilian asked.

"It must be some crazed lunatic, targeting this family, this household. Who of us might be next? What else could it be? I can't think of anyone in our lives who would do this." Lady Sarah dabbed at her eyes. "Ambrose agrees, and he knew his brother best. This had to be someone who didn't know Henry. Some political adversary or business rival."

Richard kept his head down, taking notes.

Lilian continued. "During the last few weeks, is there anything you can think of that was different or suspicious connected to Sir Henry?"

Lady Sarah took a shaky breath. "Suspicious, no. Everything was going wonderfully, especially these last few weeks. I don't know any details, but he was involved in some business deals that were going rather well. He told me he was having the best success of his life. We were planning our wedding and a wonderful honeymoon trip. He was happy. We were happy." Tears started to flow.

Lilian took a moment to pour a glass of water from a glass pitcher and put it on the side table closest to the almost-widow. "Was there anyone you can think of who was against these recent business deals? Someone who was jealous, perhaps, or a competitor?"

"No, I really didn't know what the deals were about. We never talked business."

"Was there anyone at the party who was involved in this business?"

"It's possible. There were gentlemen I didn't know who Henry spoke with much of the evening. It's possible they were business associates."

"I see. Was there anything that happened last night that wasn't business related, some family argument or tension, that you may have noticed?"

Lady Sarah looked at Lilian sharply. "If you are referring to the slight disagreement Henry and I had at the end of the evening, that was less than nothing. A lovers' spat from too much champagne, a misunderstanding that was settled as quickly as it came up."

Lilian flipped a few pages in her notebook. "So in these last few weeks he was happier and more positive than ever, and he wasn't worried or fearful about anything."

"Yes, that's correct."

They thanked her and let her go. It was clear that there would be nothing else Lady Sarah would contribute.

"What do you think are the chances it was some crazed business competitor?" Richard asked Lilian.

"Slim to none, Chief Inspector, slim to none."

"You don't think someone could have hidden in the garden and waited until the library was free?"

"I don't think anyone outside of the family or house staff knew of his morning cigar habit." Lilian shifted in her chair. "I doubt if even his whole family knew of it. They'd have to know that to get the tricky timing right. As it is, how someone was able to get into the library and make the switch without Sir Henry knowing, well, that's stumped us so far."

They agreed that every guest's whereabouts after they left the party should be checked out, and sent DC Lee to call Scotland Yard to put that in motion.

# CHAPTER 40

Juan Guerra, Philippa's husband, was next to be interviewed. Richard began with his usual questions.

"I would say, yes, that Sir Henry was in a certain mood last evening." Juan was polite and serious. "But I wouldn't place the cause on the party—he seemed to have been losing his humor lately, for more than a few weeks."

"How do you mean?"

Juan took out a gold cigarette case, removed a cigarette, and snapped the case shut, but he did not smoke. "I wouldn't have made much of it until last night, but he seemed to be even more severe in his opinions of late. Many times, we have discussed politics and disagreed, but lately he was quite, eh, militant is the word I would say."

"Can you give an example?"

Juan thought for a moment. "You know my background. I left Spain when the fascists took over. It's not a unique position here in England. But lately I have been following the union strikes. If I mentioned it to Sir Henry, that the workers should be paid better wages, deserved better working conditions, he exploded at me. And last night—" Juan suddenly stopped. He seemed to consciously make his expression placid before he spoke again.

"Last night, he introduced me to some of his fellow industrialists"— Juan said this with a subtle amount of distaste—"and he brought up the subject himself and made sure to disagree with me in front of them about my politics. They all joined him in their collective humiliation of my opinions."

"That sounds unpleasant."

"Let's just say it was a lively conversation, but I made my exit as soon as I found an excuse."

"Were you angry?" Lilian jumped in. Richard gave her a glance. *Too direct?*

"Angry? No, I wouldn't say I was angry. Sir Henry could be irksome, but he was who he was. He liked to be right, especially when it came to his family. It was impossible to disagree with him, or useless you might say." Juan looked tired. "If you disagreed with him, he would do everything he could to prove his point until whoever he was in contention with would give in. He would even withhold money or favors. Honestly, it was a waste of time to disagree with him. Much easier to just go along or change the subject."

"Yet you would entertain these contentious discussions on a regular basis."

"I would get pulled into them. Sir Henry would goad me and I sometimes would fall for it. More often than I like to admit." Juan straightened his jacket. "I won't miss it." He looked straight at Richard. "But I didn't kill him."

"Thank you, that's very helpful," Richard said without any irony. "You said he would withhold money for favors. Can you tell us what you mean by that?"

"Not from me, I am independent, but he was constantly using Philippa's allowance as a bargaining chip."

"But as the wife of an independent gentleman, did she still need her allowance?" Lilian tried to say it in a way that wasn't insulting, but she was aware it came out awkward.

Juan looked at her with tired eyes.

"Need? It wasn't a matter of need, Chief Inspector, but there was . . . pride, and a certain amount of, I don't know, merit. Let me put it this way, in our level of society, the amount of allowance or inheritance given to a child, grown or not, measures something more. Do you understand?"

Lilian nodded. She understood. And it was not the first time in her life she was glad she came from the middle class and that her parents showed their love and affection in ways other than financial.

"Can you remember anything that happened recently, or longer ago, that might've led to the baronet's death?" Richard asked.

"No. Not a specific incident. But I will say that his mood, or perhaps I'll call it his negative energy, seemed to be mounting the last few weeks." Juan looked thoughtful. "It felt like he was letting go of some of his restraint. He was always a powerful man, nothing seemed to worry him, but he could be cautious. He certainly never wanted to do anything that would damage his businesses or his reputation. Yet, lately, he seemed . . ." Juan paused to think of the right word.

"Reckless?" Richard suggested.

Juan shook his head. "No, not reckless but fearless. In a different way than he had been."

"Fearless?" Lilian asked. "What do you mean?"

"He didn't understand the danger that he might be in," Juan said. "Danger he might attract from dangerous people."

"I see, Mr. Guerra," said Richard. "And what people do you mean?"

"I do not know these people that were at the party last night," Juan said. "But I know some of them were not good people. That's all I can say."

"How did you know they weren't good people?" Lilian asked.

Juan leaned forward. "By the look in their eyes. I have met many bad people in my life. They all have the same look. I cannot explain better than that."

Somehow Lilian knew what he meant. More often than not, the bad ones showed themselves. She wondered if he was referring to the same "posh ruffians" mentioned before. Juan said he didn't know them, but it fit with what Marie had told them.

"Thank you, Mr. Guerra," Richard said. "This has been very helpful. One last question, do you know if Sir Henry was left-handed or right-handed?"

Juan thought for a moment.

"Right-handed, I believe." He stood and slowly moved toward the door, then stopped. "I just want to emphasize that Philippa loved her father very much. It wasn't a perfect relationship, but he meant a lot to her. This investigation, and how it is handled, is very important to her."

"We understand. We will do our best." Richard and Juan Guerra shook hands.

After he left, Richard remarked, "It seems the baronet was a complicated man."

"Beloved yet equally feared," Lilian added. "A tricky balance."

"So Sir Henry withheld allowance on a whim, withheld permission as ammunition, and withheld affection as a general rule."

"Delightful," Lilian mused.

Richard stood. "Look, we've been at this for hours. I think we should take a short break. Maybe Roper can get us some tea."

Lilian nodded.

"Actually, I could stretch my legs. I'll go to the kitchen." Lilian turned to Richard. "And maybe I'll indulge in some casual conversation with the house staff while the kettle boils."

# CHAPTER 41

Mrs. Anderson bustled to and fro, putting together a tea tray, while Lilian sat at the kitchen table.

"Don't trouble yourself with anything fancy, Mrs. Anderson, four hardy mugs will do for us."

"Oh, no, no, no, I'll make you a tray with a nice big pot and plenty of milk and sugar on the side. I'm sure you all need the sustenance to get you through till you have time for luncheon."

"You're too kind."

"And a small dish of biscuits wouldn't hurt."

Lilian felt rather touched. They were intruding on this household, making things tougher for everyone, especially the staff, and this woman was being perfectly lovely.

"Much appreciated, Mrs. Anderson."

Mrs. Anderson gave her a cup of still warm tea, the end of a pot, while she was waiting for the kettle to boil for the fresh one.

"Cream and sugar?"

"Oh, no, thank you, I like it plain."

"Same as me." Mrs. Anderson smiled, and she sat across from her and sipped her own cup.

Lilian had to control herself from downing the entire cup in the first sip. She hadn't realized how the morning of interviews had drained her.

"How are you holding up, Mrs. Anderson?"

"How sweet of you to ask, I'm fine, really." Her smile was tinged with sympathy. "I feel so for the children. They're not really children any more, of course, not even Miss Kate, but he was their father and this is such a terrible shock."

"Is there any one of them taking it worse than the rest?" Lilian asked, choosing her words carefully. "I want to be careful not to unduly upset anyone."

"I wouldn't say one was more upset than any other," Mrs. Anderson answered. "Although Miss Kate is always more excitable."

"That's understandable at her age. And how is the staff holding up? How is Brigid? Finding Sir Henry must've shaken her up."

"It certainly did, and I have to tell you, when I was at the library door, the sight of him was quite upsetting to me too." She shook her head. "How do you police handle the things you see in your job?"

"It isn't easy, but I think it takes a certain kind of person to do well in our job. I know police who can't stomach it, and I think it's just the wrong job for them. Perhaps I have a tougher skin than most. Seeing bad things doesn't bother me as much as when people get away with doing bad things. What I like about my job is the trying hard to do some good, if I can. It can be very satisfying."

"I never thought about it like that." Mrs. Anderson paused. "I think I know what you mean. I married very young, just a few weeks before he was sent to France in the war. I had thought my life would be dedicated to taking care of him and our children, if we were lucky enough to have them. Then he died on the battle-field, while I was busy helping with so many damaged men in a makeshift hospital, and I realized that taking care of people was what I liked to do, and it didn't have to be my own husband. My family had a small inn by the sea so I already knew about house-keeping. It was a logical direction for me after the war. What I like about my job is the taking care of people, making sure they have good food, that the house is clean and comfortable, and that they have what they need. When I feel like I'm doing a good job, it gives me great satisfaction."

"Yes." Lilian smiled to herself—even though their situations were worlds apart, she felt they understood each other.

The whistle on the kettle sounded, and Mrs. Anderson jumped up to pour the hot water in the pot she had prepared on the tray crowded with cups, cream, sugar, and a plate piled with biscuits.

# CHAPTER 42

After their tea break, Lilian, Richard, and DC Lee began their next interview.

Lady Stella Reading leaned back comfortably on the love seat, her pale green dress set off by the blue brocade of the chair. She looked at them directly with her sharp gray eyes.

"Was there anything unusual in his mood?" Lady Stella repeated their question. "Sir Henry was an interesting man. Had you ever met him?"

The detectives shook their heads.

"Yet you know of his public persona, his patriotism, his speeches on Great Britain? That was the baronet that most people knew," said Lady Stella, her dark wavy hair moving to and fro as she shook her head. "But that person was mainly a performance."

"It was synthetic?" Richard asked.

"He was certainly quite practiced at it. Was it real?" She paused. "Many would say so, even most of his family. But it was calculated. He knew what he wanted and he knew what it took to get it."

Lilian leaned forward. "What did he want?"

"To be revered, famous, admired," said Lady Stella. "To remain rich, lead the aristocracy, forever live the life of a nobleman."

This was a woman, Lilian thought, who wasn't afraid to have opinions nor to express them.

Lady Stella paused for a moment and began again. "A few years ago, when my husband died—he had been the British ambassador to the United States—I went there, to America, and I traveled by car across the country. I went by myself. I stayed in dollar-a-night lodgings. I worked as a dishwasher. I talked to people. People who were going through rough times, people who were holding on to the last shreds of hope. I wanted to understand ordinary Americans. Regular people. It gave me great insight into the human race. People like Sir Henry are easier to read after an experience like that."

Richard seemed to hide his head in his notes after hearing this. Lilian didn't know if she were shocked or impressed. *Did a journey like that take courage or folly?*

"Why did you ask him to host the fundraiser here at Hursley House?" Lilian asked.

"That's an interesting question, Chief Inspector, because I didn't." Lady Stella looked at them with gravity. "I thought the home secretary had recruited him to use Hursley House, and last night I discovered that it had actually been Sir Henry who arranged it. He had lobbied Sir Samuel, convinced him to have the gala here. But previously, Sir Henry told me that Sir Samuel had lobbied him."

This, Lilian thought with a small thrill, could be their first breakthrough, their first real clue. Perhaps there were people Sir Henry wanted to bring together or meet without having to seek them out or meet privately. These *brutes* Sir Samuel had mentioned to Marie. The bad people Juan had talked about.

"Why would Sir Henry be so interested in hosting your fundraiser here?" Lilian asked.

"I have no idea. I was quite surprised, and last night I just brushed it off. But now that he has been killed, I can't help but wonder if the two things are connected. He could have hosted the gala at any luxury resort or fancy hotel in London—that's his usual mode for his business events. He hasn't hosted a ball at Hursley House since his wife died more than a decade ago." Lady Stella sat back on the love seat and looked from one detective to the other. "He didn't have a reputation as a philanthropist. He didn't host fundraisers. He was an aristocrat. He was a successful industrialist. He was proudly nationalistic. He was very popular and respected, especially amongst his own class. He was not known for his good deeds."

Lilian mulled this over. Richard seemed struck by her frankness.

"Was there anything unusual about his mood last night?" Lilian asked.

Lady Stella sighed. "In my opinion, there was nothing unusual about Sir Henry last night. He was Sir Henry Heathcote himself, the egotist, happiest when he was getting attention, and last night he was getting plenty of attention. It was his usual popular-aristocrat-about-town kind of attention, but—" Lady Stella paused. "Come to think of it, he seemed very interested in meeting people that I knew through my charity work. Perhaps . . ." She became lost in thought.

"Anyone in particular?" Richard asked.

"Yes, people who are involved in helping with some of the projects we are putting together for the Women's Voluntary Service. We are organizing programs to prepare for the possibility of war with Germany. These people make things, or distribute things, useful things, like gas masks, transportation lorries, bulk food rations, and useful materials like canvas and aluminum," Lady Stella said. "But there was quite a large group of those people at the party. It would've been hard to avoid talking to them, I suppose."

Lilian looked at Richard and frowned.

"Are there any particular conversations or incidents you remember?" Lilian asked.

"I noticed he did have rather a snarky back and forth with Juan Guerra. Something about communism. He wasn't a fan."

"Yes, we've heard about that."

After a moment, Lady Stella cleared her throat delicately. "Sir Samuel is sending a car for me. I hadn't planned on staying past luncheon, and I'm needed in London. Is that quite all right?" She smiled charmingly and stood.

"Why, yes, of course," Richard rose quickly, looking startled. "I'm sure we'll be able to find you if we need you."

"Yes, of course, thank you so much," Lady Stella said and shook their hands. "Best of luck with the case. Don't hesitate to get in touch if you have any other questions, Wilson has my telephone number." She moved toward the door, but turned before she exited. "And if I think of anything else that might be useful, I'll contact you. I can't think of anyone in particular that would have murdered Sir Henry. But I can think of a lot of people who won't mind very much that he's dead."

Richard's face showed his surprise at this statement, but Lilian only nodded. It certainly fit the picture that was forming about Sir Henry Heathcote.

# CHAPTER 43

Wilson sipped his tea at the kitchen table, slightly drooping with fatigue. "After the detectives have their luncheon and we clear the dining room," he said, "the detectives will interview us one by one."

Brigid dropped the handful of silverware she was bringing to the sink. Mrs. Anderson looked up from her ledger and raised her eyebrows questioningly. Brigid ducked her head.

"Don't be nervous, Brigie," Bernard said and helped her pick up the spoons and forks.

"I'm not nervous, just clumsy." She smiled at him, but knew she was fooling no one, most especially herself.

"I'll be first," Wilson said. "And I'll make sure they understand everyone's position. We are faithful staff of this family, and we are constant and trustworthy."

"Of course we are, Mr. Wilson," Bernard said. "There's nothing to tell, anyway. We didn't see nothin' out of the ordinary, did we, Brigie?"

"I didn't see nothin' out of the ordinary," Brigid repeated solemnly. And she got to work washing the silverware. Cleaning things was simple and straightforward. Things were dirty, you cleaned them, you dried them, you put them away, and you moved on to the next thing that needed cleaning. You couldn't get it wrong as long as you tried your best and took your time. She hoped talking to Scotland Yard would be the same.

# CHAPTER 44

Rana Gupta couldn't have seemed more uncomfortable as he sat on the brocade loveseat for his interview. He perched on the edge, as if to be ready to run at a moment's notice. Lilian waited for Richard to begin.

"Mr. Gupta, thank you for your patience today. Just a few simple questions." Richard flipped through his notebook to a blank page. "Did you notice anything last night that might lead you to predict this horrific event this morning?"

Rana paused before he answered. He expression was one of seriousness and anxiety. "I didn't notice anything that would have led me to believe such a thing would happen."

"How well did you know the baronet?"

"I didn't know him at all. Last night was the first time I met him."

"But you knew of him, about him?"

"Of course. He's a popular public figure."

"And what was your impression of him last night?"

"My impression?" Rana looked almost confused. "He was who I always thought he would be. Rather arrogant, a definitive aristocrat, dismissive and condescending, at least to the likes of me." He suddenly stopped, perhaps surprised at his honesty.

"Then he met your expectations?"

"I suppose so." Rana relaxed slightly at Richard's response.

"And were these qualities that you heard about from others, from the home secretary, for example?"

"No, Sir Samuel never said anything of the sort. These are beliefs that are just as widespread as the opposite general opinion that is more often published in the newspapers, magazines, and newsreels, based on historical and political facts often ignored."

"I see." Richard kept his eyebrows level, although they wanted to spike straight up. "Can you share some of these ?"

"They're not secrets. Sir Henry Heathcote was well known for his disdain for the working man, his contempt for fair trade, and his high regard for nobility."

"And as a deputy to the home secretary, these facts had an impact on your job in any particular way?"

"No impact whatsoever," Rana responded. "Facts are facts and it's important to be aware of all sides in order to keep the country safe."

"Is Sir Samuel aware of all sides?"

"Of course. It's how he trained me. He's been a wonderful mentor."

"Does he share your opinions about Sir Henry?" Richard asked.

"He is aware of the facts but is perhaps less cynical in his opinions, coming from the same social circle as Sir Henry."

"I see. So, last night, you met the baronet for the first time, found him—discourteous—as expected, but did not notice any particular incident or contentious association that might lead to his murder. Anything that might help us understand what happened?"

Rana thought for a moment. "I don't think I'm the only one who saw him have a disagreement with Lady Sarah on the dance floor. And after that, his exchange with his younger daughter and her schoolmate."

"What can you tell us about those?"

Rana shifted in his seat and seemed flushed. "I don't think either incident is any of my business. They were personal to the family."

"Yes, of course, but what was your impression?"

"In the disagreement with Lady Sarah, I heard him say something about lies or lying."

"What about?"

"I have no idea. And his younger daughter and her friend, I don't know for sure, but he approached them when they were dancing and pulled them apart, physically. It was rather harsh. Both girls were quite upset. Charles came over and calmed the situation by taking them away. Sir Henry disappeared into the crowd."

"Did you see him after that?"

"Here and there. The party was still quite lively." This question seemed to make him even more uncomfortable.

"Did you have any conversations with the baronet?" Richard asked.

"I told you, he was rather dismissive of me. I wouldn't say we had anything that you might call a conversation."

Lilian wrote down his words exactly. It occurred to her that they could be interpreted in a few different ways. Richard didn't seem to have another question ready so she spoke up.

"In your opinion, Mr. Gupta, who would you say might commit such a heinous crime?" Lilian looked at him directly and waited for him to speak.

"I don't have any particular opinion, but I can only say that while he was quite popular and beloved by a large group of people, just as many had a different opinion of Sir Henry Heathcote. But as far as committing this heinous crime, it would seem to me that it would have to be deeply personal, not political."

"And why do you say that?" Davidson asked.

"There are plenty of worse political figures, why choose Sir Henry?" Rana Gupta asked. "Could his death bring about some sort of positive change? I doubt it. Yet, for someone with a personal motive, it just might be true. Inheritance, anger, emancipation? There are so many possibilities."

"Yes, so many possibilities." Lilian looked at Richard. She had no more questions.

"I think that will be all, Mr. Gupta." Richard stood.

"May I go back to London then?" Rana asked as he stood to leave the room. "I understand the home secretary and Lady Stella Reading have been released."

"I'm afraid they had special dispensation," Richard smiled charmingly. "The home secretary didn't mention that you were needed elsewhere, and we do have to keep to our protocols as much as possible. We hope to let everyone go by tonight or early tomorrow, depending."

"Depending?"

"Depending on if we feel we have the full spectrum of information." Richard looked at him expectantly. "Who knows what we might learn over the next several hours?"

"Right." Rana looked thoroughly unconvinced as he left the room.

DC Lee joined Richard and Lilian by the door as Roper came in.

"All the guests, except the four writers, have gone to their rooms, sir," he said to Davidson.

"We just have the four writers left?" DC Lee asked.

"Yes, and the house staff," Richard answered.

"I have a suggestion," Lilian said. "We should interview all four writers together. We need a better picture of what went on last night. All four are very observant, and their information could be enlightening. It occurs to me that as they give their information about last night, from their different points of view and, most likely, from different physical locations at the ball, we might be able to build a more accurate picture. And they might be more comfortable all together, they might talk more easily, remind each other of the evening's events."

Lilian knew it was unorthodox, but it might give a more organized whole to the evening, rather than the jumble of parts they had been getting so far. And perhaps if they were very helpful, she might be able to talk Richard into recruiting them to help with the investigation. He seemed to be thinking for a moment.

"Let's give it a try, shall we?" Richard said with alacrity. "In fact, Roper, you said all the guests, except the writers, have left the dining room?"

"Yes, sir."

"Splendid. Let's meet them there."

"Excellent suggestion," Lilian agreed. "We can be a bit more casual."

"And have some lunch as well?" DC Lee added.

"Good point, DC Lee, good point," Richard said. "And then we'll interview the house staff individually and look through the rooms, or vice versa. Roper, please tell the house staff we'll see them in an hour or so, and that we'd be much obliged if they would plan tea as well as dinner for the whole group. Before dinner we'll meet with the team and share where we are at that point. Hopefully we'll have made some progress by then."

Lilian wondered what possible progress they could make in that short a time, and decided some prayers were in order.

# CHAPTER 45

Constable Roper opened the double doors into the dining room and stepped aside. In walked DCIs Davidson and Wyles, with DC Lee following behind.

"Hello, ladies," he said. "May we join you for lunch?"

The four writers had finished their lunch and were sipping tea but they quickly concurred.

The Scotland Yard contingent filled their plates with cold luncheon meats, salads, and bread, and sat on one side of the table nearest to the four authors. They ate in silence for a few moments, too hungry to make small talk, the authors unsure if they should be entertaining or silent.

Wilson came in with Bernard to refresh the coffee and tea, clearing empty plates and cups from the table, with Bernard sweeping up crumbs and Wilson straightening everything to make the table look its best.

"Fresh coffee or tea?" Wilson asked, looking at the three police. They all chose tea so he brought them three clean cups and a fresh pot. They thanked him appreciatively. Lilian was the first to swallow the last of her food, followed by a long sip of tea.

"Ladies, thank you so much for your patience. It's been a long day, so far. We hope you haven't been uncomfortable," Lilian said.

"Not at all, detectives," Agatha Christie spoke up. "We understand the process, of course, and kept ourselves occupied."

"Excellent." Lilian opened her notebook. She noticed that Ngaio Marsh had a sketchbook in front of her, and both Margery Allingham and Agatha Christie had notebooks with pencils stuck into the places they last had them open. Dorothy L. Sayers apparently had been reading a thick book, the title in Italian. "Let's get started then. What we'd like to do is get a picture of last night, from your combined perspectives. If you can all talk about yesterday, from the beginning, and tell us about the day and evening, filling in the gaps between each other's stories. Is that all right?"

The four writers exchanged glances, almost seeming to communicate without speaking. Again, it was Agatha Christie who spoke up.

"Of course, shall I start?" Agatha settled herself in her seat. "We arrived early, so we would be ready to great the guests. Dorothy and I drove together, and we had lunch here and then went upstairs to get ready."

"I came on the train and then took a taxi from the station," offered Ngaio.

"I drove myself," Margery said. "I think we all arrived within an hour of each other."

"Yes, we did," Agatha agreed, and the others nodded.

"And was the family all here?" Lilian asked.

"Yes, they all lunched with us," Agatha said. "We had quite a pleasant day, in fact. Sir Henry was there, and everyone was quite lovely."

"I would agree that we had a pleasant day," Ngaio added. "Although I wouldn't say Sir Henry was lovely. I mean he was fine, but he was less than friendly."

"But that was just the way Sir Henry was," Agatha pointed out. "He certainly was much less lovely as the evening wore on. But let's not get ahead of ourselves."

"I think we get the picture," Richard said. "Was there anything between the family during the day that seemed contentious?"

There was silence for a moment, then Margery spoke up. "I don't know if contentious is the right word, but they all seemed to be, I suppose, trying to get his attention, would be one way to put it."

"I noticed that too," Dorothy said. "Charles wanted to talk about his campaign for Parliament, but Sir Henry would change the subject. Philippa seemed to want her father to talk about the house, and he would put her off to Lady Sarah."

"And Miss Kate?" Lilian asked.

Ngaio jumped in to answer "Miss Kate kept telling stories about school and things that she and her friend Sofia were involved in. Sir Henry didn't seem to be interested in any of it. It seemed to me he couldn't wait to be done with the lot of us, and he made excuses to go to his desk as soon as the plates were taken."

"Would it be fair to say he was preoccupied with something?" Richard asked.

"Self-absorbed, I would call it," Ngaio said.

"Nothing in particular came up in the luncheon discussion?"

They all shook their heads.

"Wait," Margery said, raising one finger. "There was a brief discussion that stuck out in my mind. Between Sir Henry and Juan."

"What was it?" Lilian asked.

"Juan said something about the chaos of everything with the war in Europe, and Sir Henry said something like 'Of course it is easier when the right people are in charge to sort everything out.' And that struck me as odd."

"Why?"

"It seemed that everyone assumed he meant us, you know, Britain, but somehow I had the idea that's not what he meant at all. But then someone changed the subject and it was apparently forgotten."

"And was Ambrose at the luncheon?" Lilian asked.

"Yes, he was quite lovely," Dorothy said. "Always including everyone in the conversation, and giving his attention to his nieces and nephew."

"And the home secretary, Rana Gupta, and Lady Stella?" Lilian asked.

Margery answered this one. "They didn't arrive until a couple of hours before the party. I heard them go into their rooms and they came down around the same time as we did."

"What time was that?"

"We all came down at around five and had some tea. We waited in the drawing room, except for Lady Stella, who was here and there, busy as a bee, talking to the caterers and Wilson and the musicians. Making sure everything was being taken care of."

"Where was Sir Henry at this time?" Lilian asked.

The four women all looked at each other.

"He wasn't with us," Agatha said. "I assumed he had been doing some business in his library and then he got ready late. He came down when we were all in the main hall, ready to greet the guests."

"Same for Lady Sarah?"

"No, she was with us the whole time," Agatha said.

"Then the guests began to arrive?"

"The party was in full swing in no time," Dorothy said. "Everyone was having a wonderful time. We all chatted with so many people." She smiled, seeming to remember.

"When did Sir Henry become irritable?" Lilian asked.

Ngaio looked at Agatha. "You know, I think it was after we took that break upstairs," Ngaio said. "Agatha and I found each other in the ladies' sitting room, enjoying some peace and quiet, and when we came down, Sir Henry was dancing with Lady Sarah and something went wrong."

"Could we go back for a moment?' Dorothy asked. "While you two were upstairs, I was talking with the home secretary and Rana Gupta, and they had a confusing exchange."

"How do you mean?" Lilian asked.

"Mr. Gupta mentioned he boarded at Harrow but had to return home to New Delhi in his last year due to a family issue. Then Sir Samuel asked him if he knew Sir Henry back then, because of his business there, in India, and Mr. Gupta became flustered. He said he never met him, but then he said he knew *of* him, and then there was a dark look in his eye. I don't know what that meant, but it seemed to be nothing good." Dorothy thought for a moment. "Certainly, there was no love lost there. Then he said he and his mother moved to Cambridge when his father died."

Lilian took a note to check into Rana Gupta's family. Could his father's death have something to do with Heathcote's business in India? Why would he say he had heard of him in India? Perhaps Sir Samuel would know.

"I think it was soon after that when the dance floor incident happened between Sir Henry and Lady Sarah," Dorothy said.

"Ah, I've been wanting to hear more about this." Richard sat up.

"Before we get to that," Lilian said, "was there anything else from the other corners of the room leading up to it?"

"I was dancing with Ian Colvin, just before that incident, and he seemed to be concerned about some of the people at the party," Margery answered. "I thought he was just making a joke about class, at the time, but looking back on it, perhaps he meant there were some shady characters."

"Did he mention any names?"

"No, I'm sorry, he didn't."

"Anyone else see or hear anything before the disagreement with Sir Henry and Lady Sarah?" Lilian asked.

"Charles was complaining that his father wasn't doing enough to help his parliamentary campaign," Dorothy offered. "But that seemed to be more about being ignored by his father when he wanted attention."

"Agatha and I had just come downstairs from the lounge when we all met at the buffet and refreshed our champagne," Ngaio said. "That's when we witnessed the disagreement."

"Was there anything upstairs to note?"

"No, just some servants tidying up."

"So you were all four at the buffet when it happened?" Richard asked.

"Yes," Ngaio continued. "Sir Henry and Lady Sarah were dancing, rather stiffly, I thought, and then they stopped, in the middle of the dance floor, talking lowly at first, although quite intensely."

"Could you hear what they were saying?"

"Not in the beginning, but then I caught some fragments— *why does my mother matter*, I think Lady Sarah said."

"Yes," Agatha confirmed. "I heard that as well. *What does my mother have to do with it*, something like that."

Lilian wrote in her notebook as Ngaio continued. "And then Sir Henry. I think he accused her of lying, or called her a liar?"

"I think he said, 'What other lies have you been telling me?' Yes, that was it," Margery said.

"That's what I heard," Dorothy agreed. "'What other lies have you been telling me?' He was quite heated."

"How did the row end?" Lilian asked. She glanced at Richard, who was letting her do all the talking, apparently thinking the women would be more comfortable talking with her.

"That's what was so neat," Ngaio replied, looking at Richard. "Sir Samuel came round from one side and got Sir Henry's attention away from Lady Sarah, and at the same time, Ambrose approached Lady Sarah from the other side and cut in. He danced her away so quickly, it was as if it never happened."

"It looked as if Sir Samuel told him something humorous," Dorothy added. "Because they walked away talking and smiling together. Sir Henry didn't even look back."

"You all agree with this recounting of the incident?" The four women nodded as one. "Anything to add?" They all shook their heads no.

"Something about her mother and something about lies," Lilian mused. "Did anyone see Lady Sarah after that?"

They all shook their heads again.

"She must have retired right afterward," Agatha said. "I'm sure I would have done."

"I understand that soon after that disagreement, Sir Henry sent Miss Kate to bed. Did any of you witness that?"

"I'm afraid I slipped off to bed right after the scene with Lady Sarah," Agatha reminded them.

"And I was right behind her," Ngaio said.

"Nothing else from the two of you, for the evening."

"Actually, on my way to bed, I did see the footman coming out of one of the upstairs rooms," Ngaio said. "I assumed he was checking for lost belongings or something."

"Thank you." Lilian made a note to ask Bernard about his wanderings.

"Margery and I were both in the ballroom when Sir Henry broke Kate and Sofia apart on the dance floor," Dorothy said.

"Is that how you'd describe it, 'broke apart'?" Lilian asked.

"Oh, yes," Dorothy answered. "The two girls were dancing, some new dance, nothing I'm particularly familiar with. A new band had come on sometime around midnight, modern music, the girls were thoroughly enjoying themselves. And then the music slowed down and they kept dancing. I was quite enjoying watching all the young people dance. So joyful." Dorothy smiled to herself.

"And then Sir Henry?" Lilian prodded.

"Yes, the music slowed down, the two girls kept dancing, and Sir Henry stormed over to them and pulled them apart."

"Did he say anything?"

"Something about not being children anymore. Inappropriate behavior." Dorothy paused to remember.

"He said they were embarrassing him and the family," Margery added.

"What was so embarrassing, exactly?"

Dorothy and Margery looked at each other, then at Richard and Lilian. Dorothy was the first to speak.

"I suppose he thought they were being too affectionate. You know how young girls can be, they only see the world from inside their own point of view. Perhaps he thought they were not thinking about how polite society might see them."

"And had the Misses Kate and Sofia had too much champagne?" Davidson asked.

"Champagne may have had an impact on their behavior," Dorothy replied. "But I think their youth was the larger contributor."

"Then what?" Davidson asked.

"Charles intervened and took them in hand," Dorothy continued. "On his way to the stairs Marie joined them. I was rather close behind them. I had just been about to go up, but I didn't want to follow too closely. I didn't want them to think I was listening. They were embarrassed enough."

Lilian felt sorry for the girls. Youth and affection should not be punished. *What a dark world it would be without those two things.*

"Did you see or notice anything else before you retired, Mrs. Sayers?" Lilian asked.

"Just as I was about to go up, I was in the east hall by the cloakroom, I saw Charles come down the stairs. He met his father just outside the library and they went in together. Then I went up."

"And the upper hallway, was it deserted?" Lilian asked.

"I didn't see anyone." Dorothy thought for a moment. "But I did hear doors opening and closing and some muffled voices. But I was so tired I went right to sleep."

"Thank you, Mrs. Sayers, that was quite helpful." Richard looked through his notes. "Mrs. Allingham, you were the last at the party."

"I usually am," Margery said with a smile.

"Anything to add to the Miss Kate dance floor incident?" Richard asked with a smile.

"No, I just felt so for them all. It did occur to me that if Sir Henry hadn't made such a scene of it, it would have been less embarrassing for all concerned." Margery paused. "Anyway, I do think they'd all had too much champagne. And after that, Ian Colvin found me and we wandered into the winter garden. It was quieter there for talking and comfortable sitting."

"Did you continue the conversation about 'shady characters' at the party?"

Margery shook her head. "No, we talked about journalism and literature and writing in general. He's writing a book about his experiences, and we were discussing the differences of writing fiction and nonfiction."

"I see." Richard fell silent.

"And then?" Lilian prompted.

"The footman came in, I think his name is Bernard, and subtly let us know the party was over. We realized the music had stopped," Margery continued. "I walked Ian to the cloakroom and then halfway to the front door."

"And then you went to bed?"

"Yes, but I did pass the library on my way to the stairs and I heard voices. I can't say that I recognized them. But they were men's voices, and they were elevated, otherwise I wouldn't have heard them at all.

"Do you remember the time?" asked Richard.

"When I got to my room, I noticed it was about quarter past three?" She thought for a moment. "Yes, quarter past."

"Ambrose has told us that he was in the library around that time, with his brother."

"I would say it sounded like them," Margery said. "But I could only hear the tones of their voices, not any words. There might have been a heated tone to the conversation. I'm sorry I didn't stop to eavesdrop."

Lilian thought that any number of Margery's characters would've done so. "Were they shouting?"

"No, I wouldn't say shouting, but just short of it."

"This has been very helpful, ladies," Richard said, and he stood, apparently deciding the interview was over, as did Lilian. "We appreciate your time and attention."

"Detective Chief Inspector Davidson," Ngaio stopped him before he could leave. "There's one other thing I remember, I don't know if it means anything. But earlier in the evening, I was chatting with Charles and Marie, then Marie accepted a dance with an older gentleman. Charles and I were near the buffet, and Sir Henry approached us. I think he didn't even notice me—I was on the other side of Charles. He stood next to Charles, watching Marie and her partner dance, and he leaned toward Charles and said, 'She thinks she's passing amongst our crowd, but she's not and she never will.' Then he picked up a glass of champagne and walked away."

*This was curious*, Lilian thought. "Did Charles say anything?" she asked.

"No, and I just tried to pretend I hadn't heard what Sir Henry had said. I had noticed that Sir Henry was rather cold to Marie in earlier conversations, but this was shocking. Charles was absolutely mortified. I started a new topic as quickly as possible." Ngaio felt her face flush, a flashback to the embarrassment of the moment.

"Thank you, Miss Marsh." Richard looked at her appreciatively. He looked around the group. "Can anyone else remember any other comments or something you felt was odd or stuck out in any other conversations or observations? Anything you might've heard could be relevant."

Margery spoke up. "It seemed to me that Sir Henry was rude or cold on many occasions. But there is one that sticks out in my mind. I was talking with Philippa and Juan, who were lovely, and Sir Henry was at the fringe of our group. Our conversation turned to Juan's past in Spain and he referred to Franco as 'Hitler's friend Franco,' and Sir Henry turned to Juan and said something like 'Better than being in bed with the Red Menace,' and Juan almost exploded."

"What was Juan's reply?"

"That's what was so interesting, Philippa put her hand on his arm and stopped him. She looked . . . afraid, I thought."

"Afraid? Of what?"

"Of Sir Henry, I believe," Margery responded. "She seemed to have an absolute fear of Sir Henry."

# CHAPTER 46

Bernard was outside by the back door, leaning against the building, smoking. He looked out past the trees and flicked his ashes on the ground. Brigid came out and stood looking at him.

"Smoke?" Bernard asked.

"You know I don't smoke, Bernard."

"What are you lookin' at, then?"

Brigid didn't answer him.

"Brigie, we didn't do anything wrong last night," he said. "We took a little break, we had a little dance."

"I know," she said slowly.

"So there's nothin' to tell the coppers about."

"But what if they ask?"

"Ask what, did you have a dance last night?" Bernard chuckled. "I don't think that's a question they'll be askin'." He chucked her under the chin. She laughed.

"Of course they won't ask that."

"Right, so stop worryin' and get back to work."

"You get back to work, you lazy lad!" Brigid smoothed her apron, lifted her head haughtily, and went inside.

Bernard laughed. But after he took a last drag on his cigarette, his eyes took on a worried look as he went back into Hursley House.

# CHAPTER 47

"Let me see," Lilian said, referring to her notes. "Sir Henry seemed to have been in contention with Juan over politics, with Charles about Marie's social standing, with Lady Sarah over lies and something about her mother, with Miss Kate about her public display of affection with her schoolmate, and there might be a past connection with Rana Gupta's family. Did I forget anything? Oh, yes, there were these shady characters that Ian Colvin referred to."

"That seems to sum up last night," Richard murmured. "What about this morning? Did anyone see or hear anything this morning or communicate with Sir Henry or any of the family before breakfast?"

Ngaio waited for a moment. She had something to admit that seemed completely irrelevant, something that couldn't help the case at all but that might raise an issue. *Should she say it or not?* Before she could decide, Margery Allingham jumped in.

"I was up early," Margery said. "I was just standing at the window, staring out. And I saw Sir Henry in the distance with the dogs. This was around seven fifteen."

Dorothy spoke up. "I was up early as well, actually, before six. I knew there was a chapel at the end of the garden, so I took a walk, went inside. It is a small building, quite peaceful. I was there five or ten minutes. Then I went back to my room. I came and went past the kitchen, out the back door."

"What time did you return?" Lilian asked.

"Oh, before half past six, I'm sure."

"Did you see anyone?"

"The staff was in the kitchen, but I slipped down the hallway and up the stairs." She looked embarrassed. "I doubt they even saw me."

"Anyone else engage in a morning activity?" Lilian looked at each of them. Ngaio sat up a little straighter.

"I woke up about five o'clock, ravenous." She smiled guiltily. "It happens when I drink champagne. I couldn't go back to sleep, and I knew I wouldn't unless I put something in my stomach. So I went down to the kitchen for a glass of milk."

"How long were you downstairs?" Richard asked, trying not to smile.

"Ten minutes or so. And I had some bread and butter to help wash down the milk." She smiled at him, and he couldn't help reflecting her grin.

"Did you see anyone?" He cleared his throat to erase his smile.

"No, I was completely alone." Ngaio shook her head emphatically. "I almost got lost, this house is so big and complicated. I wandered all the way from the east wing to the west to find the stairs to the kitchen."

She watched Richard think. She took a chance.

"Detective Chief Inspector," she said. "If we can help in any way, we'd be glad to."

Richard smiled. "I appreciate the offer, Miss Marsh," he said, not unkindly. He looked at Lilian. "But now we need to get on with the job. Let us know if you remember anything else."

Ngaio nodded. "Of course," she said.

"May I ask a question?" Agatha looked at both detectives. "He was poisoned, wasn't he? Cyanide?"

"Why do you think so?" Richard asked.

"The smell, the way the body looked, his red face," Agatha said. "It was on his cigar?"

The detectives looked at each other.

"We haven't gotten word back from the lab," Richard said.

"It's cyanide, I'm quite sure of it." Agatha nodded. "And someone would have put it on the only cigar he would have available to smoke first thing in the morning. We all saw that the cigar box was empty." She nodded to her friends, their faces all in agreement.

"Yes," Lilian said. Of course, Agatha Christie would know all about poisons, and it wasn't that difficult a guess.

Richard stood. "You can all move about the house freely, except for the library, the cloakroom, and the former baronet's rooms upstairs. Those will remain off limits until we finish the search. We hope to be able to release you all tomorrow, once we get the results of the tests we've sent to Scotland Yard."

"If any new information comes to light, please let us know immediately." Lilian looked at the four writers. Perhaps they would discover something that the detectives would not. As the day went on, the family might let down their guard, mention things they would never mention in front of the police.

* * *

"That went well," Agatha said after the detectives left, as she poured herself some more tea.

"Did it?" Ngaio wasn't sure if Agatha was being sarcastic or not. "DCI Davidson seemed rather dismissive."

"Why shouldn't he be?" Dorothy said. "They are professionals, we are not even amateurs, we're writers."

"But we could be helpful," Margery said. "We've been here, seen and heard things that they didn't. It seems to me we can be extremely helpful."

"Yes, why shouldn't we be?" Agatha added. "Poirot doesn't wait to be asked, he just barges right in." This made them all laugh, except Dorothy.

"How can we, if they don't want us?" Ngaio asked.

"They can't stop us from pooling our resources and talking through our theories and gathering information on our own," Agatha said.

"No, they can't, can they?" Ngaio smiled. The writers would do what they could do, and perhaps they would come up with something helpful. "Where do we start?"

# CHAPTER 48

"Davidson, we got more information from those four women than all of the interviews put together," Lilian said as she and Richard walked to the library. DC Lee had returned to the morning room to begin typing up the statements. "I think we should enlist them to help us."

He stopped walking and looked at her.

"Hear me out—they would more easily have the trust of the family, and could be much more spontaneous. They could have more casual conversations with the family members and Rana Gupta than we could. Anytime we chat with any of them, they'll just shut down, like they did in the interviews."

"Absolutely not." Richard resumed walking. "We could never do something that unprofessional, especially not on a case with the home secretary breathing down our necks."

Lilian was surprised at his vehemence.

"But—"

"No, it's too risky." Richard turned back to her. "We get to the truth with the good old investigatory process, as always. Fingerprints, footprints, tracing the poison. The real clues and evidence that make up a real investigation."

"Yes, of course," Lilian admitted. "But we don't even know what direction to go."

"Are you forgetting that one of the writers might just as well be the murderer?" Richard said. "Miss Marsh was running through the house before the sun was up, Mrs. Sayers rose at the crack of dawn to allegedly visit the chapel, passing the kitchen. Mrs. Allingham watched Sir Henry trot off with his dogs from her window, she could've gone to the library at that moment."

"If she had a key."

"And Mrs. Christie knew about the cyanide. She could be the poisoner."

Lilian was surprised he was taking this tack. "Rather unlikely, isn't it? They didn't know about the morning cigar ritual before they found him."

"Maybe they did, maybe someone mentioned it last night at the party. Maybe they were in it together." He kept walking and she followed him.

"And they were just waiting for the perfect opportunity to poison someone they didn't know, without a motive?" Lilian pointed out.

"Perhaps the motive was to invent an unsolvable crime that would make for a best-selling novel." Richard's footsteps sounded more like stomping as they went down the main hall.

Lilian blinked. She wanted to ask him, *Are you serious?*

"In which they would then reveal that they were the murderer?"

"Each of them had a moment when they could have stolen the cigars and planted the poisoned one."

"Except Agatha Christie," Lilian said.

"Who knows about cyanide. She knew how it was done."

"And she told you so that you'd know she did it?" Lilian said. "If there's one thing we know about real crime, it's that it always makes some kind of sense in the end. Albeit twisted."

They had arrived at the library, and Richard took out the keys Wilson had given him "Either way, they are still suspects, and that's the best reason not to enlist their help finding the murderer."

"What happened to 'I respect your instincts'?"

Richard turned to her. His eyebrows shot up. "I—"

"You what?" Lilian felt her face grow warm. "It's all well and good to tell me you're going to treat me as an equal, but the proof is in the pudding."

She took the keys from him and opened the door.

# CHAPTER 49

Lilian paced around the library, still fuming inside, trying to clear her head. Being angry wasn't going to help her think clearly. In some ways she was used to being treated as second fiddle at Scotland Yard, but she had garnered respect from her colleagues over the years and had left most of her frustration behind. She hadn't worked this kind of case with DCI Davidson before and, although she wasn't surprised when he pulled rank, she wasn't willing to let it stand in the way of solving the case. Even if he thought he knew best, not using the writers to help them was shortsighted.

She would do what it took to get the job done, whether he agreed with her or not. But now, she had to observe everything she could about the library and not let Davidson's shortsightedness muddle her concentration.

She took her time and scanned the library, which seemed just as the investigation team had left it. The sky had cleared, and a soft sunny glow filled the room from the French windows that faced the north garden. Lilian looked at the four walls covered in books, the deep red and gold patterned carpet, the heavy mahogany furniture. The room was a classic, if not clichéd, nobleman's library. She had known they existed, outside of books and films, but she had never been inside one. The difference between this room and the libraries that lived inside her imagination was the variety of books, old mixed with modern, and that made the room look off to her. Not untidy, exactly, but as if the original collection had been interspersed with incongruous stock. It made her feel as if the room were off balance.

She turned to the sofa that had held Sir Henry as he smoked his last cigar. She could see the impression his body had left in the cushions of rich brocade. Next to the sofa was a coffee table and on one side an end table, both with piles of books. On the other end of the room was the magnificent leather-topped desk, with some neatly piled papers and some in disarray. Lilian walked to the desk and began to shuffle through them. Maybe she would find something that would lead her to understand this violent death.

Across the room, Richard stood at the French windows and examined the lock. It didn't seem to have been tampered with. He looked through Sir Henry's keys and fit the smallest key into the lock and turned it. It worked smoothly. He opened the door to the gentle sound of dripping from the eaves and the sweet smell of wet grass from the earlier rain. He fitted the key from the outside, turning it back and forth, the mechanism working fluidly. He pondered the series of events. *In the morning, Sir Henry had his coffee, left though this door to run his dogs, then returned to smoke the deathly cigar.* Richard turned toward Lilian and spoke. "If he left the door unlocked while he was out, someone could've come in this way, stolen the freshly filled cigars and left the poisoned one."

"Everyone seems to think he couldn't possibly have left any door unlocked. Maybe they came through the main library door with a key. Wilson's key or Sir Henry's," Lilian said, trying not to sound irked.

"It would've been devilish tricky to take the keys off him and then return them," Richard said.

Lilian was used to bouncing theories back and forth with a colleague, but now she felt annoyed. Why did it bother her so much that he disagreed with her about asking the writers to assist? She'd dealt with plenty of opposition over the years with her male police colleagues, from many levels, but she had thought Richard was on her side. She shook her head to release her mind from the feeling. *It didn't matter if he didn't trust her instincts.* She'd dealt with worse. It was her own sensibilities that she had to battle. She had to tell herself that she didn't care what Richard Davidson thought of her.

Lilian concentrated on the papers on the desk, trying to make some sort of sense of them. They were all about Sir Henry's businesses—manufacturing, shipping, importing, exporting. He seemed to be into a little bit of everything.

"I think we should take these papers. Study them for any significance."

There was nothing interesting in the drawers: pens, ink, clean paper and envelopes, pencils, paper clips. Sir Henry apparently hadn't kept anything personal where anyone could easily find it, even if he had kept the room locked. She supposed there was always a chance that a maid or even Wilson could come across something.

The desk was near the fireplace, and she turned toward it. There was a good deal of ash in the grate, which seemed rather odd for the month of June. She knelt in front of it and sorted through the ashes with a pencil. It was white ash, certainly from paper, not logs, and she found a few corners of stationery to prove her point. She took an envelope from her pocket and gathered what she could.

"It looks like someone was burning papers here." She stood and folded the envelope. "Something they didn't want anyone to find, I suppose."

"Or just papers they no longer needed."

"We'll have to ask Ambrose if he can tell if any papers are missing."

"He should be able to tell us something," Richard agreed.

"Only if he wants us to know who the murderer is," Lilian added.

"Precisely."

"Let's let the house staff know we'll be ready for them soon so they don't wander too far. In about half an hour, after we look through Sir Henry's bedroom."

"I'll go," Lilian said quickly. She could use the short break, and she'd found that chatting with staff could be fruitful.

# CHAPTER 50

Lilian made her way below stairs to the kitchen. She found herself looking forward to seeing Mrs. Anderson—she needed a friendly face. When you were working at the Yard you could always take a walk and find a distraction with a colleague on another case, get your mind off the case and give it a rest, converse about something completely different. Then when you came back, your mind was fresh and things might seem clearer. Here, stuck in this house, she was getting shortsighted. She needed perspective. She arrived in the lower hallway and made her way to Mrs. Anderson's office. The door was ajar and, careful not to peek inside, Lilian knocked on the doorjamb.

"Come!" Mrs. Anderson's melodic voice answered.

"Sorry to disturb you," Lilian began.

"Not at all, please come in and make yourself comfortable. I was just adding up some figures, and this is a pleasant interruption." Mrs. Anderson sat at her desk, a ledger book open in front of her.

Lilian perched on the edge of a comfortable overstuffed chair to the side of Mrs. Anderson's desk. The room was a cheerful mix of pale pink, yellow, and ivory that put Lilian in the mind of summer ice creams and sweets.

"I just wanted to let you know we'll be ready for the staff interviews soon, one at a time."

"Of course, I'll tell Mr. Wilson."

"It's no rush," Lilian said quickly. "I don't mind a short pause, if I'm honest. And this room is a lovely place to take a moment."

"Thank you," Mrs. Anderson said. "It's my little oasis from the chaos." She laughed a soothing laugh.

"Mrs. Anderson—"

"Please, won't you call me Elspeth? I spend most of my time being formal without having a choice for any other way."

"Certainly, Elspeth. Call me Lilian." Lilian had been surprised at Mrs. Anderson's offer and answered before she could think better of it. She had wanted to construct a relationship to achieve a kind of trust to help with the interviews but hadn't expected this.

"Well, then, Lilian, I can't tell you how many questions I have about what it must be like to be a detective, especially as a woman, but perhaps that would be inappropriate?"

"Not at all, I'd be happy to answer your questions, but perhaps it might wait until the conclusion of the case."

"I understand, but let me just ask you one thing—actually, two things."

"Very well." Lilian smiled.

"All right." Elspeth Anderson turned her chair more comfortably to face Lilian. "Firstly, do you read detective novels?"

Lilian was surprised and for a second wondered if she should answer truthfully, being embarrassed to admit that she did. But she brushed away the thought.

"Yes, I do. I enjoy a good whodunit now and then."

"Wonderful, so do I," Elspeth responded. "And secondly, do you find that they relate at all to the job that you do?"

Lilian thought for a moment. Fiction was certainly quite different from real life. The books she enjoyed, like the novels of the writers who were sitting right upstairs, were clever puzzles but were rather unrealistic in every way. Yet working them out, or trying to, was ultimately satisfying.

"I wouldn't say the mysteries themselves relate to the cases I've worked on," Lilian replied. "But the depth of detail in the characters makes sense to me, and I think those fictional people are relatable to what I experience in my work."

Elspeth Anderson looked at her quizzically for a moment. "Do you mean that, even though the mystery might be unrealistic, the people in the books feel like real people?"

"Yes, they do," Lilian answered. "I meet so many different people in my work, and the people in mystery books seem like people I might meet. Except for some of the detectives themselves, if I'm honest."

This made Elspeth laugh, and Lilian smiled and sat back comfortably in the embrace of the soft chair. She allowed herself a few more moments of repose before tearing herself away from the cheery room. *Back to the real work of policing.*

# CHAPTER 51

"I've never seen so many neckties in one place outside of a shop." Lilian stood in front of an open armoire in Sir Henry Heathcote's dressing room. "Why would one man have so many ties?" She looked over at Richard, who was carefully searching through Sir Henry Heathcote's dresser drawers.

"I wouldn't know. I have a black one for weddings and funerals, and a blue one, a red one, and a striped one for work, and a paisley my sister gave me for my last birthday. Never needed more than that."

Lilian was sorry she asked. She would not be able to avoid noticing his tie rotation now that he'd laid it out so plainly. She finished rustling through all of Sir Henry's ties, felt around the edges of the armoire, bottom, top and sides and back, then knelt down and looked underneath. Nothing.

"Here are some letters from Lady Sarah." Richard had them in his hand but wasn't looking at them.

"Read them," she said, noting his obvious reluctance. "We've got to."

"I know, it's just not my favorite part of this job," Richard muttered. "I don't really want to know the private thoughts of a loving couple."

"If they *were* a loving couple," Lilian commented, moving toward the bedside table as Richard scanned the letters. "For some coppers it's the favorite part of the job. Nosing into people's business."

"Is it yours?"

"No. But it doesn't bother me either." Lilian opened the top drawer. "I've seen and heard enough in my life that nothing surprises me anymore."

"That's a shame." Richard opened a mahogany chest at the foot of the sturdy hardwood bedstead.

"Is it?" Lilian closed the top drawer and opened the next one. "I never really liked surprises."

"Don't you like to open a present at Christmas and feel that delicious anticipation before you know what it is?" Richard carefully removed the blankets and linens from the chest, one at a time, checked the chest, and then replaced them.

"You mean the moment before you see it's something you didn't want or can't use and most certainly is not to your taste?" Lilian closed the drawer and reached under the side table.

Richard chuckled and closed the chest and moved to searching the bed, folding back the linens and feeling between them.

Lilian moved to the writing desk in the corner and opened the one long drawer under the writing surface. Engaging in the search, she felt her ire begin to subside at Richard's opposition. But the frustration remained. She shuffled through the pens, paper, and other writing supplies. It almost looked as if the desk was never used. At least not for writing. But Sir Henry had had that big desk in the library where he must've spent more time.

"I hadn't pegged you as so jaded," Richard said, folding the linens back into place.

"I'm not jaded, just—" Lilian paused, looking for the right word. "Experienced." She almost brought up recruiting the writers, but she decided it was best not to bring it up again for the time being. She didn't like the idea of keeping her thoughts about the case from him, but he wasn't leaving her much choice.

There was a row of pigeonholes along the case top of the desk and two pairs of smaller drawers just below. The pigeonholes were empty. She opened the top drawer.

"What's this?" She pulled the drawer all the way out of its slot and put it on the writing surface. A leather cigarette case filled the entire space of the small drawer. "Oh, it's just a cigarette case, I think."

Lilian pried the case out of the drawer and opened it. Richard came over to see what she had found. Stamped into the inside of the leather cigarette case, on the bottom edge, was a swastika. Lilian looked at Richard and saw the same reaction on his face that she knew was on hers.

Inside was a row of cigarettes, but she noticed the leather lining was peeling up at one corner. She pulled at it, and the back opened like a book, revealing a space behind the cigarettes. Nestled in the leather were two brass cylinders and a space for one more. She took one out, unscrewed the top and turned it upside down onto her palm. A sealed ampule filled with clear liquid slid onto her hand. They both stood still.

"Leave it," Richard said. "Put it back, carefully. We'll send it right to the lab."

"But you know what it is," Lilian said.

"Probably cyanide."

"I've heard about this. Nazis give them to their spies. So they can commit suicide if they are caught and interrogated."

"This doesn't necessarily mean he was a Nazi spy." Richard didn't sound convinced.

"Doesn't it?" Lilian asked.

"Do you think he committed suicide?"

"No, he wasn't arrested," she scoffed. "He wasn't about to be interrogated."

"Or it could have been planted here for us to find to steer us in the wrong direction."

"Either way, anyone could have had access to this poison and used it on Sir Henry's cigar."

Lilian closed the case and slid it into an envelope, reminding herself to go wash her hands thoroughly—she knew how dangerous cyanide could be and didn't want to take any chances. How could Richard be so dense? It seemed logical to her that Sir Henry had political connections or some sort of affiliation with the Nazis. Richard's posh background was prejudicing his thinking. And anyone in the family or on the staff could've known about this leather case, which meant they knew about his Nazi sympathies. And if they knew, maybe that's why they weren't talking. "No one mentioned knowing about this."

"Either way, this must be where the poison came from," Richard said.

"Obviously, but it doesn't winnow down any suspects," Lilian said. "Anyone in the house could've had access."

"Let's get to the interviews with the house staff," Richard said. "At least we have more questions to ask now."

They had plenty of questions, Lilian thought. What they needed was more answers.

# CHAPTER 52

Agatha Christie sat in a high-backed upholstered chair in the drawing room, facing the window. She needed a break from the chatting, planning, and collaborating. She preferred to think things through on her own, let her brain do its work in silence, use her own little gray cells, as Hercule Poirot would say. The view of the garden was inspiring. She missed her own garden, and looking at the rainbow of roses just outside the window gave her joy. She slid down in the chair and let her whole body relax. Her brain kept working. *Who might've done it?* Poison a baronet? Who would do such a thing? It made her think of a Shakespeare line, *The web of our life is of a mingled yarn, good and ill together.* Even to someone as unpleasant as Sir Henry, it was a dreadful act for any human to commit. They would've had to have a very good reason, or be a horrible person. Or both. She heard footsteps enter the drawing room, but she couldn't see who it was and she knew she couldn't be seen, as the back of the chair was so tall. She was fully hidden.

"But Sarah, darling," Ambrose cajoled. "He couldn't have meant it."

"You don't understand," Sarah said.

"Then explain it to me."

Agatha heard a rustle of fabric and pictured them sitting on the love seat behind her. She closed her eyes. If they happen to find her, she could pretend to be asleep, to save them any embarrassment. Meanwhile, she listened keenly.

"He asked me to dance and I noticed he seemed tense."

"He'd had quite a lot of champagne."

"He wasn't tipsy, Ambrose, he was angry."

"All right, all right."

"He was clutching me too tight and I said, 'Henry, you're hurting me.' And he said, 'You know what really hurts? When you find out someone's been lying to you.' And I said, 'Whatever do you mean?' and then he put his face right in mine and said, 'About your mother.'"

"Your mother?"

"That's what I said, and he said, 'You never told me about your mother.' And I said, 'Why should my mother matter?'" Sarah's voice broke, and they were silent for a moment. Agatha restrained herself from peeking around the side of the chair and found herself holding her breath.

"What did he say?" Ambrose asked.

"He said, 'It matters that your mother was a Jew, and now I wonder what other lies you've told me.'" Agatha could hear Sarah weeping quietly.

"Darling, I'm so sorry." Ambrose sounded genuinely sympathetic.

"And then he broke the engagement. Right then and there." Sarah's voice now sounded angry. "He told me the wedding was off and that he wanted me out of the house first thing in the morning."

"What did you say?"

"What could I say? He'd made everything perfectly clear." Sarah sniffed. "I would've left right then and there if I could have."

"When I danced you away, you did look ghastly."

"I was in shock. Once I got to my room it felt like I'd been punched. I cried, then I pulled myself together and packed my things. I barely slept. Then in the morning—"

"In the morning we found him dead," Ambrose finished her sentence.

"I didn't kill him, Ambrose." Agatha heard the fear in Sarah's voice. "You've got to believe me."

"I believe you, darling." His voice was kind. "I've never been more sure of anything in my life."

"He accused me of lying, but how would I know that my mother's mother's religion would matter to him? I never heard him speak like that. It's this bloody impending war, it's turning everyone inside out."

"Not everyone."

They were silent, and Agatha wondered what she was missing. Ambrose's voice was huskier now.

"Darling, do you remember the night we met? Just before you'd met Henry? Before he stole you away from me?"

"Oh, Ambrose." Sarah sounded embarrassed. "That was ages ago."

"It doesn't feel like that long to me."

"I could never go back to that time, Ambrose."

They were quiet again, and Agatha began to wonder if she was going to be trapped there forever. But she heard that rustling noise again, and their voices came from a higher elevation so she knew they were standing.

"Don't tell the police, whatever you do," Ambrose warned her.

"Of course not, it would just give them the wrong impression."

"It doesn't matter now, whether he broke the engagement last night or not." Ambrose's voice got fainter as they moved toward the door. "It's over for good now."

Agatha heard their footfalls move off the carpet to the marble floor of the hallway. She slowly peeked around the chair to make sure they'd gone. *Ha! Don't tell the police, indeed!*

# CHAPTER 53

L ilian sat across from Mr. Wilson in the elegant morning room that they had been using for their interviews. He'd gone through his account of the whole evening, all the way through to when he filled the cigar box and went to bed. DC Lee dutifully took notes and Richard waited patiently, only prodding and asking questions in order to move him forward. Lilian had been uncharacteristically quiet during the interview so far. She was gauging whether Wilson would respond to DCI Davidson, man to man, or if her working-class style would do better. And perhaps it wouldn't be a bad idea to let Richard rely on his own instincts for a while, since he hadn't faith in hers.

"Thank you, Mr. Wilson, I think we have everything down from your point of view." Richard smiled congenially. "Just a few more questions." He glanced at Lilian, but she just nodded, and he went on. "Mr. Wilson, were you in the habit as acting as valet for the baronet?"

"Rarely, Chief Inspector," Wilson began. "His lordship preferred to dress himself. Of course, Mrs. Anderson and I made sure his wardrobe and accessories were in perfect condition and ready when needed."

"Were you familiar with everything in his rooms?"

"I would say so, yes."

"In and out of his drawers and cabinets, were you?"

"Yes, sir. Everything in his room was something to do with dressing himself. Mrs. Anderson and I had to keep things clean, neat, polished, well stocked."

"And had you noticed anything unusual, perhaps recently?" Richard asked.

"Unusual?" Wilson looked perplexed. "I don't know what you might mean, sir."

Richard removed the leather cigarette case from the envelope and showed it to Wilson.

"Is this familiar to you?"

"That cigarette case, sir?" Wilson asked. "Sir Henry usually carried one of the silver ones with his monogram, but that one was occasionally in use. Usually for the hunt or when he went out riding. Sometimes I'd see it in the library or he might have it with him at breakfast."

"Do you remember when and where you last saw it? Did you see it last night?"

Wilson paused. He looked pensive, and he shifted uneasily. "Last night? I didn't see him with it."

Richard opened it, revealing the swastika stamped onto the leather. Wilson looked at it, then at the detectives. Richard waited, but Wilson said nothing. Richard was sure that Wilson knew the swastika was the symbol of the Nazi party, but he couldn't tell if Wilson had known it was stamped on the inside of his master's case.

"Any idea where it came from, Mr. Wilson?" Lilian asked gently. Maybe she could make better progress. "Or who might've given it to him?"

"I haven't the foggiest," Wilson said after a beat. He seemed to shut down at that moment. His posture stiffened, and the expression on his soft wrinkled face went blank.

Lilian wondered what he really knew and if he was protecting his lord and master, or if the leather cigarette case with the Nazi symbol actually meant nothing to him. Either way, it was obvious that he would not engage in any negativity about Sir Henry Heathcote. She tried a new tactic.

"Mr. Wilson," Lilian began again. "Obviously this item is no reflection on you, we're just wondering about it. Maybe it has recently come to the house, or perhaps it was some relic that Sir Henry had collected years ago. Any ideas?"

"None at all, ma'am."

Lilian knew the interview was as good as over. They had hit a wall and any additional questioning would be a waste of time. She glanced at Richard, who looked as if he was having the same thoughts. Richard slipped the leather case back into the envelope and put it in his pocket. But Lilian wasn't ready to give up.

"Back to last night, Mr. Wilson, or early this morning, rather. Would you please describe your exact movements from the moment you locked the library until you fell asleep?"

Wilson looked at her strangely, but complied, describing going to his room, emptying his pockets, undressing and dressing for bed.

"And where do you keep the house keys overnight? Specifically, the key to the library?"

"I always keep the keys in my bedside table drawer."

"Is this well known?"

"Amongst the house staff, I suppose so."

"And the family?"

"Perhaps, I couldn't be sure."

"And your bedroom door, is it kept locked while you sleep?" Lilian asked.

"No, actually, I'm a heavy sleeper and Mrs. Anderson or Bernard wake me each morning."

"And who woke you this morning?"

"Mrs. Anderson."

"In fact, anyone could've entered your room, if they were rather quiet, and borrowed the keys?" Lilian asked.

"I doubt that anyone from my house staff would do something of that nature, risking the security of their job, and for that matter their reputation for a future job in service." Wilson's face was turning red. It was the first time Lilian had seen him close to losing his restraint.

"Yes, it certainly would be a dangerous piece of business," Richard remarked. "Of course, someone in the family wouldn't be risking their reputation."

"I can assure the both of you, no one entered my room early this morning, borrowed the keys, and returned them before I woke." Wilson regained his unreproachable butler's manner.

"How could you know?" Lilian asked innocently.

"For one thing, no one would." Wilson couldn't hide his indignance. "For another, my keys were undisturbed. They were exactly as I left them."

Lilian doubted he would notice the exact position of his key ring as it lay in his drawer, but she gave him no argument.

"Thank you, Mr. Wilson," Richard said. "I think we're finished for now. Please send Mrs. Anderson in, if you don't mind."

They all stood. Mr. Wilson gave a curt nod and left the room.

"That could be the mystery of the locked room solved," Davidson said wryly. "In the drawer next to a known heavy sleeper?"

"Possibly," Lilian mused. "But I still wonder why Sir Henry's keys were in the wrong pocket of his trousers when his body was found."

"It would be difficult to get the keys from Sir Henry while he was awake or even napping," Richard said. "And as you said, perhaps he just slipped them in the other pocket because his right hand was busy doing something else."

"Possibly." Lilian wasn't convinced. She felt less patient at his alternate theories than usual, still irked from their disagreement. As soon as they were done with the house staff, she just might try to find a way to speak with the mystery writers on her own. She glanced at DC Lee, who quickly looked back down to her notes, organizing her papers for the next interview. Had Lee noticed their tension?

# CHAPTER 54

Dorothy found the two young women, Kate and Sofia, in the winter garden. The warm June sun coming into the room made of glass created a tropical feeling.

"May I join you?" Dorothy asked.

"Oh, yes, Mrs. Sayers, please come and sit by me, it's quite comfortable on this settee."

"Very well, but how many times do I have to say, please call me Dorothy."

Kate's eyes were wet with grateful tears.

Sofia had been leaning over some deep purple orchids. "I love orchids, they're so perfect, such a pure art form from nature." She stood up straight. "But they have so little scent! So disappointing. How could something so beautiful be without an equal magnificence of perfume?" Sofia dropped on the settee on the other side of Kate, her arm draped casually around her friend's shoulders. She was turned sideways enough to speak to Dorothy. "Do you like orchids, Dorothy?"

"I prefer English roses."

"Oh, yes! So do I! What an aroma, the best of all flowers." Sofia wrinkled her nose. "The Italian national flower is the lily, but I find its fragrance too heavy. So thick, it chokes you. It reminds me of funerals."

At this, Kate put her handkerchief to her nose and sniffed.

"Cara mia, you must be strong," Sofia said softly.

"It can't be easy, my dear Kate," Dorothy soothed her. "Why don't we talk about something else. Tell me about school, what do you enjoy studying best?"

Kate didn't answer right away—she seemed too stuck in the sadness of her father's death to change the subject. But soon her face lit up.

"Poetry, literature, drama." Her eyes shone. "We read so many beautiful books."

"Who do you like?" Dorothy asked.

"Oh, Virginia Woolf, Edith Wharton, Daphne du Maurier, and older books like the Brontë sisters and Jane Austen. Oh, and George Eliot."

"My, you have a variety of tastes."

"I'd rather read than anything, wouldn't you?"

"Yes, read, and write, of course," Dorothy admitted.

"Oh, yes, and I've read all your books, Dorothy! Of course. I love them all."

"Why, thank you." Dorothy smiled. "I hardly compare to Virginia Woolf, of course."

Kate quickly spoke up. "Different books for different moods," she said sincerely. "Why limit our appetite?"

Sofia nudged Kate, and the two girls smiled at each other.

"Is that what you want to study at Oxford, literature?" Dorothy asked.

"Yes, I'm sure that would be the best sort of life."

"Is it the same for you, Sofia, do you want to study literature?"

"Yes, but both the Italian and the English authors."

"I study Italian literature as well," Dorothy added.

"It's full of so much beauty and drama." Sofia gazed toward the glass wall of the winter garden, out to the green lawn of the Hursley House Park.

"And after university?"

"I definitely want a career." Kate's eyes turned dark. "I'm not going to marry some man for his money and live in a house like this."

"No?" Dorothy asked.

"No, I'm going to live in London, in a townhouse, or a flat, and maybe work in a publishing house or teach literature or I don't know, anything else! As long I don't have to live in the country or get married."

Dorothy stopped herself from smiling. *Ah, youth!* To follow your passion no matter the consequences.

"Earlier you mentioned some doubt about your father letting you continue your education." Dorothy broached the topic carefully. "Was he against you going to university?"

Kate shifted in her seat and looked at Sofia, who took her hand.

"He didn't believe women should go to university. Women were meant for marriage and babies." Kate glanced at Sofia. "He was always talking about marrying me off. He had so many old-fashioned ideas."

"He didn't like *me* very much," Sofia added.

"He did at first. Until he realized how modern we were." Kate turned to Dorothy. "Do you know he actually thought Sofia was a bad influence on me? As if I didn't have my own thoughts and ideas."

"As if many of the women our age weren't like us." Sofia laughed.

"Will Charles let you go to university now that he is head of the family?"

Kate's mood shifted, and Dorothy couldn't read her. She looked toward the orchids. "He says he will. He's not like Father that way, and Marie's wonderful." Kate suddenly smiled and looked at Dorothy. "She went to university, you know."

"I think she's a good influence on him," Sofia said. And they laughed and locked hands.

Dorothy smiled. Going to university was important to Kate, and now she didn't have to worry about not being allowed to go.

Would she have been desperate enough to kill her father for that reason? Hard to imagine, but patricide was not out of the question. It was also obvious that Sofia cared for her deeply. Perhaps Sofia would be capable of doing something as despicable as murder in the name of love.

# Chapter 55

There was a timid knock at the door, and Mrs. Anderson entered.

"You sent for me, Chief Inspectors?"

"Come in, please, Mrs. Anderson." Lilian reverted to using her formal name for the interview. "Make yourself comfortable."

They asked her to describe the evening, anything that would include or be relevant to Sir Henry, anything unusual. Her recounting of the party had no new twists or turns.

"And this morning, when you woke Mr. Wilson, nothing was amiss?"

"Nothing at all," Mrs. Anderson said pleasantly. "The poor man only had a few hours of sleep. Not that any of us got a full night. We're all having quite a difficult day."

"I'm sure, Mrs. Anderson, and our sincere apologies for making it any more difficult," Lilian said. "Did you notice any of the family or house guests come below stairs this morning, or last night before you retired for the evening?"

"Not that I noticed." She gave her usual calm smile. "Except for Mr. Juan Guerra, this morning."

"This morning?" Lilian asked.

"Yes, it was just Cook and myself. He wanted to check what we were preparing for Lady Philippa. As if we didn't know her every want and need." Mrs. Anderson clucked. "I've been housekeeper here since before Lady Philippa came out." She smiled and shook her head.

"Why do you think he felt the need to check with you?"

"I really couldn't say," Mrs. Anderson said.

"And did you notice where he came from, exactly?" Lilian asked.

"He came right in the door to the kitchen."

"Did you see him come down the back stairs or did he come from the hall?"

"I didn't notice." Mrs. Anderson remained completely calm and pleasant, as if they were talking about what sandwiches to serve for tea. Lilian couldn't help wondering if she might get more from her later if they were alone. She felt she had been forging a fruitful relationship with Mrs. Anderson, but here with DCI Davidson and DC Lee, it had all gone flat.

They could think of nothing else for Mrs. Anderson, so they asked her to send Bernard.

Lilian Wyles and Richard Davidson wandered over to the window, closer to DC Lee.

"Do you need a break, Detective Constable?" Lilian asked.

"No, ma'am. I'm fine."

The three of them stood in silence for a moment.

"Could be something, Juan Guerra being below stairs," Richard said.

"He could've been sneaking the keys," Lilian added.

"Or returning them," DC Lee said.

"I suppose we have to entertain the possibility of a partnership in this murder."

"Or even more than two people," Lilian continued. "Juan and Philippa, perhaps with Charles."

"Or Juan and Charles," DC Lee suggested.

"Poison is a woman's weapon," Richard said. "Maybe Philippa and Kate."

"I can't see those two collaborating on anything. They don't seem to get on."

"Maybe it was collaborating on the murder that put a wedge between them," Richard said. Lilian was unconvinced.

"We're not getting enough from any of these interviews, Davidson." Lilian turned to him. "I still think we should recruit the writers to do what they do best. Ask leading questions or eavesdrop and get what they can for us."

"It's unprofessional," he protested.

"Don't you use sources on the street?" Lilian asked, trying to seem more convincing than annoyed. "I get some of the most useful information from people you wouldn't think could help."

"We don't know if it will be reliable."

"But it might give us some direction. We're nowhere right now."

"Nowhere is better than bungled." Richard shook his head.

Lilian looked at DC Lee who had her nose buried in her notes, pretending not to hear the conversation she surely couldn't help but hear.

Lilian Wyles looked out the window. It was a lovely spring day. Everything was shiny after the rain. Then something occurred to her. It didn't matter if he trusted her instincts, because she did.

# CHAPTER 56

Ngaio had decided to take a walk in the garden. She thought that maybe whoever had stolen the cigars might've hidden them outside, buried them, or chucked them under some shrubbery. She walked along the grass by the inner hedgerow looking for freshly turned earth. When she got to the farthest part of the lawn, she heard some voices on the other side of the hedge just ahead of her.

"I didn't want you to know," Charles was saying.

"But I knew something was wrong," Marie responded. "He was nothing but charming to me at first and then lately, especially last night at the party, he wouldn't even look at me."

"Better than the daggers that I felt every time he looked at me," Charles said.

Ngaio froze. This was a private conversation. She shouldn't be listening. Were they sitting or walking? She couldn't see them through the greenery. There was a marble bench a few feet away on her side of the hedge. She sat and tried not to lean into the shrubbery.

"What . . . *mumble*?" Marie's voice was low.

"I'm not sure, but near the start of the party I saw him talking with a man I didn't know, and as they were talking, they both kept glancing at the two of us. After that, his whole attitude changed."

"Yes . . . *mumble*." Again Ngaio missed what Marie was saying, but Charles's voice was louder.

"I felt like I was chasing him around all night, I wanted him to introduce me to some of the important people, but he was avoiding me. When I would almost catch up, he'd make some snide remark, or *mumble, mumble* and his row with Sarah and his ridiculous display with Kate and Sofia, I knew I had to get him alone. You'd gone to bed, so I followed him into the library."

"Right after *mumble mumble*?"

"Yes, and then he let it all out."

"*Mumble* he *mumble*?"

Ngaio was frustrated—what was the point in eavesdropping if you couldn't hear it?

"I never wanted you to know, Marie." Charles lowered his voice. Ngaio leaned into the hedge, making a crackling sound. She froze in an uncomfortable position and held her breath. "He brought up your background. Your grandfather."

Marie didn't say anything for a moment. Ngaio held her breath.

"Go on, Charles. It's nothing I haven't heard before." Her voice was steely.

"He said that I couldn't marry anyone with African-Caribbean blood. That our children would be tainted and that he wouldn't have the thirteenth baronet—"

"Go on, say it," Marie prodded.

"—not be white." Charles couldn't have sounded more ashamed. "He said he'd cut me out of the will if we married."

"What did you say?" Marie's voice had a strange edge to it. Ngaio felt for them both.

"I told him to go right ahead, that we'd be married no matter what he did."

Ngaio hoped that was what he had said. But something like this could plant a seed of doubt into Marie's mind and grow into the kind of mistrust that could break them apart. Ngaio suddenly felt conscience-stricken and slowly stepped away from the hedgerow. She stole back to the house quickly.

A father doing something like that could certainly instill anger in a son. Enough anger to do something desperate, she thought.

# CHAPTER 57

Margery Allingham was starting to get peckish. She looked at her wristwatch as she wandered down the expansive main hall. She hadn't eaten much at lunch, but it wasn't close to teatime. She felt a little guilty to expect the house staff to function as normal amidst all the drama. How did they feel about the death of Sir Henry Heathcote? Had they found him as objectionable as she did? Would they go so far as to murder their lord and master?

She went into the drawing room and found Philippa sitting by the window, staring out at the garden. Margery tried to walk heavily so that Philippa would hear her and not feel she was being spied upon. Philippa turned her head at the sound of the footfalls.

"Hello," she said listlessly.

"Hello." Margery wandered closer to where Philippa was sitting, wondering how to start a conversation. She shouldn't have worried.

"I don't know if I'm more sad or afraid," Philippa said, and then burst into tears.

Margery was at a loss for what to do in the moment. Philippa produced her own handkerchief and dabbed at her eyes and nose. Margery sat near her.

"I'm so sorry, this is inexcusable," Philippa murmured.

"No, not at all," Margery protested. "I can't imagine a more excusable situation." She smiled, hoping to lighten the mood.

"You're very kind." Philippa finished wiping her tears and tried to smile at Margery.

"Do you mind if I ask, what are you afraid of, exactly?" Margery asked.

"That the murderer isn't finished."

"What do you mean?"

"Whoever killed my father, perhaps they have something against the whole family." Philippa explained. "We might all be in danger."

Margery thought about that. She was rather convinced that it was one of the family who killed the baronet, and she doubted they had the same grudge against someone else. Sir Henry's death seemed to solve a few problems for the family in general, and she couldn't think of any lingering issues with others in the family.

"What do you think they had against your father?" Margery asked.

"Juan's politics were so different than my father's. I mean, I didn't think it was an issue until recently. I thought they used to enjoy their debates; they were quite lively. But these last few weeks, and especially last night, there was too much ire behind my father's words."

"Did Juan stop engaging your father in political discussion?"

Philippa paused and looked at Margery, frowning. "Juan is a perfect gentleman and a wonderful husband," she said. "He always thinks of me first. When I mentioned my fears last night, he did his best to make the evening pleasant."

"Right." Margery took a breath. "And your father didn't pour any petrol on the fire?"

"There was no fire." Philippa forced a light laugh. "And my father was much too busy with his business associates to follow Juan around and start rows with him." Philippa smoothed her skirt. "But speaking of rows, Mr. Rana Gupta could've been ready to start one." When Margery smiled encouragingly, Philippa went on. "He doesn't think I know, but years ago my father had business in India. New Delhi, in fact, where Mr. Gupta's family is from, and there was something between our fathers back then."

"Yes?"

"I don't know exactly what it was, but I believe his father accused my father of cheating him out of some business or land, or something like that."

Margery's eyes widened. "What do you think happened?"

"I know my father is a savvy businessman and often bought and sold businesses, manufacturing plants, plantations, such like that." Philippa tossed off this as if every father had similar business dealings.

"And you think one of those business deals proved negative for Rana Gupta's father?"

"I really don't know the details, but last night he mentioned his background, and thinking about it this afternoon, it came to me who he is. I'm sure that he talked Sir Samuel into bringing him along just so he could get to my father." Philippa nodded vigorously. "Why else would he be here except for some kind of recrimination?"

Margery rubbed her hands together. *This was a twist.* "Have you told the detectives?"

"I just put it together a few minutes ago, and then I was struck with fear. What if he wants revenge on all of us?" Philippa looked at Margery, eyes wide, her mouth trembling.

"I think we should go talk to the police as soon as possible." Margery stood, and as she did, Rana Gupta entered the drawing room. Philippa gave a little squeak as she stood, and Margery noted that Rana looked embarrassed. Wilson entered behind him.

"Lady Philippa, shall we serve tea here in the drawing room as usual or would you prefer the dining room?" Wilson asked.

"Here in the drawing room is fine, Wilson. I think we all need a break from the dining room. Could you please invite Chief Inspectors Wyles and Davidson to join us when you gather the others? And if you don't mind, please serve the constables in the morning room."

"Very good, my lady," Wilson responded and backed out politely.

Margery hadn't spent much time around the aristocratic world and couldn't help feeling slightly amused. Margery saw Philippa look at Rana and then at her.

"Margery, let's find your compatriots and let them know tea will be served soon, shall we?" She took her arm and almost marched past Rana Gupta, who seemed rather surprised. Margery tried to smile at him as they passed, but she was sure her expression wasn't natural. She didn't know what to think about what Philippa had told her, but it was obvious Philippa didn't want to be near the man. They would have to tell the detectives as soon as possible.

# CHAPTER 58

"Mr. Wilson needs me back soon, sir," Bernard was saying as he stood in front of Lilian Wyles and Richard Davidson. "It's teatime."

"Please sit down, Bernard." Richard held an open hand toward the blue love seat.

Bernard looked at him questioningly and perched on the edge of the seat. "If you say so, sir." With prompting, he walked them through his version of the evening. Lilian noticed that his description was more colorful than some of the others, with an emphasis on the music and his impression of the men in the catering group. She thought he was quite observant, in an amusing way, but offered nothing that added to their investigation. Was he leaving something out, or had he really witnessed nothing of significance? Had he really heard nothing of any of the conflicts they had already heard about?

"A few of the guests mentioned seeing you upstairs during the party," Lilian asked.

"Yes, Brigid and I went upstairs a few times to fill matches and cigarettes, and to tidy up the sitting-out rooms," Bernard explained. "And toward the end of the night to check for any belongings anyone might've left lying about. Sometimes ladies leave their gloves or gentlemen forget they left a lighter or cigarette case."

"I see," Lilian said. "You checked every room upstairs?"

"Except the rooms of the family or the weekend guests that were locked, ma'am," Bernard answered.

"Did you happen to see anything out of the ordinary as you went through the rooms?"

"No, ma'am."

"Did you look through anywhere else?"

"The ground floor as well, people tend to wander about."

"The library?"

"That's always locked, ma'am."

"But you have access to the keys, don't you?"

"Only if Mr. Wilson requires us to do something there."

"Yes, I understand." Lilian felt as if he were reading from a list, giving the proper answers, but leaving something out. She went on. "During the party, where did you spend most of your time?"

Bernard shrugged one shoulder. "There was a lot to do, helping the caterers, keeping an eye on things. Mr. Wilson wanted us, Brigid and me, to keep watch on the household. You never know if some catering mug gets an idea in his head, you know what I mean?"

"I certainly do," Lilian replied.

"And did any catering mug get an idea in his head?" Richard asked.

"No, sir, not with us watchin', there were no real problems, just some messes to clean up." Bernard was affable in all his responses. Lilian couldn't think of a way to knock him off balance, off his script.

"Are you almost done with me, Chief Inspectors?" Bernard's smile didn't fade. "I'll be needed to serve tea."

As if on cue, Wilson knocked, then opened the door, and Bernard jumped to his feet and was gone in the blink of any eye.

Wilson nodded to them. "I just wanted to let you know that Lady Philippa has invited both of you, Chief Inspectors, to the drawing room for tea. And tea will be served here in the morning room for the rest of your colleagues."

"Thank you, Mr. Wilson," Lilian responded. "That's very kind. Please send Miss Brigid in. After that we'll join the family in the drawing room."

Wilson ducked out and closed the door.

"Bernard's not telling us something." Lilian looked at Richard. "Did you get that impression?"

"He certainly had the party line down pat." Richard stretched his legs and leaned back on the chair. "A faithful servant, through and through."

"Yes, that's what I meant."

★ ★ ★

Brigid started off the same as Bernard, cheerfully describing a lovely party. Everyone having a good time. Busy helping Mr. Wilson and Mrs. Anderson supervise the catering team.

"I've never served at such a party." Brigid practically had stars in her eyes. "The music was so lovely. And then at midnight a new band came on and played the most wonderful dance music. Everyone was having a good time, especially the young folks."

"Did you notice any disagreements or arguments on the dance floor?" Lilian asked.

"No, ma'am, nothing like that." Brigid looked taken aback. "It was so fun watching everyone dance. I—" She stopped suddenly.

"Were you allowed to dance?"

"Oh, no, of course not, we were working." Brigid's voice got softer.

"You and Bernard didn't take a short break and enjoy the music?" Lilian saw something in Brigid's eyes. Maybe she'd hit on something here.

"We couldn't do that. If we got caught, we could lose our jobs."

Lilian lowered her voice. "We wouldn't tell anyone, Brigid. But if I were serving a big party like that, I'd certainly find a hiding place to have a little dance to the music, when I could."

Brigid's brown eyes grew big. She sat up straighter and looked from Lilian to Richard. "Did Bernard say something?"

"We can't comment on what was said in the other interviews," Lilian said. "Is there something you want to tell us?"

"You don't tell no one else what any of us have said?" Brigid asked nervously.

"Never. But if we find that you've lied to us, it would be very serious," Richard added.

Lilian watched Brigid carefully. Her eyes were moist. She twisted her hands together.

"I never lie," Brigid said. "Lying is wrong."

"Yes, of course," Lilian agreed. "Perhaps you forgot to tell us something. Is there something else you remember?"

"Well," Brigid started. "If it's private, between us, I mean, that is, if you won't be telling Mr. Wilson or Sir Charles."

"No, Brigid, anything you tell us is confidential." Lilian waited. Brigid's posture slumped and then she took a deep breath.

"The dance music was so fun." She clasped her hands in front of her, and her eyes took on a dreamy cast. "I love to dance, and Bernard said why shouldn't we dance if we want to."

"Of course," Lilian agreed amiably.

"But I was afraid of getting caught. There were so many people around, wandering everywhere, anyone could've walked in on us if we used the winter garden or the dining room."

"Yes?"

"So, Bernard had just gotten the keys from Mr. Wilson, to get matches and cigarettes from the storeroom and—"

"And?" Lilian prodded.

"And we had the library key on the ring so we let ourselves in. We knew we'd hear the music well enough, it's so close to the ballroom and there was plenty of room to dance, and no one would dare come in."

"I see."

"Bernard is a wonderful dancer! We had such fun. But then—" Brigid twisted her fingers.

"Did someone come in?"

"Yes. We heard the key in the lock. It was Sir Henry." Brigid's remembered fear shone darkly in her eyes. "We hid behind the curtains by the French windows."

Lilian felt her pulse quicken but spoke calmly. "Was Sir Henry alone?"

"No, he was with another man, I don't know who he was." Now that Brigid had gotten started, she seemed anxious to confess. "I couldn't see them and I didn't recognize his voice."

"Did you hear what they were talking about?"

"I could hear them rustling some papers about, and I think they said something about a factory." Brigid wrinkled her forehead. "I didn't really understand what they were saying. It didn't make sense. They were talking about someone's auntie. But it was a funny name. Auntie Mary-something, not Mary Anne, though, something different. I thought maybe it was French."

"Auntie Mary?"

"Auntie Mary-something. I don't know, Auntie Meredith or Mary Beth?" Brigid was frustrated. "Definitely something about Auntie someone," she said definitively.

Lilian and Richard looked at each other.

"I couldn't hear very well behind the curtain, and I couldn't see them at all," said Brigid. "I just recognized his lordship's voice, and my heart was pounding so loud in my chest, I could barely hear anything else. I was so afraid we'd get caught. I can't lose this job, ma'am. You won't tell Mr. Wilson, will you? Or Sir Charles or Lady Philippa?"

"Don't worry," Lilian comforted her. Brigid was practically levitating with anxiety. "Your interview is confidential, I promise."

Brigid calmed down a little, her big brown eyes still wide.

"What happened then, Brigid? How long were you hiding before they left the library?"

"Maybe five minutes? But it felt like an hour!" Brigid sat back on the love seat. "By the time we escaped, I was sure Mr. Wilson had seen we were missing and was having a cow."

"Had he?"

"No. He hadn't noticed. We went straight to find him and told him we were on our way to the upstairs lounges, to fill the matches and cigarettes." Brigid put on a shy smile. "He never did know the difference."

"And the keys?" Lilian asked.

"We gave them right back to Mr. Wilson as soon as we escaped."

Lilian looked down at her notes. A factory, some papers, Auntie Mary-something. It wasn't making sense, not yet.

They let Brigid go.

"What do you think she was talking about, Auntie Mary-something?" DC Lee asked. "Not sure how I should make the note for the report."

"Write it out the way she said it for now, DC Lee," Lilian answered.

"I can't imagine he was talking about a real aunt of his," Richard said. "It must be some kind of code name."

"Or perhaps it just sounded like auntie," Lilian added.

"I think we need to speak to Bernard again. Perhaps he heard more than Brigid did." Richard stood. "But for now let's join the family for tea. We could use it, and maybe something will come up in conversation."

Lilian turned to DC Lee. "We'll tell Roper to gather the others for your tea in here. We'll continue with any other necessary interviews later."

Richard held the door open for Lilian, and she went out ahead of him. Lilian doubted the family would drop their guard over tea and sandwiches, but one could always hope.

# CHAPTER 59

The drawing room was full of family and guests, yet the only sounds were teacups clinking in their saucers and spoons stirring sugar into tea.

Everyone nodded to them with strained smiles, and by the time Lilian and Richard had poured their tea and chosen sandwiches and biscuits, family members were dabbing their mouths with napkins and quietly leaving the room. Soon it was only the two detectives and the four writers left. Richard ate quickly.

"I've got to ring the Yard," Richard said to Lilian. "Perhaps they'll have some results."

"Do you need me?" Lilian looked at her unfinished plate.

"No, no, you stay." Richard looked distractedly at his notebook. "Finish your tea. I'll come back when I'm done." He turned and nodded to them all as he left the room.

Lilian refilled her cup and sat back in her chair. She waited until she reckoned Richard was far enough down the hall. She looked at the writers, and they looked at her.

"Ladies," Lilian began. "I believe you offered to help."

"Yes?" Agatha placed her cup in its saucer with a clink.

"If you don't mind, I'd like to talk about how you might do just that."

The four women tried not to look overtly pleased. But they each perked up in their own inimitable way and gave Lilian their attention.

"Perhaps, if you are able to engage in casual conversation with the family and guests, you might gather some information they left out of the interviews."

The writers looked at each other and smiled.

"Funny you should mention it," Ngaio said, and they all moved closer to where Lilian was sitting.

★ ★ ★

"Sir Samuel, yes, sir, I just finished speaking to the Yard," Richard said into the phone on the hall table. "Nothing useful, sir, in regards to fingerprints." Richard flipped through the pages of his notebook. "Yes, cyanide confirmed, the end of his cigar was soaked in it. He died very quickly."

Richard looked down the hall to make sure he was alone. "Sir, one thing you should know. We found a leather cigarette case in his bedroom, with a Nazi symbol stamped onto the inside. Yes, sir, a swastika. And inside the case, in a compartment behind the cigarettes, were two unopened ampules of liquid, most likely cyanide, with space for a third." Richard fiddled with the lace doily under the phone, smoothing the edges. "You'd know better than I, sir, if you've seen something like it before, I understand. Did he have a file with the Home Office?"

Richard moved the phone closer to the edge of the telephone table and sat on the padded bench that was placed for that purpose. "Rana Gupta's family? That's very interesting. Did you know about that previous to his appointment? No. Of course not." Richard stood again, straight as a rail. "You will? Very good, sir. Your presence will be very welcome here, sir. Yes, we'll expect you in a couple of hours or so. Thank you, sir." He hung up the phone and stood thinking for a moment. Then he scratched away in his notebook, put it back in his pocket, and stalked down the hall toward the drawing room.

★ ★ ★

"So, let me make sure I have this all down correctly." Lilian flipped back a few pages in her notebook and read from her notes. "Agatha heard Ambrose and Sarah discuss that the row with Henry was about the fact that her mother's mother was Jewish and that Sir Henry broke off the engagement. And did Ambrose know about this?"

"He didn't seem to," Agatha said. "But I couldn't be sure. He didn't say either way."

"Right. And then, Dorothy, you were with Miss Kate, and Miss Sofia confirmed that Sir Henry wasn't going to let her go to university, is that right?"

"Yes, he seemed to be more interested in finding her a husband," Dorothy answered. "And he wasn't thrilled about her relationship with Sofia."

"And Ngaio, you overheard Charles tell Marie that Sir Henry was going to disinherit him if he married her because of her racial background?"

"Her African ancestry, yes," Ngaio said. "They were quite upset."

"Was Charles very angry?"

"I would say he sounded so, yes, but I couldn't see his face," Ngaio said, a little embarrassed, "um, through the hedge."

"Margery, Philippa let it slip that her husband had a political dispute with Sir Henry?"

"Yes, but she played it down and tried to change the subject by telling me about Mr. Gupta's family. She seemed to think her father had some business dealings with the Guptas in New Delhi that went bad for his family. I don't know if she didn't know the details or just didn't want to reveal them."

"Perhaps I can find out more." Lilian checked through her notebook. "Ladies, I can't tell you how helpful you've been. This is all very useful."

"It seems everyone had some sort of motive," Agatha said. "But did they all have the opportunity?"

"That's what we're trying to ascertain," Lilian said. "Who could've gotten hold of the keys and switched the cigars between three thirty and seven forty in the morning?"

The writers looked at each other, shaking their heads. This was one piece of the puzzle none of them had made progress on.

"Maybe this has nothing to do with the murder, but Sir Henry had a private meeting with a man in the library during the party," Lilian told them. "They were discussing something and sharing some papers."

"How did you come to know this?" Agatha asked.

"Please don't mention this to anyone in the family, but Wilson gave Brigid and Bernard the keys to go to the storeroom at one point during the party, and they let themselves into the library to have a bit of a dance party of their own."

Margery laughed while the others smiled.

"They hid behind the curtains when Sir Henry and the other man came in."

"Did they hear what they were talking about?" Ngaio asked.

"That's the odd thing, Brigid heard Sir Henry say something about his Auntie Mary, or Auntie Meredith, or some name she didn't recognize," Lilian said.

"Auntie Meredith?" Dorothy remarked. "That seems arbitrary."

"And no one found any relevant papers?" Margery asked.

"Just plenty of ash in the grate." Lilian frowned.

"Blast," Ngaio muttered.

"Precisely," Lilian agreed. "But again, please keep this confidential. Brigid is afraid of losing her position."

"Of course, but what of the missing cigars?" Agatha asked. "If Wilson filled the box at half three and someone replaced those cigars with just one poisoned cigar sometime before seven, what happened to all those cigars?"

"That's what I've been wondering," Lilian added. "A pile of cigars hasn't turned up anywhere."

"And who knew that he'd smoke that cigar?" Margery asked.

"It would have to be someone who knew his routine," Lilian said. "He smoked one every morning after he ran his dogs."

"His family would know, certainly, and the house staff," Agatha mused aloud. "But would Rana Gupta? Or even Marie or Sofia?"

"It may have been mentioned at any time," Lilian answered. "I'm more puzzled at how someone got into the library, as he kept it locked and only Sir Henry and Wilson had keys."

"He never left it open?" Ngaio asked.

"That's what they say," Lilian answered.

"But—" Ngaio stopped mid thought. Something was in the back of her mind, wanting to come out.

"But what?" Lilian asked.

"When I woke up at five o'clock and wandered through the house looking for the kitchen stairs," Ngaio began. "I didn't see or hear anyone. But the library door may have been open."

"What?" Lilian sat up.

"Yes, now I remember, I'm sure of it. I came through the main hall, looking for an entrance to the lower staircase. I looked at each door as I passed, noting whether it would lead me to the stairs or not. I knew it would be by the dining room, so when I went by the library, I knew it wasn't close enough to that end of the house, but the image of it didn't really register. I was a bit sleepy and, well, still under the effects of champagne." She looked embarrassed.

"But you're sure now, the door was open?" Lilian asked.

"Yes, I can picture it now," Ngaio said. "I hadn't been in the library before, but I saw the shelves of books from the door and logged it in my brain, *that's the library.*"

They all sat in silence for a moment, contemplating the possibilities.

"That might explain why we found his jacket and tie in the sitting room." Lilian mused. "He must've felt the house was all put to bed, and he wandered around without bothering to lock the door, as he usually did. He went into the cloakroom, took off his jacket and tie, perhaps smoked a cigarette or took a nap."

"So the library wasn't actually a locked room the whole time, after all." Agatha smiled. "That gives a window of opportunity for someone to switch the cigars, but it doesn't give a clue as to where they are hidden."

"We should all keep searching." Ngaio stood.

"Absolutely," Margery agreed.

"And keep listening." Agatha looked at Lilian.

"Yes, please keep listening," Lilian responded. "And chatting."

"And thinking," Dorothy said.

"Five heads are better than one." Lilian looked around the room at them. "Or six, if we count DCI Davidson."

"Of course we must." Ngaio smiled. He had a lovely head on his shoulders, she thought to herself, for drawing and thinking.

Then, as if on cue, DCI Richard Davidson walked into the drawing room.

# CHAPTER 60

"Thanks for the chat, ladies," Lilian said as she stood. She smiled and nodded to each of them.

The writers smiled in return and silently filed out of the room, each nodding to Richard Davidson on the way out.

"Hello, Davidson," Lilian said. "Brilliant timing."

"As usual," Richard said sardonically. "Can we talk here?"

"I have a few things to tell you."

"First, I have to report that no fingerprints other than Sir Henry's were found in the library, and that Sir Samuel is on his way back to Hursley House."

"I hope he can be helpful," Lilian said.

"I think he wants to do anything he can to speed things up." Richard straightened his tie.

Lilian settled on a sofa. Richard sat near her and poured a cup of tea. He wouldn't be able to deny that the writers had been useful when she told him what she knew.

★ ★ ★

Lilian updated Richard on everything the writers had told her, including Ngaio's discovery of the open library. He took notes and asked few questions, occasionally lifting one eyebrow or pulling at his chin.

"It seems they may be helpful after all."

"Yes." She looked at him expectantly.

"What do you want me to say?"

"Oh, something like 'Good instincts, DCI Wyles' might do."

His cheeks went pink. "It's the biggest case I've ever been on—I've been rather averse to taking any risks."

"I understand, but if there's one thing I've learned, it's that you don't solve cases without taking risks." Lilian felt some sympathy toward him. "And always trust your instincts."

They were quiet for a moment.

"Can we start again?" Richard asked.

Lilian gave him an appreciative nod, but she knew her trust in him would take time to mend.

"In connection to what Lady Philippa said about Rana Gupta," Richard went on, "Sir Henry found some new information he hadn't known about Rana. Some business dealings that Sir Henry had in New Delhi that ruined the Gupta family."

"Ruined?"

"They lost a plantation that had been in the family for generations. Rana was almost at the end of his last year at school here in England. Back in New Delhi, his father took his own life."

"Dear God!" Lilian exclaimed.

"Yes, it was quite serious. He returned to New Delhi to be with his mother."

"That does fit with what Philippa told Margery."

"Let's bring him back for questioning. This could be the strongest motive so far," Richard said. "And we need to speak with Bernard as well. He might've heard more than Brigid did from behind those curtains."

As Richard Davidson drained his teacup, Lilian wondered who "Auntie Meredith" was.

★ ★ ★

The four writers huddled in the winter garden.

"Shall we each find our own scheme or give out assignments?" Margery asked excitedly.

"Letting it happen organically has been working so far," Agatha said.

"I'm for that," Ngaio agreed.

"I might just take myself to the drawing room and have a think," Dorothy murmured.

"But wait." Margery stopped them before they dispersed. "Let's discuss the possibility of using clues or events here in our own books. I have a proposal."

"A proposal?" Ngaio asked.

"We don't know all the details of this mystery yet, or who might want to use what parts of it. But I propose that whoever gets closest to finding the murderer gets first choice of the story details." Margery looked at the others expectantly.

"Why not?" Agatha said. "It'll help pass the time."

Margery clasped her hands together and rocked back and forth on her heels.

# Chapter 61

"It's no use, Bernard," Richard said. "Brigid told us the two of you were in the library and had to hide behind the curtains."

Bernard's expression hadn't changed, but his face turned pink and grew darker red as DCI Davidson spoke.

"Lying to Scotland Yard is not recommended," Richard went on. "We'll wait right here until you come clean and tell us anything you might've forgotten to tell us in our last interview."

Bernard sat for a moment, unmoving. Then he rubbed his palm across his mouth and forced a cooperative smile.

"Of course, sir, it just didn't seem to be anything important, and we're trained not to eavesdrop on our employers as we move about on the job."

"You were hardly on the job at that moment." Richard looked at him pointedly. "Be that as it may, please repeat whatever you heard, however accidentally."

"I don't know what Brigid said, but it was hard to hear anything behind that thick velvet curtain."

"Any fragments would be of interest to us."

Bernard screwed up his face. "It didn't make sense, sir, them talking about an auntie."

"Did he say it was his auntie, or someone else's?" Lilian asked. "Can you repeat exactly what you thought you heard?"

Bernard looked down at his feet as he shuffled them.

"He said, 'It'll be the Auntie Meredith, or some name like that. That's the one. The Auntie Meredith.' And then we just heard them moving papers around and waited for them to go." Bernard opened his hands, palms up, in defeat.

"So it was *the* Auntie Meredith, not *his* Auntie Meredith?" Lilian confirmed.

"Yes, ma'am, but it wasn't exactly Meredith," Bernard admitted. "It was something like Meredith, but different."

"All right, Bernard. Was there anything else you wanted to tell us?" Lilian asked.

"No, nothing. I swear that's the lot of it."

"We can only hope so," Davidson said in an arch tone. "Make sure you come straight to us if you remember anything else, or hear anything else. Do you understand?"

"Yes, sir."

"We're done with you for now."

Bernard took his leave, almost knocking down Constable Roper on his way out.

"Mr. Rana Gupta is nowhere to be found in the house, sir," Roper said with humility.

"Is that so?" Davidson replied. Rana's disappearance did not bode well. "I need to stretch my legs, in any case. Wyles, let's call this a break with a purpose. We can keep our eyes open for Gupta or anything else that might be useful. I'll take the back garden."

"Very well," Lilian stood. "I'll take the front."

# CHAPTER 62

Ngaio knew that whoever had done the deed would've needed to dispose of the cigars that had been in the mahogany box before they put the poisoned one in place. Therefore, she decided to continue to look for the missing cigars. It was a path to take, at least, since she couldn't think how else to carry on with the investigation.

She wandered through the back garden, walking in a logical pattern so she didn't miss a spot, looking for freshly dug earth. She zigzagged the long, sloped lawn until she came to the chapel. It was a beautiful building, small, built from stone. The tall narrow windows lifted her eyes to the heavens, as they were meant to do. The heavy wooden door was ajar, and she slipped inside soundlessly.

She stood for a moment looking at the late afternoon summer light coming through the slender pointed-arched windows. It was a soft glow, leaving a great deal of vague shadows and mysterious corners. A dramatic shaft of light fell across the altar, making her wish she'd brought her sketchbook. Ngaio breathed in the fragrance of incense and ancient dust. She began to move forward and then suddenly sneezed violently.

Richard Davidson popped up from below the front row of pews.

"Bloody hell!" Ngaio jumped back, bumped into a pew, and almost fell over.

"Pardon me," Richard said quickly.

"Were you trying to give me a heart attack?" Ngaio attempted to recover from being flustered, but she felt that she had looked the fool and that irked her.

"I didn't hear you come in." Richard was as surprised as Ngaio, and even more defensive.

"What were you doing under the pew? Hiding?" Ngaio began to get her composure back.

"I was just searching for, erm, anything."

"To do with the case?"

"Yes, of course to do with the case."

They stood there silently for a moment, staring at each other. The moment passed. Richard ventured an apologetic smile.

"I didn't mean to be objectionable." Ngaio smiled back. "Shall we start again?"

"Please, Miss Marsh."

"Call me Ngaio, won't you?" She reached her hand forward for shaking. He took it in his, gentle but firm. "May I call you Richard?"

"I'd be delighted," Richard paused. "Ngaio."

"Well done, us." Ngaio dropped his hand and laughed. "Have you found anything here in the chapel?"

"No, unfortunately. I was really using the excuse of a search to take a break from interviewing. It can drain you, talking to people for hours."

"Oh," Ngaio ran her hand through her short dark hair. "I'll leave you to it, then."

"No, no, I didn't mean—" Richard stopped, wondering why he felt tongue-tied with her. "Interrogating people is different than, erm, just talking."

"Of course, but don't let me keep you," Ngaio gestured feebly toward the spot where Richard had emerged. "From your search."

Richard didn't know how to respond. Was she dismissing him? Was she being polite? Or shy?

"Did you come in for some quiet?" he asked.

"If I'm honest"—Ngaio tried not to smile too broadly—
"I've actually been searching as well. You see, I was wondering,
what happened to all those cigars? Wilson had just filled the
box."

"Precisely my thoughts," Richard agreed. "That's what I hoped
I might find."

"If we found their hiding place, perhaps that would give us
some sort of indication about who replaced them."

"Yes, but . . ."

"What?"

"It's just that, technically, I don't think I can sanction or at least
approve of you searching for anything about the case. But anything
you happened to find on your own, and then would bring to us,
would be fine, of course."

"Just—unsanctioned," she said.

"Yes." Richard put his hands in his pockets.

"I see." Ngaio folded her arms across her chest. "And if we
were to search together?"

He seemed to wince at this notion. Then he shrugged.

"Too unorthodox?" Ngaio ventured.

"It's just, to—to employ a possible witness in the case, to engage
in the investigation, it's not exactly the accepted procedure . . ."

"At Scotland Yard," Ngaio finished. Richard shook his head
apologetically.

"Well, Richard," Ngaio smiled and started to walk casually
down the center aisle, looking one way, then the other. "I'm in the
mood for a walk, and I'm a very observant person, you know. I
have a trained eye, as both an artist and a writer. One never knows
what I might find, casually, that is, in an unsanctioned sort of way,
while I just happened to be walking about."

"I say." Richard began to walk back through the pews. "That
sounds like a pleasant way to pass the afternoon. Taking a casual
walk." He began to feel under each pew, to look in each prayer
book rack, and behind every cushion meant for kneeling. Ngaio
followed his lead and did the same on the other side of the aisle.

When they each got to the last of the pews on their own side, they arrived at the back of the room at almost the same time.

"Nothing," Richard said.

"Nothing," Ngaio echoed.

"By the way, I can't tell you how much it means to the case that you noticed the library door was unlocked and open at five in the morning," Richard said. "In fact, all your observations have been very helpful and much appreciated." Suddenly he felt embarrassed by his effusiveness. "I admit, I am a stickler for the rules, and you, all of you, could've easily kept to yourselves, and then we would've missed out on some important information. I just wanted to say thank you."

Ngaio didn't know how to respond. She was pleased, not just by his admission, but with his genuine and honest presentation.

"You're very welcome, Richard. It's my pleasure." They smiled at each other for a moment, then both felt like idiots and laughed.

"Fancy a walk by the hedges?"

"I thought you'd never ask."

He held the heavy wooden door open for her, and she walked through into the late afternoon sunlight.

# Chapter 63

Margery took her time to think as she sat on the bench in the winter garden after the others had gone. She noted how the low angle of the sun glared through the glass and made ominous shadows of the plants that surrounded her. She was thinking about how Lilian had said that Brigid had been hiding behind the curtains and heard two voices, Sir Henry and another man. And they'd been rustling papers. In the library.

She popped up off the bench and went down the main hall. While the library had been kept locked during Sir Henry's lifetime, now that it had been searched, it had been left unlocked and unattended. Margery stood by the door, her hand on the knob, looking down the hall one way, then the other. No one had told them they couldn't go in the library, had they? Internally, she shrugged to herself and went in, leaving the door open behind her.

It was a dim room, even after she switched on the reading lamp by the sofa and the desk lamp across the room. The sun was getting lower in the sky and only a faint glow came through the glass. She moved to the French windows and then slipped behind the curtains. Standing there for a moment, she listened. What had Brigid heard? Margery could hear nothing but the wind outside and an occasional bird call.

She came out from behind the curtains into the room and walked to the sofa, around it, once, then twice and stopped between the coffee table and the side table. Both surfaces had tall stacks of books—what a collector Sir Henry had been, she thought. She turned to look around the room, at the ceiling-high shelves completely full of books, every shape and size. She had many books herself, but this was a collection that rivaled the Bodleian at Oxford. She turned to the coffee table and glanced at the books there. Maybe they had significance. She leaned over to look more closely and in doing so she bumped the stack of books on the side table. She felt the shift of the weight behind her and swung around, just as the stack of books fell over and hit the floor.

"My hat! That was clumsy." She looked around, realized no one was listening, and smiled at herself. She began to pick up the books to stack them back on the table when some papers fell out of one of them, apparently architectural drawings of some kind. She unfolded them and turned them around, this way and that, to try and understand what she was looking at. But the light was too dim. Margery moved toward the reading lamp and, just as she could finally see the correct orientation of the figures on the paper, she heard a step behind her. But before she could turn to see who it was, something hit her on the back of the head and everything went black.

# CHAPTER 64

"But, Dorothy," Kate was in the middle of an impassioned speech as she sat next to Dorothy in the drawing room. "I just don't *know* what I feel."

"But that's normal, Kate," Dorothy responded. "You're still in shock. Your heart and mind haven't had enough time to let it sink in and make sense of it,"

"But *none* of it makes sense, don't you *see*?" Kate sighed rather dramatically. "I know I feel sad, deep down. But after last night all I can think about is that now I'll be able to go to university next year and I can be with Sofia whenever I want."

"That's all right."

"But I also feel so guilty, so incredibly guilty."

"What for?"

"For not caring so much that Father is gone. And that everyone might find out that I feel that way." She looked at Dorothy, her big blue eyes getting waterier by the second.

"Kate, do you know what I think?"

"I *don't* know what you think, Dorothy, and I'm *dying* to."

"I think you care more than you'll allow yourself to admit." Dorothy put her hand on Kate's. "And I also think that you are allowed to be happy, in fact you deserve to be. And you should never feel guilty about that."

Kate threw her arms around Dorothy and let the tears flow. But Dorothy couldn't help wondering if this admission was close to a confession.

# CHAPTER 65

"Where have you been, Bernard?" Brigid was polishing crystal glasses in the butler's pantry as Bernard rushed in from the main hall. He stopped at the sound of her voice.

"I had to speak to the coppers again, since you gave away our secret." He folded his arms and leaned against the counter. Brigid handed him a clean towel and gestured to the platoon of unpolished glasses on the counter.

"You took your time getting back here when they were done with you. Are you sure you didn't stop somewhere on your way back?"

"Wouldn't have been with them at all if you'd held your tongue." Bernard gave her a reproving look, then picked up a glass and rubbed away at it, spinning the class by its stem.

"I couldn't very well lie to Scotland Yard!" She looked at the sparkling glass she had finished, put it down and picked up another. "I'm not ending up in jail."

"They wouldn't put us in jail. They just make threats to get what they can out of us."

"I'm not taking any chances." She looked closely at the glass. Then she glanced up at Bernard and blinked. "You're not cross?"

"No, Brigie." Bernard flicked the towel at her. "I could never be cross with you."

She smiled. She didn't want a row with Bernard, but she also didn't want to get in trouble with the police. Something was making her queasy, but she tried to push it away. She gazed through the perfect crystal glass for any errant spots and hoped the police detectives would catch the murderer soon.

*How else would she ever feel safe in Hursley House?*

# CHAPTER 66

Lilian had spent some time thinking in the main hall before she followed Richard's suggestion to take a walk, but her thoughts seem to just go round in circles. Each time she seemed to follow a thread of logic, Richard's lack of trust derailed her thought process. He had admitted the writers had helped, but she couldn't let go of it. Now she stood in front of Hursley House, hands on hips, looking out across the drive to the expanse of the green park. This is what she needed, fresh air.

What had happened to Rana Gupta? Just when they were going to reinterview him, he disappeared. Had he fled or was he just avoiding them? Roper said none of Rana Gupta's personal items were missing, so she reckoned he had taken a walk in the park and was not too far away. Perhaps he had just needed a break. They hadn't told the guests not to wander, just not to leave. Although a guilty man would've taken this chance to escape.

She walked across the drive and veered left toward a group of trees that looked like a nice shady spot. Perhaps this would help clear her head. She hadn't any particular opinion about who could've done it yet—everyone's motives and opportunities seemed about equal. Rana might've wanted revenge for what Sir Henry Heathcote had done to his family, but how would he know about the morning cigar ritual? Sir Samuel had left in a hurry, but she couldn't think of any motive he might have. Lady Sarah would know about Sir Henry's cigar habit, but how would killing him benefit her? He'd already broken the engagement, she wasn't in the will, and it was too risky to get caught in such a scandal. Would she take the risk just for reprisal? Or perhaps Ambrose wanted Henry out of the way so he could be with Sarah? But Sarah didn't seem to return his feelings, according to what Agatha had overheard. *And who would have known about the poison?* Almost any family or house staff could have found the leather case. But would they look inside as she had? Or perhaps the family knew more about Sir Henry's dealings than they were letting on.

Charles was baronet now, but he had been counting on his father's influence to help his Parliamentary campaign. Although if his father was going to disinherit him for marrying Marie, that would've ended everything he'd hoped for in terms of career. Of all of them, Charles had the most to lose. That theory was making the most sense so far. Or Marie—if she knew what Sir Henry was planning—to save Charles's campaign and future?

Or perhaps Kate felt her freedom was worth murder. Or Kate and Sofia, working together?

Lilian paused in the middle of the lawn, her thoughts taking precedence over her muscle functions. Would Kate really kill her own father just because he wouldn't let her go to university, or live the life she wanted with Sofia? And Juan, could he have been so angry at Henry, so moved by their disagreements that night? But that would've been more of a face-to-face encounter, an in-the-moment lashing out. To have the calm to make the plan of switching the cigars was a different mood altogether.

Unless Philippa did it to protect her husband. She seemed like she could be a cold, calm killer. And what about the ampules of cyanide in Sir Henry's room? Motives were one thing, but to know about the poison, and to steal one without being seen—she shook her head. Could that be family or staff? Perhaps there was some unknown reason for Mr. Wilson to want Sir Henry dead. No, *the butler did it* was simply too cliché.

Lilian came around the clump of trees into the shade and found Rana, sitting under an oak, reading a book.

"Hello, Mr. Gupta," Lilian said.

"Oh, Chief Inspector." Rana scrambled to his feet. "I didn't hear you approaching."

"I didn't mean to startle you." Lilian noticed his hair was damp at the temples and his breath was quick. Had he run there from somewhere?

"What are you reading?" she asked.

"Oh, just something that was on the side table in my room." He turned the cover to show her. *A Gun for Sale* by Graham Greene. "Someone must've left it there."

"Interesting?"

"It's one of those modern thrillers." Rana turned it over in his hands. "A 'page turner.'" He smiled wryly. "It passes the time."

"I prefer a puzzle solver, myself." Lilian looked at him expectantly. "If you don't mind, Mr. Gupta, DCI Davidson and I would like to pass some time with you in another interview."

"Right." He closed the book, put it under his arm, and mopped the sweat on his brow with his handkerchief as they walked back into Hursley House. Lilian noticed he hadn't met her eye as they spoke, and she wondered if it was natural nervousness or genuine guilt.

# CHAPTER 67

"Margery! Marge, can you hear me, dear? Margery?" Agatha was holding Margery's hand and patting her wrist. She had found her on the floor in the library after seeing someone run out of the library and disappear down the main hall. She'd been too far down the hall to see who it was, but she had been curious as to why someone would run out of the library and leave the door open, so she investigated. And a good thing too.

"Oh, my head." Margery moved slowly and then reached to the back of her head. "Ow."

"Dear girl, are you all right?" Agatha helped her on to the sofa. "It seems like any time I come into this room I have to help someone off the floor."

"Ooh," Margery winced. "Don't joke, it only hurts when I laugh."

"You sound normal, anyway. What happened?"

"I don't know exactly, I—" Margery stopped for a moment, looked around, saw the books on the floor. "I knocked those books over and some papers fell out. I was just looking at them when someone gave me a thwack on the head."

"What were the papers?" Agatha asked.

"Some sort of architectural drawings." Margery rubbed the back of her head. "I don't know what they were drawings of, I had just gotten them round the right way, when everything went black."

"Let me get the chief inspectors."

"No, don't leave." Margery clutched her hand and gave Agatha a weak smile. She didn't want to be left alone at that precise moment. Not yet.

★ ★ ★

"I covered the whole of the back lawn between the hedges," Ngaio was saying as she walked back toward Hursley House with Richard. "Not a single rip in the turf."

"I searched the ground all around the chapel," Richard added. "And the full perimeter of the main house, nothing. Not a bump."

"I suppose they could've gone much farther afield."

"Or perhaps they didn't bury them at all."

"That could be the case. And they couldn't have burned them, the whole estate would've smelled of cigars." Ngaio wrinkled her nose, and Richard watched a light breeze whip back her short dark hair, emphasizing the delicate bones of her face. A face that said so much about the thinking brain that was behind it. She turned toward him suddenly, before Richard had time to look away, and their gaze met. She smiled, as if to suggest *what fun, being in this together, don't you think?* He felt himself start to turn red as he smiled in return.

"A clutch of constables has searched the house and grounds," Richard said. Ngaio took note of the term; it pleased her. Richard continued. "I suppose I could send them out to look again, from here to the woods, drag the lake, climb every tree, but it's just occurred to me, even if we do find the cigars, what might they tell us? Nothing else we've found had any fingerprints besides Sir Henry's. We could be on a wild goose chase. This murderer knew what he was doing."

"Do you think it was a man?"

"It's always hard for me to imagine a woman committing murder."

"Yet there have been plenty."

"True. I have had some of those cases."

"And poison is often a woman's choice when planning a murder," Ngaio said.

"So I've read," Richard said. "If it's a woman, it could be one of his daughters."

"Or Lady Sarah."

"Yes, or Marie Sinclair."

"Not Marie." Ngaio looked at him.

"Why not?"

"No motive. Marie didn't know that Sir Henry had prejudice against her until after he was dead."

"Yes, DCI Wyles told me about the conversation you overheard," Richard said. "But she could've overheard Sir Henry's conversation with Charles and then pretended she didn't know."

"I suppose that's a possibility." Ngaio chose not to be contentious. "But she sounded sincere. If we're sticking to women, it's more likely that Sarah did it since he broke the engagement."

"For revenge?" They stopped at the door. They had walked all the way up the back lawn and around to the front of Hursley House.

"A crime of passion," Ngaio proclaimed.

"What about Kate?" Richard suggested. "Is she a possibility in your clever mind?"

"Kate's very low on my list," Ngaio replied. "The murder was planned out, and Kate strikes me as more impetuous."

"Perhaps, but she may be more calculating than we can see." Richard reached for the door and opened it, giving a slight bow to Ngaio so she would enter first. She smiled at his formality.

Inside the house they walked toward the drawing room together. Ngaio was about to continue the conversation debating the suspects, but the hush of the interior of Hursley House gave her momentary pause. It was a grand space, but its voluminous atmosphere had turned ominous for her. Such a contrast to the joyous ball of the night before. They walked in silence, their footfalls hardly registering on the thick carpet. As they passed the library, Agatha Christie saw them and called out.

"Chief Inspector!"

★ ★ ★

Dorothy and Kate could hear voices outside the drawing room, and they rose at the same time and moved toward the open doors into the main hall.

"What's happened?" Kate asked no one in particular.

They saw the small gathering outside the library, and Kate and Dorothy hurried to join them.

Agatha Christie was pointing down the hall toward the front entrance and speaking to Ngaio and DCI Davidson.

"I saw someone run out of the library and disappear toward the front door," Agatha said.

"Could you see who it was?" Richard asked.

"No, I was coming from the winter garden, I was too far away," Agatha said. "A man, I think, not too tall, but not short."

"What's happened?" Dorothy asked as she and Kate caught up to the group.

"Margery was bashed on the head in the library," Ngaio answered.

"What?" Dorothy pushed her way into the room. "Where is she?"

"I'm here, Dorothy. I'm all right," Margery said from the sofa. Dorothy moved to her quickly and sat down.

"Are you sure?"

"Yes, just a small lump on the back of my head." She gave an embarrassed smile. "Just nosing around the wrong spot, I suppose."

"Someone thought so, anyway." Dorothy patted her hand. Kate had come to stand beside them.

DCI Wyles joined the group at the doorway with Rana Gupta.

"Ah, Mr. Gupta," Richard said. "We were wondering where you'd gone."

"He was out front under a shady tree reading a book." Lilian looked at Richard with a nod, as if to say, *more to tell later.* "What's the commotion here?"

"Margery found some papers in a book she knocked over and then someone gave her a knock on the head," Agatha explained. "I saw someone run out of here, I was at the other end of the main hall, and I came in and found Margery unconscious."

DCI Davidson approached Margery.

"Are you quite all right, Mrs. Allingham?" he asked.

"Yes, I really am, I wish everyone would stop making such a fuss."

"All right then, so where are these papers you found?"

"They're gone, but they were some sort of architectural drawings."

"Were there any familiar markings?"

"No, it was nothing I'd seen before, and I'd just got it turned round the right way to read the heading when I got bashed. I wasn't able to read anything useful, I'm afraid."

"Is there anything you remember about the drawings, what type of building it might've been or where?" Richard asked.

"Not where, certainly, but it did seem like some sort of factory." She screwed up her face thinking. "Big open spaces and some hallways? That was my impression, at least."

"That might be helpful, Mrs. Allingham," Richard said. "Miss Kate, does that sound at all familiar to you?"

"No, Chief Inspector," Kate shook her head. "I didn't know anything about my father's business. He would never discuss such things with me."

"He had plenty of business interests in factories and operations of that nature," Rana offered, his eyes dark. "Here and in India."

"Yes, thank you, Mr. Gupta." Richard looked at Lilian and made a motion with his head for her to clear the room. She subtly corralled the group toward the door.

"Thank you so much, Mrs. Allingham," Richard said to her with a slight bow as he backed away. "I imagine you'd like to rest."

"Thank you." Margery reclined back on the sofa, careful not to lean on her sore spot. She was thinking that her position was almost exactly the same as Sir Henry's body had been that very morning. She sat up.

"Perhaps the drawing room might be more comfortable?" Margery looked at Dorothy.

"Yes, let's," Dorothy said. They rose to leave. Lilian and Richard were the last at the door.

"Davidson, let's lock up the library and have the constables give it another thorough search," Lilian said. "Perhaps something else got missed that the murderer is still looking for. They may need to look in every single one of these books." She looked at the tall shelves. It was going to take a while.

*　*　*

Six of them were in the hall: Agatha Christie, Ngaio Marsh, Dorothy L. Sayers, Margery Allingham, Rana Gupta, and Kate Heathcote. They were moving in a clump toward the drawing room when the two chief inspectors came out of the library.

"Mrs. Christie," Richard said. "Would you wait for a moment?"

She did so and stood near him.

Lilian turned to Rana Gupta. "Mr. Gupta, if you would be so kind as to stay within the house so we could call on you when we are ready for you, it would be much appreciated."

"Certainly." Rana looked at his watch. "It's time to dress for dinner, at any rate." He left them and disappeared toward the main stairs.

*Time to dress for dinner*, Lilian thought, of course. These aristocrats! Even a murder investigation couldn't stop the upper class from following protocol.

Richard, Lilian, and Agatha Christie were left alone in the main hall. Agatha felt a kind of anxiety she wasn't used to. Her new friend Margery, whom she greatly admired, had been in danger. While the other writers and some of the family had mentioned their fear of the possibility of the murderer amongst them, Agatha had to admit she hadn't taken it seriously. The crime must have been committed for a particular reason, and she thought that the motive had been satisfied. However, like in their many books, whoever got close to discovering the truth might incite a reason to continue the violence.

"Chief Inspectors," Agatha began. "I am beginning to worry that if we do not find the murderer soon, we could have another death on our hands."

"Your concerns are appreciated, Mrs. Christie," Richard said. "And we are fully aware of the possible danger. You can help us by describing, to the best of your ability, who you saw running from the library just before you found Mrs. Allingham."

"I was too far to really see any detail," Agatha responded, a little cross with herself for not being able to provide a better answer. "Dressed as a man, certainly, medium height. Dark hair. It could've been Charles, or Juan, or Rana, or even Bernard for that matter."

"At least that narrows the suspect down to a man," Lilian remarked.

"Unless it was a woman dressed as a man, or a man colluding with one or more of the others," Richard added.

They stood in silence for a moment. Ambrose came down the main hall from the direction of the grand staircase.

"Has something happened?" Ambrose asked. His face showed genuine concern.

"Margery Allingham was knocked out in the library," Richard told him.

"Knocked out? What do you mean? By whom?" Ambrose asked, his eyebrows lifting.

"She didn't see, someone came from behind," Lilian answered.

"Why would someone do such a thing? Is she all right?"

"I think she's fine, more shaken up than hurt." Lilian remembered what she had wanted to ask Ambrose. "Sir Ambrose, did you notice if there were any papers missing from the library?"

"Papers?" Ambrose paused, his brow furrowing. "No, why?"

"There was a lot of ash in the grate, and whoever attacked Margery stole the papers she'd found."

"What kind of papers?"

"She hadn't really gotten a good look."

Ambrose pulled at his chin. "Very concerning, Chief Inspectors, very concerning."

Wilson approached them from the opposite end of the hallway, from the dining room wing.

"Excuse me, Chief Inspectors," he began. "Dinner will be served in half an hour, if that isn't inconvenient."

Lilian and Richard looked at each other. The day had slipped away.

"Thank you, Wilson," Richard replied. Wilson moved toward the drawing room, and Ambrose accompanied him.

Lilian turned to Agatha and Richard. "I've built my career on the careful and methodical gathering of evidence to find the perpetrator and build a strong case against them. But this case is impossible. There's been no real telltale clues. Just vague suggestions of suspects that lead us nowhere." Lilian pulled at the cuffs of her blouse from under her jacket in frustration. She had to take a risk, and they needed a new tactic. "We're going to have to try something different. The dinner gathering might be a good time to get a few things out into the open. Perhaps we'll get some reactions from the others when they hear the details we've discovered."

"Talk about the case openly?" Richard said.

"If I may," Agatha added. "Everyone knows the main details of the murder, and I agree with DCI Wyles, if we can help get them talking, we might bring out some information we haven't heard before and lead to some conversation that will force someone to reveal their actions."

"Exactly." Lilian and Agatha looked at Richard. He was obviously still uncomfortable.

"I can't say that I agree this is the best way to proceed." Richard shook his head.

"Do you have an alternative strategy?" Lilian asked. She felt bad that they were having this discussion in front of Agatha. "We are out of options. The home secretary is on his way, and the dinner may be our last chance."

# Chapter 68

Kate didn't feel like dressing for dinner. But she should at least find Sofia, who was probably reading in her room. She took the stairs slowly, thinking about Margery getting bashed and wondering about the papers that the murderer had found so important and how everything seemed to be spinning out of control.

Just as she reached Sofia's room, the door across the hall opened. Philippa was in the doorway, gesturing to her and whispering.

"Kate. Come through, Kate. Come."

Kate paused for a moment, looked at Sofia's closed door, then back at Philippa who was still motioning for her to join her in her room. Now what? Kate thought. But she followed Philippa.

Inside Philippa's room there seemed to be a family meeting in progress.

"What's all this?" Kate asked as she looked at her brother, Marie, Philippa, and Juan. "Meeting without me?"

"We were looking for you, little sister," Philippa answered. "But we didn't want anyone to realize we were gathering."

"Why not? It isn't against the law." Kate clearly thought they were being ridiculous.

"Don't be cheeky," Charles said. "We need to talk. Can we work together as a family for once?"

They looked meekly at each other without answering.

"All right, then." Charles perched on the arm of the uphol-stered chair where Marie was sitting. The others took a moment to find places to sit, Philippa and Juan sharing the love seat, Kate on the chair in front of the dressing table. They looked at him expectantly. Charles continued. "The important thing is to get the police and Scotland Yard out of here before the press gets wind of it."

"How do you propose we get Scotland Yard out of the house?" Juan asked. "I can't imagine they'll leave until they think they have enough information to help their investigation."

"They can't stay forever," Charles said. "I think it's within our rights to have our house back to ourselves. Sir Samuel left a message that he's returning tonight. He'll be here in time for dinner."

"Maybe he has information." Juan glanced at Philippa, and she touched his arm.

"Perhaps," Charles continued. "Be that as it may, when he gets here, I propose we ask him to rid the house of police presence."

"Can he do that?" Philippa asked.

"He can and he will, if we ask him to," Charles replied. "Maybe he can clear them out before dinner."

"That would be quite a relief." Philippa sighed.

Marie took Charles's hand. "I have a thought, Charles," Marie said. "Let's have a civilized dinner with the two chief inspectors, all of us on our best behavior, and show them that we have nothing to fear from their investigation. Then they will see the sense of taking the investigation back to their offices."

"Well said, and well reasoned, as usual, my dear." Charles looked from Marie to the group. "Presenting ourselves as a calm, united front. Yes, that's the best way to proceed."

"That could be risky," Juan said.

"I don't suppose it can make things worse," Philippa said.

"Although it may be a challenge for this family," Kate remarked as she leaned toward the mirror on the dressing table, fixing her golden curls. Charles looked as if he was about to give his sister a rebuke. She sat up straight and gave a conciliatory smile. "Calm and united we shall be, brother, calm and united."

# CHAPTER 69

Lilian paced in the main hall by the front door, waiting for the home secretary, thinking about her journey in law enforcement. She had been studying law when the Great War broke out and interrupted her studies to take up hospital work, as was very much needed in those years. This had disappointed her father. As his only daughter he had indulged her, and while it was not common for women to study the law, he had been proud and supportive. He would have loved to see Lilian become a barrister, as he had always wanted to practice the law himself, but being the eldest son, he had entered the family business as a brewer.

Lilian remembered the beginning of her career fondly—she had met so many other wonderful women when she joined the Women's Patrol. Their function was to help and protect girls who by their own folly and inexperience might get into trouble of one kind or another. Young women, often just girls and certainly unaware as to what awaited them in London, would come from the country, hoping to make their fortunes. Many would quickly be recruited or tricked into some sort of beastly service, unable to find their way out and admit to their families the humiliating, illegal, and illicit experiences they'd had. If they could be led away from this sort of thing, before they became deadened to their own instincts for the right path, they could be saved from the emotional trauma and the exile from their families. That was the goal, but often the job became trying to pull them from the system when they were already too far gone, sometimes in denial or too damaged to admit that they were in a bad place.

Lilian believed that law enforcement should be a preventative, rather than focusing on penalties, and that it was a righteous community service. Especially since it was mainly helping young women who had little support or choice in their lives. She had been lucky to have her family's support to find a career and build a life for herself. Most women didn't.

When she joined the CID and was promoted, she was proud to be recognized as a Detective Chief Inspector, working on all sorts of cases, every one of them interesting to her and giving her purpose. She had not been on a murder case before, but as long as she learned something, she felt she was on the right road. She had worked on cases involving the upper class before and found all people interesting. Every interaction was a new experience and taught her something that would help her with the next case. This could be the same—people were people and understanding all people helped her do her job better.

This situation was certainly unique. Not just the aristocratic background of the family but the political aspect. The world was changing as the possibility of a new war loomed. There seemed to be a different kind of division between people. Or maybe it was just more emphasized now that Hitler had articulated his twisted beliefs. Lilian knew that he was dangerous. She had witnessed dewy-eyed young women being so easily talked into following the wrong path, and realized it wasn't just their youth and inexperience that allowed them to be drawn into such immoral ideology. She had seen and heard the propaganda, watched brainwashing and indoctrination change minds. And now, as whole countries were being tricked into supporting the idea that some people were lesser than others, and that it was perfectly all right to do evil deeds, she saw how powerful propaganda could be even over intelligent and pious people. And how those misbegotten beliefs could lead to death and destruction.

The question that she had to ask herself now was, did these politics have something to do with this family and the murder of Sir Henry Heathcote? It seemed that Sir Henry had two sides to him. In his popular public persona, he had made patriotic speeches about British citizenry and how important it was to be supportive of king and country. But now she could see evidence of his other side. For Sir Henry, being pro-British apparently meant being against so many other things. Like different racial or ethnic backgrounds, freedom of choice for women, or even having different political stances. He had alienated all of his children and broken up with his fiancée over these things.

It was possible, Lilian thought, that Sir Henry believed if Hitler won Europe, he would be allowed to keep his wealth, while if Russia helped fight the Nazis, Europe might become communist and then aristocrats like him would not be allowed to keep their worldly goods and property. How could he have been that gullible to think that Hitler would allow the aristocracy to remain if Germany prevailed? It seemed to Lilian that the influential Nazi propaganda had worked its way all the way up the line.

It was more possible that someone in the family or one of the weekend guests—or perhaps more than one of them—wanted Sir Henry dead. They all had benefited from it. Which motive was more likely? Revenge, freedom from oppression, a crime of passion, money and property? And who took the poison from the cigarette case?

How could someone have gotten into the library to switch the cigars? If the door had been left open by Sir Henry as he wandered the house, someone had to have been awake and watching for their chance.

At dinner, they could focus on that. If they could get them talking about their movements early in the morning, perhaps one of them would slip up or remember something that would lead to finding the murderer.

Lilian saw the large black sedan pull up outside. *The home secretary.* Had he known about Sir Henry's other side? He was part of the aristocracy, and Lilian was beginning to realize that anyone could be a victim of propaganda. He would certainly know about Nazi cyanide capsules. She shuddered and almost wished she hadn't been brought on this case. Slogging away at catching or preventing crimes in London was a completely different world. If she took a wrong step, with the home secretary watching, or if he was somehow a part of it, this case could sink their careers at Scotland Yard. Richard was right. *Politics, what a mire.* She should be wearing Wellingtons. She pushed aside her confusion of thoughts.

Just then Elspeth Anderson approached her. "Hello," she said. "I'm glad I caught you alone."

"How can I help, Elspeth?" Lilian detected a note of desperation in the housekeeper's tone.

"It's just that, I wanted to ask you—" Elspeth paused for a moment. "Maybe it's not my place."

"You can say anything to me, Elspeth, really." Maybe she's ready to tell me something she was reluctant to say before, Lilian thought.

"It's just that, I—" Elspeth looked directly at her, searchingly, her voice emotional. "I can't believe that any one of the staff or the family members could've possibly done this horrible thing. And—"

"Elspeth—"

"No, wait, I just want to say it straight out before I lose my nerve. Please remember, they are all, every one of them, like family to me. To imagine any of them doing this, poisoning Sir Henry." Tears sprang into her eyes. "It's breaking my heart."

"I understand, but what are you saying?" Lilian was bewildered.

Elspeth shook her head and wiped her eyes. "You said before, meeting people, understanding them is a satisfying part of your job. Please remember that all these people, imperfect as we all are, we're a family."

"Do you know something, Elspeth?" Lilian asked. She realized that Rana Gupta was the only suspect that Elspeth seemed to be leaving out of this equation. "Is there something you're not telling me? Do you know something about Mr. Gupta?"

"No! I—" Elspeth said. "That's not it, I just wanted to tell you, to ask you, to take it into consideration, what I've said about the family."

Did Elspeth see her as an injudicious copper who would arrest anyone to close a case? Lilian felt herself stiffen. "I always strive to be fair and thorough," she said carefully, waiting to see if the housekeeper would say more.

But Mrs. Anderson turned away, apparently having said her piece. Lilian shook her head and went to wait with Richard Davidson, ready to greet the home secretary.

★ ★ ★

Richard had been pacing outside, and when the home secretary's sedan drove up, he stood in place like a servant waiting for his master. He chided himself for that, but he blamed his own upbringing. While his family hadn't any great wealth, his family had a distant legacy of landed gentry. Though it was more than a few generations ago and they no longer owned an estate, they had handed down the traditions and conventions. It was the only inheritance he had. He was grateful his family had gone into the law, although he was the first to join Scotland Yard. Most of them were barristers, and there was an uncle who was a judge. He didn't think of his family as aristocratic, although Lilian and the other detective inspectors often teased him on his background. It had taken him years to free himself of what he thought of as his upper-class naïveté. Being a good copper meant understanding people and what they might be capable of. In the early years of his career more cases had involved the kind of people that he had much to learn about than the kind of people he had always known.

But this case, this was more his territory. He knew these people. And while they were not born of higher moral ground than the working classes—in fact he found them often much darker—he understood their motives and mentality. He could crack this case, he knew it, without the help of amateurs. He blushed at the thought. Foolish pride? After all, he had enjoyed talking over the case with Ngaio, and while he didn't condone actual collaboration, he felt a kindred spirit in her, and that gave him a boost of confidence.

Lilian stepped up next to him, and they watched Sir Samuel climb out of his automobile. He looked impatient. Richard knew that if he didn't solve this case or if his efforts angered the Heathcote family, Sir Samuel Hoare would make sure he would lose all the gains he had made at Scotland Yard, or worse. Richard straightened up. He was just going to have to make sure that wouldn't happen.

# CHAPTER 70

A fter the two DCIs had updated the home secretary on the details of the case, they brought him to the drawing room. Everyone was having drinks while they waited for dinner to be announced.

"Mr. Gupta," Richard said. "Can we have you for just a few moments?" Richard looked at the home secretary who nodded to him, then poured himself a drink and sat near Charles.

Rana Gupta put down his cocktail and followed them to the morning room they had been using as an office. The two chief inspectors waited for Rana to sit, and for DC Lee to settle herself at the desk, before they began.

"Mr. Gupta," Richard started. "We have learned that you have a connection to this family, from your past in New Delhi. While you were boarding at school here in England, your family business went to ruin and your father took his own life." Richard looked at his notebook while he spoke, but glanced up at Rana's face at the last few words. "You returned to New Delhi, then a few years later, moved to England, with your mother, and you entered university. Is that correct."

"You have the broad strokes." Rana Gupta sat rigidly on the sofa.

"Care to add any details?" Richard asked. Lilian watched Rana closely. His eyes were locked on Richard's face, his hands grasped together.

"You are already aware that Sir Henry Heathcote was responsible for ruining our family business. He made certain deals with the government that forced my father to lose his land."

"I understand."

"Do you understand?" Rana's face was stony. "Do you understand what it might be like for a seventeen-year-old at school to be told that his father was dead and that his family had lost the land that had been in the family for generations?"

"I understand that all these years later you might still be angry enough to take revenge on Sir Henry for what he did to your family." Richard kept his tone even. "And arrange to come to the gala in order to do so."

"I would never be that foolish," Rana huffed. "Nor did I know of this morning cigar habit of his. It makes no sense."

"Why else would you be at Hursley House?"

"Ask Sir Samuel. He invited me without any prompting." Rana gestured toward the door as if the home secretary was just on the other side. "In fact, I found the idea abhorrent, entering Hursley House of Heathcote, but he insisted. There were people he needed to see, and he wanted me here to help with any arrangements or to note any information he might gather."

"What people, what arrangements?" Lilian asked.

"This is not information I am at liberty to discuss," Rana responded.

"And since you were here," Lilian continued. "Did you engage in any conversation with the baronet, about your past or otherwise?"

He was silent for a moment.

"There was a moment during the party that I went outside to smoke, and on my way back to the ballroom I found Heathcote alone by the library. Part of my direction from Sir Samuel, you see, was to note who Heathcote was speaking with and overhear anything if I could. I tried to find myself close to him at any time possible in the evening in order to do so."

"Did you hear anything or see anything useful?" Richard asked.

"I have reported any findings to the home secretary. There's nothing I can think of that connects to his murder, specifically."

"Specifically?" Lilian repeated.

"I'll just say this, Sir Henry Heathcote seemed to be doing business as usual. And by that I mean making deals with immoral brutes and arranging business in every way possible, including stepping on anyone he needed to, in order to make him richer." He spoke tersely.

"None of this seemed to have anything to do with his murder?" Lilian asked.

"Not that I know of." Rana straightened his posture. "You may not be aware that it was all business as usual for Heathcote and those like him. The men he spent the most time with last night were rich industrialists, like Heathcote, and they all put money above anything else. It was nothing new. Why someone should murder him now, rather than ten years ago, or ten years hence, I can't imagine."

Lilian and Richard let that sink in for a moment. Lilian thought if Sir Henry and his type put money above everything else, then perhaps that was the root of this case. Had they missed something? Lilian looked at her wristwatch. Eight o'clock. Wilson would be announcing that dinner is served.

"That will be all for now, Mr. Gupta," she said. "We thank you for your time."

Rana stood and stalked out of the room.

Lilian looked at her partner. "I think our best chance is to get everyone talking about the night before and see if anyone has any new information that they forgot to mention or hope something slips out that they didn't mean for us to know."

"We can't interrogate them at dinner—Sir Samuel would have our heads," Richard said.

"I know that. That's not what I meant." Lilian took a breath. "The writers have made friends with the family, and they feel more relaxed around them. If the writers keep them talking, something new may come to light. We can keep to ourselves and listen. See what comes out."

"And if it doesn't work?"

"If it doesn't work, then we rehash everything with them all after the pudding." Lilian looked at him expectantly. She hadn't seen his confidence lag like this before. She suddenly realized that his opposition to her ideas was rooted in his absence of conviction in his own abilities. He needed her bolstering, not her defiance. "Davidson, we can do this. We are going to find out who the murderer is, whatever it takes."

"As long as it doesn't all take us down."

"The law is what matters," Lilian reminded him. "Articulating the line between right and wrong."

"Sometimes that line moves."

"Then we just have to keep up with it, don't we?" Her mouth was set. They had to keep at it until it was solved. That was the job. She felt a tiny flutter. She understood that Richard was trying to balance the job against his career and his relationship with the home secretary. She knew that was a struggle; she'd seen it before. She'd had her own occasional doubts on her journey but had thought she put that behind her. Her thoughts drifted to Elspeth Anderson, the housekeeper.

What had she been asking of her? Had she wanted her to compromise her integrity? Had she been questioning her good nature? Either way, Lilian felt deflated by their last conversation.

She looked at Richard; his struggle wasn't so different from hers. He wanted to make something of his life and he had hopes that gave him doubts. But doubts could ruin a case. She couldn't let him or Elspeth or anyone else put that in her head, and she couldn't let Richard doubt himself. "We use our cunning and imagination, Richard, like always. Don't let the rest of the noise muddle your brain," Lilian said

"It's all part of the game, I suppose."

"And it's our game and we play by our rules." Then Lilian remembered her father's words. "We do good *and* do well. That's all that matters."

"Yes, that's all that matters." He smiled at her with more certainty.

"Now, let's have a quick word with the writers before we all sit down for dinner." Lilian motioned for Richard to follow her out the door.

# CHAPTER 71

As they marched toward the drawing room, they passed the family going to the dining room. Behind them was the home secretary, Rana Gupta, and the four Queens of Crime. Just as Lilian and Richard approached Sir Samuel, Dorothy Sayers came closer.

"Excuse me, Chief Inspectors," Dorothy began. "I've been thinking about the Auntie Meredith."

"The what?" Sir Samuel asked.

"It was something the servants overheard Sir Henry say, sir," Richard explained. "He said something about the Auntie Mary-something. Or Auntie Meredith."

"Does he have one? An Aunt Mary something?"

"No, sir," Richard replied.

"I kept thinking that 'Auntie Meredith' sounded familiar, and I think I know what it reminded me of," Dorothy spoke softly.

"Tell us."

"In Latin, *ante meridiem* means before noon," Dorothy continued. "So I thought maybe that's what they heard, and without being familiar with Latin, they heard it as Auntie Meredith or Maryann."

"Did you say ante meridiem?" Sir Samuel asked.

"Yes, ante meridiem," Dorothy said.

Sir Samuel looked at Rana Gupta, both with surprised expressions on their faces.

"What is it, sir?" Lilian asked.

"Ante meridiem is the name of a government project," Sir Samuel said. "It's to do with munitions. If he knew about it, if he was talking to someone about it, that wouldn't have been on the up and up. I can't really say more than that." He looked at Rana, who nodded.

"Understood, sir," Richard said. "Thank you, Mrs. Sayers. Brilliant connection. Latin was never my strongest subject. We appreciate your help."

"Davidson, why don't you take Mr. Gupta and Sir Samuel into the dining room. We'll follow right behind after a quick word," Lilian said.

Davidson nodded and gestured to the two government officials to precede him.

When they had disappeared down the main hall, Lilian turned to the four writers. "I have one last favor to ask."

"At your service, Chief Inspector," Agatha Christie said. "At your service."

\* \* \*

The writers entered the dining room just as everyone was taking their seats. Richard was still at the door and stepped aside to let them in. Ngaio was the last, and she smiled at him. He took her arm and stole her back out into the hallway.

"Ngaio, before we go in," Richard glanced back at the door.

"What is it?"

Richard paused. "Shall I commit an impropriety?"

"You've discovered who the murderer is?" Ngaio asked.

"If tonight's dinner goes the right way, we hope that will be the revelation." He saw her expression change. "What is it?"

"You just reminded me of the reality," Ngaio shuddered, "that someone will hang for this murder."

"And . . ."

"It's only that the thought of capital punishment is so horrible."
She looked at him, her eyes serious. "I sometimes wonder how can
you do a job like this knowing you might be sending someone to
the gallows."

"What should the punishment be for murder?"

"I don't know. But I've never seen the point in an eye for an
eye, and so forth."

Richard paused. His thoughts seem to carry him away for a
moment. "What if the murder of one man could prevent the death
of thousands, maybe millions of innocent people?"

"How?" Ngaio asked.

"I'm sorry, ignore that. It's just something I've been thinking
about lately."

"Why?"

"This may be my last murder case, of this type," Richard said.
"For a while at least."

"What do you mean?"

"I'm going into the special branch soon."

"The special—" Ngaio looked confused. "Oh, I see. Sometimes I fool myself into thinking we're not on the brink of war."

"Yes. Nothing like a murder to distract you from imminent
invasion."

They both fell silent. It wasn't awkward, on the contrary, they
seemed to feel a mutual comfort in the moment.

"I really just wanted to tell you," Richard began, "that if the
case does come to a head tonight, things may happen rather quickly
after that."

"Yes, I understand."

"And I wanted to say," Richard paused. "Thank you."

"For what?"

"For," he seemed embarrassed, "for your collaboration.
This . . . alliance has helped more than you know."

She smiled, not knowing what to say. She'd felt such an unusual
connection to him from the moment she saw him and was shy to
admit it.

"May I see you in London?" Richard asked.

"That would be lovely," Ngaio smiled. "Although I'll be leaving for New Zealand soon. My father is not well and I must travel home."

"I'm so sorry." Richard took her right hand in his, as if to shake it formally. But his touch was gentle, and he covered her hand with his other one. "Perhaps we can write while you're away."

Ngaio couldn't have been more pleased. This man consistently surprised her. She added her other hand to their grasp.

"Writing is what I do best." They released their hands, looked at each other shyly, and then turned to go into the dining room.

Richard and Ngaio walked past Lilian standing inside the door of the dining room. She smiled to herself at the connection Richard seemed to have made with the writer. It had certainly seemed to help him calm down about collaborating, she mused. She watched Ngaio settle in her chair at the far end of the table. Richard stood near her at the top of the table and glanced back at Lilian. Just as she was about to join Richard at the table, Wilson and Mrs. Anderson arrived. Wilson stood by the sideboard, ready to serve. Mrs. Anderson stood in the doorway, raised her eyebrows and gave a subtle nod to Lilian. Then she took a step back into the main hall. Lilian held up one finger to Richard, signaling to him that she'd be a moment, and followed Mrs. Anderson into the hall. She still felt prickly at how the housekeeper had spoken to her earlier, and realized she had counted on this new friendship more than she had realized.

"What is it, Elspeth?" Lilian spoke softly so no one would hear. She noticed that Elspeth seemed anxious. "Is something the matter?"

"It's just that, I'm beginning to understand how hard it is to do what you have to do, and I just wanted to say—" Elspeth paused for a moment. She inhaled a nervous breath and then her face changed and she smiled encouragingly. "I wanted to say, I'm sorry if I sounded like I didn't trust your judgment earlier. I was just so worried for the children. I felt a kind of panic for them. I know they're not my own, but sometimes I feel as if they are. But whatever happens tonight, I count on your good nature, I know you'll do the right thing. I know you'll do good."

Lilian had steeled herself from the spark of sentiment she had begun to feel. But to have Elspeth's confidence meant a lot.

"Thank you, Elspeth," Lilian said. "That means the world." She touched her arm briefly and turned back into the dining room. Nothing would muddle her course. She would do the right thing, she thought to herself, no matter what.

# Chapter 72

The writers had inserted themselves between family members at the elegantly set table, Dorothy near Kate and Sofia, Agatha near Sarah and Ambrose, Margery sitting by Philippa and Juan, and Ngaio arriving last to sit near Marie and Charles, who were next to Rana Gupta and Sir Samuel. Lilian Wyles and Richard Davidson sat nearest the door on the other side of Sir Samuel. They all engaged in stilted but polite chatter as they got comfortable.

What little conversation they had faded out as Bernard and Wilson served the soup from an elegant tureen. Lilian could see that it was cream of something-or-other and was reluctant to taste it, in case it was some strange fish she hadn't had before. But she was relieved to find it was only potato leek, and delicious at that. She tried to catch Agatha Christie's eye, to egg her on to start some conversation, but Agatha was focused on her soup. Lilian looked toward Margery Allingham, who seemed the most outgoing of them all. Lilian caught her eye.

"This is quite delicious," Margery began. "You know I always say, soup is sustenance. That's why I like a real sit-down dinner better than a buffet. You can hardly serve soup at a buffet." She laughed at her own joke, garnering a few forced smiles from the group. "Last night the buffet was excellent, though. Philippa, did you choose the menu?"

Philippa started but quickly regained her composure, remembering their goal for the evening. Calm and united.

"I'm so glad you enjoyed it." Philippa dabbed at her lips with her linen napkin. "But I can't take the credit. Sarah and Stella worked with the caterers, and Mrs. Anderson, of course."

"Lady Stella is an amazing woman," Margery turned to Sarah. "Don't you agree?"

"Oh, yes," Sarah said, her voice quiet in the substantial space of the dining room. "I think so highly of Lady Stella. I enjoyed working with her on the event, she's so congenial. Henry and I—" Her voice broke, and she cleared her throat. "Henry admired her. He had hoped to do more for the Women's Voluntary Service."

"In what way?" Agatha asked.

"Oh, you know, more fundraising, I suppose. He had told me that he was looking forward to the gala so he could meet Lady Stella's friends and contacts."

Agatha thought that didn't sound right. "I would imagine Lady Stella would have already enlisted her own contacts to give money to the cause. If Sir Henry was looking forward to meeting her friends and acquaintances, perhaps it was for another reason."

"I didn't think of it that way." Sarah sounded unsure.

"Perhaps he thought Lady Stella's contacts would be useful to one of his businesses," Margery suggested. "What types of business was Sir Henry in?"

"I didn't really know anything about his businesses," Sarah said, deflecting. "Charles, would know better, wouldn't you, Charles?"

"Somewhat," Charles said. "His investments included companies that were mainly to do with refining natural materials for manufacturing, and there were some that did shipping, import-export, that type of thing. I really hadn't been that involved in the day-to-day business."

"You'll have to get involved now," Kate remarked. "Whether you like it or not. But could you be a member of Parliament and help with business at the same time?" Kate put her soup spoon aside and looked at Charles with innocent alacrity.

"Yes, I suppose I could." Charles focused on keeping his calm. He wasn't going to let Kate fluster him tonight. "Uncle Ambrose will be by my side, won't you, Uncle?"

"Of course, Charles." Ambrose's deep voice was comforting. "We'll work out everything together."

"Oh, were you involved in Sir Henry's pursuits?" Margery inquired. "What kind of business did he do?"

"I was just included in the legal paperwork aspect, contracts, et cetera." Ambrose stirred his soup distractedly. "He had investments in refineries, metals and such, and in the transporting of goods, lorries and cargo trains, that sort of thing. He kept his papers in perfect order, we won't miss a beat, even with him gone. There's no reason to give up your campaign, Charles. We need you there. The country is lacking without a Heathcote in Parliament."

"Thank you, Uncle."

Margery thought Charles seemed genuinely touched. Ambrose was far and away more attentive and supportive than Henry Heathcote had been, in her short observation. She didn't see how Henry's death was a real tragedy to anyone in the family.

"Did you meet anyone last night who had to do with your father's business?" Margery asked.

"I think Father wanted me to concentrate on my campaign." Charles smile was wry. "He didn't introduce me to anyone at the party last night. But that wasn't unusual. He never wanted to burden me with business. He knew I was busy with other activities." He looked at Marie.

Lilian thought he sounded like he was convincing himself. It was odd, when someone died, how quickly history was rewritten. She guessed that Sir Henry kept his son out of his business out of his need to control everything, not in regard for his son.

"Charles always has plenty of his own concerns keeping him occupied," Marie remarked. "He's so busy with the campaign, we'll be lucky to find a date for the wedding." She laughed lightly.

"There's nothing in the world that could make me too busy for that, my darling." Charles kissed her hand.

"Henry was a busy one last night," Ambrose jumped in. "So many people to speak with, he hardly even danced, and he loved to dance, didn't he, Sarah?"

"He was an excellent dancer," she replied. "And he loved people to see him on the dance floor. But you are correct, he didn't have much time to dance last night. He kept dashing off with one business acquaintance or another to the library or outside to the garden."

"Do you remember anyone in particular?" Richard asked.

Sarah looked at him as if she had forgotten he was there.

"No," she answered. "I really didn't know any of them, actually. And I was so busy with Lady Stella, I wasn't even introduced to most of them." She took a sip of wine. A long sip. "It was an exhausting night followed by an exhausting day." She looked at Richard. "I'm looking forward to returning home tomorrow and taking a long rest."

"I'm sure you're all quite tired of Scotland Yard, at this point," Sir Samuel Hoare remarked as Wilson and Bernard began to gather the soup bowls. "I'm sure they'll all be out of your way tomorrow." He cleared his throat, finished his wine, and signaled Wilson for more.

Lilian thought his statement was premature, but she took it as a sign of positive reinforcement.

"Yes, the police are rather like the distant relatives that come for a visit and outstay their welcome," she smiled. "But we should have everything we need by tomorrow." If they were lucky, she thought to herself, they would be able to catch a few hours of sleep at the local pub. More likely they'd be up all night, not unusual for hardy coppers on a case.

The meaning of her statement fell differently on the ears of the people in the room. No one broke the silence for a long moment while Wilson and Bernard settled plates of roast beef and vegetables in front of each of them.

"I enjoyed dancing last night," Margery said, spearing a forkful of roasted parsnips. "Both bands were quite good."

"I found the first one rather old-fashioned." Kate smiled at Sofia.

"Some of us old-fashioned people like to dance too, my darling Kate," Ambrose teased. "But I knew the young people would have more fun after midnight with the second band, that's why I suggested it."

"You're so thoughtful, Uncle Ambrose," Kate replied.

"I only think of you," Ambrose looked around the table. "All of the Heathcotes. You all mean the world to me, you know that."

"I have to admit, when the second band began," Philippa said with an embarrassed smile, "it was so loud I found it necessary to take a break upstairs."

"I confess I did the same," Agatha said. "I didn't see you, although Ngaio joined me for a cigarette."

Philippa looked at Agatha for a moment. "I went to our own rooms to freshen up," Philippa responded blankly. "And I wanted to fill Juan's cigarette case with his own brand."

"I had to freshen up myself around that time," Ambrose said. "I spilled something on my shirt front and had to change. Some gentleman I am." He chuckled self-consciously.

Lilian took note of this. Either of them, she thought, could've been in Sir Henry's room and accessed the leather cigarette case without anyone seeing them.

"Sofia and I were having such a grand time at the party," Kate said. "We didn't go upstairs for a moment until we had to." Her statement had begun with joy, but by the end of the sentence, the whole weight of the memory was in her words. She looked at Sofia with tears in her eyes. Sofia squeezed her hand and mumbled something. Kate pushed her plate away. "I only want to remember the beginning of the party, when everything was fun. I don't want to remember anything bad. I want it to be a happy memory. One last happy memory of Father." Her voice was husky, and she used her dinner napkin to dab at her eyes.

"Then it shall be a happy memory," Dorothy broke in. "A happy memory of generous charity for the Women's Voluntary Service, a happy memory of dancing, delicious delicacies, and bubbling champagne. A happy memory of being with lovely people." She raised her glass to them and then took a sip of her wine.

"Hear, hear," said Sir Samuel, and the others echoed the sentiment. Lilian noticed that Rana Gupta did not echo the toast. But the party couldn't be a happy memory for him, she thought. He had met the man who had ruined his family and, by hearing his business conversations during the party, confirmed the kind of beastly businessman that man was. Lilian searched Rana's face for any sign of guilt.

Wilson and Bernard cleared the last of the dinner plates and served coffee and tea. Elegant plates of fruit and cheese were passed around the table.

"I'm almost sorry I went to bed so early," Agatha said as she chose some French cheese. "Everyone was having such a good time. But I'll admit I couldn't sleep right away. I spent some time reading. I could actually still hear the music in my room."

"I'm so sorry, did it keep you awake?" Charles asked.

"No, no, it wasn't loud, I just have very good hearing," Agatha said. "I don't know why I didn't remember this before, but I thought I recognized a song the band was playing so I stuck my head out into the hallway to hear it better, and I saw Miss Kate go into her room."

"I didn't see you, Mrs. Christie." Kate seemed surprised.

"You were coming from the west end of the hallway so I was at your back."

Lilian looked at Kate—*this was new.* Was Kate just wandering about, or had she been in Heathcote's room?

"I must have gone to the toilets, I suppose." Kate was flustered. "I really don't remember."

The toilet rooms were in the other direction, Lilian was sure, toward the east. The west end was Sir Henry's room. This bit of news meant that Kate also had the opportunity to access the leather cigarette case in his room. Philippa, Ambrose, or Kate? Or were they working together? This was progress, the writers were keeping up the conversation in just the right way, pulling in bits and pieces of new information. Lilian said a silent prayer, please, let it all come out. *Let the murderer be revealed.*

# CHAPTER 73

"I didn't hear the music at all, I actually went out like a light as soon as my head hit the pillow," Ngaio said. "But I meant to confess that last night, or rather early this morning, I woke up starving and couldn't go back to sleep. I snuck down into the kitchen and helped myself to a glass of milk." She smiled toward Wilson, who pretended he wasn't listening. "And some bread and butter. It was just before five o'clock. I almost got lost, wandering down the main stairs, through the main hall from the east wing to the west wing and finally finding the staircase to the kitchen. I'm not used to such a big house." She smiled at Ambrose. He had a funny look on his face.

"We were all quite sound asleep at that time, I suppose," Ambrose said, leaning slightly as Wilson poured him tea. "I'm glad you were able to find what you needed."

"It put me right back to sleep," Ngaio added.

"We had no trouble sleeping," Juan said. "Did we, my dear? Although I woke early and wandered down into the kitchen myself for an early cup of coffee and to check on your tray."

"You're so thoughtful, darling." Philippa looked at him.

Lilian still thought Juan might've gone below stairs to get hold of the keys, but the timing was tricky.

"I couldn't sleep right away so I went into Sofia's room for a while." Kate threw a glance at Sofia. "We read and talked till late."

"Yes, I saw you when I went up at about half three," Ambrose said. "I fell asleep as soon as my head hit the pillow."

"Yes," Kate said warmly. "I thought you looked completely exhausted when you came up." She took a delicate bite of trifle and a sip of tea. "I think we were so excited by the party, we just couldn't fall asleep."

"Too much excitement for everyone," Philippa said. The conversation stalled, and there was just the clinking of spoons on crystal scooping up trifle.

Lilian looked around the table. They were running out of time.

The writers had done their best and had turned up new information, but they needed more. She and Davidson had to push harder before they all retired for the evening. She looked at Richard and gave a nod to prod him. He stood.

"Sir Samuel," Richard looked at him, then around the table. "Ladies and gentlemen, if you don't mind, we'd like to ask you to allow us one more conversation about the details of Sir Henry's death."

"There's nothing we want more than to be as helpful as we can," Charles said. "And to get to the bottom of this despicable crime." His voice was clear and firm although somewhat mechanical.

"In that spirit, Sir Charles," Richard said, "we'd like to go through the details of the last twenty-four hours. Perhaps we'll find some connections we missed that will lead us to an, as yet, unforeseen revelation." Richard looked at Lilian. She stood with her notebook.

"Thank you, DCI Davidson," Lilian began. "I'm going to run through the time line of everything we know, from about midnight until Sir Henry was found. I beg your pardon for anything that might seem insensitive, but as we confirm all the details, we can make any corrections or connections." She looked at the faces around the table. Some were more anxious than others. She continued.

Lilian opened her notebook and glanced at Sir Samuel. He nodded back.

"At midnight, the new dance band started to play. Agatha Christie went upstairs to the ladies' sitting room, and was soon joined by Ngaio Marsh. Soon after, Lady Philippa went to her rooms to rest for a short period, and Ambrose visited his rooms to change his stained shirt."

She looked at Philippa and Ambrose, and they nodded.

"At approximately one twenty, Lady Sarah danced with Sir Henry, which ended abruptly, and then she danced with Sir Ambrose, but feeling a headache, retired to her room for the evening. Shortly after this, Agatha Christie retired to her room, Ngaio Marsh close behind her. At approximately half past one, Sir Henry was seen going to the library with an unknown gentleman, where they looked over some papers that we have yet to find."

Lilian glanced at Bernard who stared straight ahead, unmoving.

"About that time, Bernard and Brigid checked the upstairs sitting rooms to tidy up and fill cigarettes and matches. Shortly before two o'clock, Sir Henry met Miss Kate and Miss Sofia on the dance floor, stopped them from dancing and told them to go to their rooms. Sir Charles and Miss Marie escorted the two young ladies upstairs. Miss Kate, Miss Sofia, and Miss Marie went to their rooms for the night and shortly thereafter, Agatha Christie saw Miss Kate in the hallway."

Kate put her cup back into its saucer a little too loudly.

"At about this same time," Lilian continued. "Dorothy Sayers was on her way to her room when she saw Sir Charles go in the library with his father. At two thirty Sir Samuel and Lady Stella retired for the night. Mr. Rana Gupta also went to his room about this time and as he walked by the library, he heard the raised voices of Sir Henry and Sir Charles."

Charles looked at Rana with a blank expression.

"At about two forty-five, Miss Marie heard Sir Charles return to his room. Close to three, Bernard noticed Margery Allingham and Ian Colvin in the winter garden. Margery and Ian walked to the cloakroom, and then Ian Colvin left the party. On her way to the stairs, Margery Allingham also heard voices in the library, men's voices."

Lilian went on to note Philippa and Juan saying good night to the guests, the caterers packing and leaving, and Wilson telling the rest of the staff they could go to bed.

"Between three and three thirty, Sir Ambrose and Sir Henry had cigars in the library. At about three thirty, Mr. Wilson looked in at the library, and Sir Henry asked him to fill the cigar box. Sir Ambrose left them and went upstairs, Miss Kate saw him in the corridor at about three thirty as he saw her go into her room."

At this statement, Sofia whispered to Kate and she shook her head.

"I'm sorry, but the time is wrong," Sofia said to Lilian.

"Correct me, please," Lilian said to Sofia.

"It was four thirty, not three thirty. Kate was coming into my room, not to her room, at that time. I heard her say good night to her uncle in the corridor, and when she came in, I looked at the clock." Sofia couldn't have been more confident in her statement. Kate looked embarrassed but nodded in agreement.

"Oh, yes, of course, of course, I remember now," Ambrose offered. "I couldn't fall asleep right away, and I knew there would be some aspirin in the hall closet."

Lilian made a note, but wondered why this had not come up before. Perhaps Kate did not want to admit that she was going into Sofia's room at such an hour.

"Thank you, Miss Sofia, Sir Ambrose." She finished writing in her notebook. "When Mr. Wilson returned to the library with the fresh cigars, the library was empty. He let himself in with his key, filled the cigar box, checked that the lock on the French windows was secure and locked the library when he left. Now we're at about three forty." Lilian looked at her audience—they were rapt. She turned a page in her notebook.

"We do not know where Sir Henry was at this time. The next report we have is Ngaio Marsh passing the library before five o'clock, on her way to the kitchen for a glass of milk. The library door was open." Lilian paused. "Miss Marsh, did you notice if the library door was open on your way back to your room?"

"Why, no, since I found the west wing stairs, I went straight up to my room that way without passing the library again."

"Thank you," Lilian continued. "We can only assume that Sir Henry was still up and somewhere on the ground floor, since the library was open. We found his jacket and tie in the room used as the cloakroom, so he may have wandered there."

"Perhaps he was looking for cigarettes, if he didn't have his case with him," Sarah said. "The cloakroom is really the men's smoking room, next to the drawing room. He would've found the cigarettes he liked there."

"Thank you, Lady Sarah, extremely helpful." Lilian paused to make a note. "Did anyone see Sir Henry's cigarette case that night?"

There was silence for a moment. Then Wilson spoke. "Perhaps I forgot to mention, the baronet gave me his silver case when I was in the library at half three, for polishing."

"Thank you, Wilson," Davidson said. "Did anyone see his leather cigarette case that night?"

"The brown leather one?" Sarah asked. "He had it at teatime. Didn't he, Ambrose? I think I saw him use it."

"Yes," Ambrose said quietly. "I think you're right, my dear."

"Was it a dark brown leather case?" Agatha asked.

"Yes, that's the one," Lilian confirmed.

"I saw him use it, also, at tea." Agatha looked thoughtful. "I think it might've still been on the table when he left. He excused himself before the rest of us were finished. I think there was a phone call, some business he had to attend to. Yes, the leather cigarette case was still on the table after he left."

Lilian turned to Wilson and Bernard. "Was it there when you cleared up?" she asked them. They both shook their heads.

"Did anyone else see it, or know what happened to it?" Lilian asked. Heads shook.

"Why does a cigarette case matter?" Kate asked. "Is it terribly important? It was an ugly old thing. I don't even know where it came from."

"Does anyone know how Sir Henry came to own it?" Lilian asked. She purposely ignored Kate's question. "No? Or how long Sir Henry had it?"

"He's had it as long as I've known him," Lady Sarah answered. "More than a year. I always thought it was some kind of cigarette case for hunting. An old thing he'd use when he didn't want to carry one of his silver or gold cases. But he used it round the house also."

No one else offered any information. But it was clear to Lilian that this was when someone had the chance to take it, remove one ampule of cyanide, and then stow it in the desk in Sir Henry's bedroom. But it was not clear who knew about the secret compartment behind the cigarettes or who might've moved it. No help in solving the case, but an important detail, nonetheless. Lilian continued.

"At six o'clock, the house staff arose, began making coffee and fixing breakfast. At seven o'clock, Brigid brought Sir Henry his coffee tray in the library. He was alive and well at his time and as far as we know, it's the last time anyone saw him as such."

She looked at their faces. There was a mix of emotions. No one disputed this statement.

"At seven fifteen, Mr. Juan Guerra stopped by the kitchen to check on his wife's tray. At eight o'clock, the dining room was ready for breakfast, and at eight o'clock, Brigid brought Lady Philippa her tray. Between eight and nine o'clock, guests were having breakfast in the dining room. At about nine o'clock, Brigid entered the library to clear the coffee tray and found Sir Henry Heathcote's body."

Lilian had tried to sound as matter of fact and indeed, as scientific, as possible. But she could see the effect on the family. Their faces showed that her words brought the emotional trauma back to them, the shock of his death, the loss of his life. Lilian felt sympathy for them, but it couldn't be helped.

"I'd also like to mention that this afternoon, Margery Allingham was in the library and after accidentally knocking over some books, found some papers that had been hidden in one of them.

Just as she was getting a look at the papers to see what they were, someone came up behind her and hit her on the head, knocking her out and stealing the papers."

There was some surprised muttering—not everyone had heard about this incident.

"Luckily, Agatha Christie was just coming out of the winter garden and saw someone run from the library." Lilian looked at their reactions. "She couldn't quite see who it was, but it was a medium height man with dark hair."

Everyone looked around the room at each other. It was obvious that Rana Gupta, Ambrose Heathcote, Charles Heathcote, Juan Guerra, even Bernard the footman were possibilities.

"If the gentlemen wouldn't mind going over their movements this afternoon," said Richard. "We'll start with you, Mr. Gupta."

"I was outside in the park, reading under a tree. DCI Wyles saw me." He nervously pushed his coffee cup away.

"I don't know how long you were there, Mr. Gupta," Lilian said. "And I noticed you were perspiring, perhaps as if you had just run there."

"I took a walk before settling under that tree," Rana exclaimed. "It was a warm day."

"And Sir Charles," Richard said. "Where were you this afternoon?"

"After teatime?" Charles asked. "I had papers to read for the campaign, I was upstairs in my sitting room." He looked at Marie. "Marie was with me."

"Yes, he was working, I was reading a book," Marie confirmed. "Right up till dinner."

"And Mr. Juan Guerra?" Richard continued. "Where were you this afternoon?"

"We were in our rooms, as well," Juan answered confidently, looking at his wife. "Together."

"From teatime till dinner," Philippa concurred. "We had no desire to be social."

"Sir Ambrose?" Richard turned to him.

"I was in my room after tea," Ambrose said. "I started making a list of everyone I'd have to notify about Henry's death. There's a lot to be done."

"Did you see anyone, or did anyone see you?" Richard asked.

"No, I was alone," Ambrose said calmly. Then he turned to the home secretary, his eyes dark. "Sir Samuel, this is ridiculous."

"Just following protocol, Ambrose," Sir Samuel Hoare said and looked at him with sympathetic eyebrows. "Nothing to worry about."

Richard felt a wave of relief. He didn't want the home secretary to accuse him of badgering these friends of his, but he had to do his job. Richard turned to Bernard.

"And Bernard," he said. "Where were you after teatime?"

"Me, sir?" Bernard couldn't have been more shocked. "I was clearing up in the kitchen, and speaking with you and the lady chief inspector. Then polishing crystal with Brigid. You can ask her."

"I will, thank you."

Lilian spoke. "I'd like to say, alibis for this afternoon notwithstanding, it is possible that more than one person was involved in this crime. It could be that whoever knocked out Margery Allingham was working with someone else. In fact, everyone at this table has a motive, and it's a matter of the details to get down to the truth."

# CHAPTER 74

Lilian took a deep breath. The others, including Richard and the home secretary, might not like what she was about to do next, but it was essential. If the home secretary was going to let everyone leave after dinner, this might be her last chance to get to the truth.

"Very well," Lilian said. "Let's run through all the possible motives."

Gasps, raised eyebrows, nervous laughter—she had startled the room. Richard looked at her questioningly. They hadn't talked about announcing everyone's motives, out loud, in front of everyone. He glanced at Sir Samuel, then back at Lilian. She gave him a steely look and turned a page in her notebook, but she had no need to check her notes.

She started at one end, prepared to go round the whole table. "Miss Kate, isn't it true that your father refused to allow you to continue your education and go to university?"

"Yes, it's true. But I hadn't stopped trying to talk him into it," Kate spoke confidently. "I was hopeful that by this time next year he would have changed his mind."

"Tell us what happened when he removed you and Miss Sofia from the dance floor?" Lilian asked.

Kate paused for a moment, and then tossed her head and described the incident.

"It was silly, we were just dancing. We'd been practicing a fast Suzie Q dance step back at school and had gotten quite good at it. The music the band played was perfect for it. We were having so much fun that when the song ended, we hugged each other, quite out of breath. The next tune was a ballad, so we naturally changed to a slow dance. We didn't care what the music was, we just love to dance.

"Suddenly, Father stormed onto the dance floor and pulled us apart. I didn't even know what was happening. Then he stuck his face close to my ear."

"What do you think you're doing?"
    "What do you mean?"
    "This is a public place, not the back rooms of your emancipated school."
    'How can you say such a thing?'
    "I should've pulled you out of there long ago."

"Then he grabbed my wrist and marched me to the buffet, Sofia followed us. We were upset. Charles and Marie came over to calm Father down. They took us to bed. It was humiliating."

Lilian waited a beat before speaking. "So your father was against you continuing school and also against your friendship with Miss Sofia?"

"He was against a lot of things, but he couldn't stop me from having friends." Kate looked at Sofia, then back at Lilian. "Hardly a motive for murder."

"No, darling," Ambrose said. "And I will support you, completely. We all will."

Lilian thought, definitely, without Sir Henry around, a few things will go easier for this family. She turned to Sarah.

"Lady Sarah, in the argument you had with Sir Henry on the dance floor he made some accusations?"

"He was quite out of control. Too much to drink I thought, at first."

"Would you tell us the full exchange?"

Lady Sarah looked at Ambrose. He nodded, and she began speaking.

"When he asked me to dance, I was almost surprised. He'd been so busy all evening, I wasn't sure we'd get another chance. But I was pleased and I was enjoying the moment. Then he got so strange. He was clutching me too tight."

"Henry, you're hurting me."

"You know what really hurts? When you find out someone's been lying to you."

"Whatever do you mean?"

"Do you think you've been fooling me about your mother?"

"What are you talking about, Henry? I haven't been hiding anything from you. Are you drunk?"

"Your mother, and your mother's mother. Don't pretend you don't know."

"What are you on about?"

"Your maternal line is Jewish and you've been hiding that from me this whole time."

"That was generations ago. Why should it matter?"

"It matters because I would never marry a Jew."

Sarah shook her head, blinking back tears. "Then he pulled away from me and stopped dancing. We were standing there, in the middle of the dance floor. He said something like 'I wonder what other lies you've told me.' He wasn't shouting, but I felt like everyone could hear us and I was paralyzed. He said the wedding was off and he wanted me out of the house. Thankfully Ambrose appeared and danced me away."

Sarah still had tears in her eyes, but her demeanor was relatively calm. "I had no idea that would be something that would matter to him, that my grandmother had been Jewish. I never thought about it." She held her head high.

"So, the wedding was off." Lilian prompted.

"Yes, he broke the engagement." Sarah twisted her linen napkin in her hands. "But that was just fine with me. He was not the man I thought he was. I would never have married him after what he said. I went to bed immediately. I even packed, so I would be ready to leave first thing in the morning. But then—" She stopped. Charles and Philippa couldn't look at her. Kate couldn't look away.

Lilian nodded and then glanced at Sir Samuel. She knew she was entering dangerous territory, but this might be the only way to put all the pieces together.

"Mr. Gupta," Lilian began. "When you were in your last year at Harrow, Sir Henry Heathcote made some business arrangements with the local government in New Delhi that caused hardship for your family, did he not?"

"Hardship?" Rana's scoff was darkly sarcastic. "His 'business arrangements' resulted in the loss of land that had been in my family for generations. My father was devastated. He took his own life as a result."

Kate and Sofia looked horrified. There were shocked faces all around the table.

Lilian continued. "Did you purposely come here to Hursley House to confront Sir Henry Heathcote?"

"Absolutely not!" Rana stood and looked at Sir Samuel. "I did everything I could *not* to attend this event, but Sir Samuel insisted I accompany him. Tell them, Sir Samuel."

"It's true, he didn't want to come with me, but I didn't know why. Rana, I had no idea what had happened to your family." The home secretary looked genuinely apologetic. "If you had told me, I never would have insisted—"

"I had no intention of divulging my family's most shameful and confidential history." Rana looked back at Lilian. "Only Scotland Yard would do such a thing."

"But since you were here in the house of the man who ruined your family," Lilian continued. "You made sure Sir Henry knew who you were."

"It wasn't planned," Rana said. "But I found myself next to him at the buffet. And when he spoke I had to respond."

"Enjoying the party? An impressive crowd, don't you agree? I'm sure you've never seen so many people of this stature in one room."

"Do you have any idea who I am? My family in India had more status than your family will ever have. We rubbed elbows with royalty, we lived in splendor with a level of culture and intellectual achievements beyond what any Englishman could comprehend. But when you came to New Delhi and made your despicable deals, you caused my family to lose their land, land that had been in our family for thousands of years."

"I don't know what you're talking about."

"My father was so devastated he took his own life. You'll never understand that family is more important than greed or position. Your party guests do not impress me, Sir Henry."

"He looked at me as if I'd gone mad." Rana sat back down. "I admit my tone was deeply caustic and I walked away quickly. I did not see him again that evening, and I was not proud of myself. I hadn't wanted to give him the satisfaction of knowing he had ruined my family. I'm sure he only found pleasure in it."

The room was without sound. No one in the family apparently had known about this. They could not even look in Rana's direction.

"And before you ask, Chief Inspector, no, I did not murder Sir Henry," Rana added. "He certainly wasn't worth the risk of ruining the life I've built for myself, by myself." Rana pushed his chair farther from the table and crossed his arms.

Sir Samuel cleared his throat. "There's nothing to be ashamed of, Rana. Your life is beyond criticism, irreproachable. I know your mother is very proud of you. I'm proud of you."

Richard looked at his detective partner. He wondered if she'd gone mad. If this tactic didn't reveal the killer, the home secretary would have their jobs. They'd both be back in uniform, patrolling the worst sections of London, if they were still coppers at all.

Lilian avoided Richard's eye—there was no way she could stop now. She had to keep going until she revealed the murderer.

"Sir Charles," she continued. "Isn't it true that on the night of the party you had an argument with your father in the library, and he threatened to disinherit you if you married Marie Sinclair?"

Marie gripped his hand.

"He said as much," Charles answered.

"Would you tell us about your conversation in the library between two thirty and two forty-five in the morning?

Charles paused for a moment and then looked at Marie.

"It's all right, Charles," his fiancée said steadily. "I want you to tell them everything."

Charles took a breath and began. "I saw him go into the library and I followed him. He had been acting strangely all evening and had been very cold to Marie since she arrived. I wanted to know why. I confronted him. He asked me point-blank."

"How could you marry that girl?"

"What are you talking about? You encouraged me to go to the Caribbean to meet Marie's family."

"I didn't know about her background at the time. How did you grow up in this family and think it would be all right to marry a person of mixed blood?"

"Marie is from a good family, educated and kind, she'll make a wonderful wife and mother."

"The thirteenth baronet will not be of mixed blood, I will cut you out of this family, out of my will, out of the estate."

"I'd rather live happily with Marie for the rest of my life than have your money or title. We'll move to the Caribbean and never come back."

Charles looked into Marie's eyes and held her hands. "When he said I'd be out of the family, after a moment of shock, I wasn't sad or angry. I realized that all my life I'd been trying to gain his approval. But no matter what I did, I never felt that I was good enough for him. But when he spoke to me like that, when he asked me to choose Marie or him, I told him I chose Marie. And I felt the most satisfying feeling of relief. I felt free of his overbearing personality for the first time in my life. I felt joyful. I had no reason to murder my father, Chief Inspector. He was already as good as dead to me."

Philippa was crying, holding a lace handkerchief to her mouth, clutching Juan's arm, her face filled with commiseration and support. Her brother looked at her and gave a subtle bow, his hand on his heart.

"He never would've gone through with it," Ambrose declared. "The honor of our family name meant too much to us. There's nothing more important. His death was a tragedy, but nothing will break us apart and fracture this family. The Heathcote name is too strong. Henry believed that. He wasn't himself that night."

Lilian was beginning to feel a mounting release, a feeling of cleansing, coming from each person in the room. Except Ambrose, who seemed in denial, everyone else was releasing themselves from familial bondage that they might not have known had been so heavy to them. She took a breath and continued. "Mr. Guerra, you were overheard having an argument with Sir Henry over politics."

Juan almost chuckled. "Sir Henry and I often jousted about politics."

"But was there something more serious last night?" Lilian asked.

Juan looked at Philippa, seeing fear in her eyes. He put a hand on hers and spoke. "It started in the usual way. Sir Henry tried to goad me into an argument."

"Juan, I know you are not a stupid man, so how can you side with the Russians over the Germans?"

"It's not all Germans, just the Nazis."

"They're all Nazis now."

"You're wrong, Sir Henry, many do not agree with the current government, like those of us that fought Franco. Their time will come and as Hitler gets closer, you will see, it might be the Russians that save us from the same fate."

"I find it disgusting that the man married to my daughter is involved with the red menace."

"Leave my wife out of it."

"If you don't watch out, Juan, she'll be widowed before she has her first child."

"Sir Henry didn't scare me, I knew he was doing it to get at Philippa and I hated him for it."

Lilian watched tears slide down Philippa's cheeks.

"But it is not a motive for murder, Chief Inspector," Juan put his arm around his wife and her weeping slowed. "We always disagreed about politics. I had no reason to kill him. I would never do that to my wife, she cared deeply for him, even if he was often horrible to her. But I will tell you one thing, he was becoming a dangerous man."

"What do you mean?" Lilian asked.

"He was confusing his 'king and country' enthusiasm with Hitler's latest policies, as you heard about tonight, and that was something that worried me."

Ambrose suddenly stood up and looked at Juan. "That's not true, Juan, it's not true." Ambrose was shaking with emotion. "Henry was the most patriotic Englishman you could ever meet. He cared about his country and his family more than life itself."

"He was mixing his own propaganda with that of the Third Reich," Juan's voice grew louder. "He was meeting with brutes from the Fifth Column. People in league with Hitler. Did you know those people at the party last night? They were dangerous people, and he was becoming a dangerous man."

"I won't have this!" Ambrose cried. "I won't have our family name dragged through the mud. Henry can't even defend himself.

Even if he was mixed up in something he didn't understand, it's over now. It's all over and he can't take this family down. Nothing is more important than our family and our family name. I would never let him take us down, I would never let him do that to us. Never."

# CHAPTER 75

The room had fallen silent. Lilian looked at Ambrose Heathcote. He couldn't possibly believe that Henry was as innocent as that. Not after hearing all the conversations with Sir Henry from the night before. How could Ambrose be the only person who did not see what Sir Henry had become? He stood there, perspiring and shaking. Then she remembered what Sofia had said, how Ambrose had been seen at four-thirty. He had not gone to bed at three-thirty as he had claimed.

Lilian didn't pause—she let her instincts take over.

"Ambrose Heathcote, in your statement to Scotland Yard you said you went directly to bed after your conversation with your brother at three thirty in the morning. Yet, Miss Sofia bore witness this evening that it was actually at four thirty this morning that you were in the upstairs corridor. And we know that sometime between four and six o'clock this morning, the library door was wide open and available for anyone who was downstairs to empty the cigar box and leave one poisoned cigar. You are the only one without an alibi for this time."

"Henry was confused last night, he didn't know—he didn't mean—he would never—" Ambrose stammered.

Lilian didn't let up.

"You knew of his morning ritual of smoking his first cigar after he ran his dogs. Only you knew that he had broken his engagement with Lady Sarah. You knew that he was going to disinherit Charles if he married Marie Sinclair and, despite your advocacy, you knew that he wouldn't allow Miss Kate to go to university. In fact, he told you he was considering pulling her out of school because of her friendship with Miss Sofia, didn't he?"

Lilian was guessing at the last bit, but it was not outside the realm of possibilities. Ambrose's last conversation with Henry must have contained so many objectionable elements that Ambrose felt he had no choice. Ambrose gasped for breath, his face drained of color.

"And, Sir Ambrose, you knew of his affiliations with the Fifth Column and his plans to use his business and influence to support Nazi objectives."

"No, you don't understand, you have it all wrong. I didn't know before last night. There were all these bits and pieces of things that I noticed or heard about for weeks that didn't make sense, or maybe I just didn't want them to make sense. And yesterday, when he left his cigarette case on the table at tea, I took it to give it to him, but then I saw what was inside it, the ampules of poison, and that mark on the inside—the Nazi symbol! I couldn't believe it. And then last night, I knew about some of those people he was talking to, I knew what they were about. The Fifth Column! They were brutes that would do anything to keep their wealth and position, collaborate with Nazis over country, over reputation. I couldn't deny it anymore. And then I heard what he said to Sarah, I saw how he acted with Kate, how he treated Marie, it all hit me like a bolt of lightning. But I was sure I could talk him out of it. He was my brother."

Ambrose wiped his brow with a trembling hand. "I confronted him in the library. I was sure I could make him see what he was doing to our family, that he would understand he was wrong."

"So you went to the library and found him alone," Lilian prompted.

"Yes." And then Ambrose continued. "I entered the library, and Henry offered me a cigar. We began smoking as I thought about how to approach the subject. Wilson knocked and peeked inside."

"Anything else before I retire, my lord?"

"Yes, this cigar box needs filling, Wilson."

"My apologies, my lord. I'll get a fresh box right away."

"Wait." Henry handed his empty silver cigarette case to Wilson. "Might as well take this for polishing."

"Shall I bring you a new case, sir?"

"No, Wilson, just the cigars." I could tell when my brother was in a foul mood and, at the moment, he was barely trying to hide it.

"Why Wilson can't keep this box full is beyond me." He slammed the lid shut. "You'd think he was brand new to the job. Weak intellect!"

"Henry, what happened tonight? You had words with Sarah and you've been on a tear ever since."

"It's hardly your business, Ambrose."

"Isn't it? Sarah went to bed upset. I saw that myself. Did you speak with her in the last hour or so?"

"Not at the end of the evening, no. There was nothing to say."

"All right, you don't want to talk about it. But how can I help? What can I do to patch things up between you?" Henry laughed. It was a mean-sounding burst. I felt a sudden chill. My brother had never seemed so unlike himself.

"There won't be any patching up, old boy. The wedding is off, and if we didn't have so many honored guests this weekend, I'd be making sure Sarah was packed and out of the house at first light."

"Henry, what can you possibly mean?"

"I'm not going to talk about it. If Sarah wants to go public with our discussion, that's up to her. Gentlemen don't disclose details."

"Even with your own brother?" Henry puffed on his cigar as if he hadn't heard me. He walked to the French windows, unlocked and opened them. Fresh air mixed with the cigar smoke. I knew better than to poke the lion any further. I had more important things to discuss. I had no idea they would all be connected. But Henry continued.

"And there's something else, I'm pulling Kate out of that subversive school she's going to. It's a bad influence on her."

"Don't be ridiculous, Henry, she's happy there."

"It's perverting her."

"There's something else I want to discuss with you." My brother looked at me blankly, as if he barely saw me. "I heard you speaking with Juan and Philippa this evening, something about the Nazis versus the Communists."

"What about it?"

"Do you really believe that the Communists are worse than the Nazis? Hitler's about to knock on our door and at least the Communists are on our side against him."

"Is that what you think, little brother?" His condescension was blatant. "Hitler may be closer to our backyard than Stalin, but what makes you think either of them wouldn't take over Great Britain given half a chance?"

"Maybe you're right, but only Hitler is trying to at the moment."

"Not yet he's not, and if we play ball with him, then why would he?"

"Play ball?" I was so shocked at what he was saying, I was trying not to believe what I heard.

"Listen, Communists believe in distributing all the wealth. How do you think that would fare with an aristocratic family like ours? The Nazis believe in order and hierarchy, and so do we. What's the real difference?"

"The difference is we aren't killing anyone who is different than we are—"

"Stop exaggerating, Ambrose, and think. If we fight the Nazis alongside the Communists, what do you think will happen if we win? The Communists will take over, just like you fear Hitler will, and that will be a worse fate for this family, not to mention many of our friends. The Germans are not our enemies. People like Juan are."

My head was spinning. I couldn't believe he was saying those words. My brother, an honored public speaker for Great Britain, the man everyone respected as the model of an upstanding English citizen. *What was he thinking?*

"Henry, you don't know what you're saying. I know we have many German friends, our family married Germans centuries ago, but this antisemitism, you can't agree."

"Jews are not British, brother, certainly even you can see that. And since you've pushed me to the edge, I'll tell you about Sarah. Her grandmother is a Jew, did you know that? She was hiding that little fact from me. That's why we can't marry."

I just stared at him. I couldn't believe what I was hearing. He was out of his mind. "I'm surprised to see that you've lost the meaning of humanity and you've let something else take power over your heart."

"I'm not surprised to hear my brother turn into a mealy-mouthed sap."

"How can you say that? England is at the brink of war with these fascists."

"And I'll do what I can to help this country understand our proper place and how to keep peace with Germany. We join them. There are many people at high levels of government that agree with me, and we won't be left behind as this war escalates."

"If you think Hitler is going to welcome you into his club and let you keep your land and riches, you aren't the intelligent person I always thought you were. You—" I broke off what I was saying. *What did he mean, he'd do what he could to help Hitler?* What did he have planned? It suddenly occurred to me that this was all more than theoretical. "What are you planning, Henry? What are you playing at? Don't you know what kind of danger you might come up against?"

"Don't you worry, little brother, I'm not naïve like you. I know what I'm doing." He closed the French windows, locked them and turned to me.

"What exactly are you going to do?" I suddenly felt panicked. What was he mixed up in? I wasn't just worried about Henry and what might happen to him, I was realizing that the whole family could be disgraced. If Henry did something stupid, and it became public, all of our lives would be ruined. Charles would never get into Parliament. Philippa and Juan would have to leave the country. And poor Kate, her life would be over before it even started. Everywhere they went they would be pariahs.

"I won't tell you my plans, but you know my businesses. Supplies, warehouses, transporting goods. And after tonight, it's all set up perfectly. I had some very important meetings and it's all going as planned." He waved his cigar at me and dropped his keys. I bent to get them, but he grabbed them with his left hand and slipped them into his pocket. That's when I began to realize I had to do something.

"Henry, please think this through. Think of your family."

"I am thinking of my family, Ambrose, more than you. I'm saving our life as we know it. What could be more important?"

"Unless it all goes the other way, and then we'll be ruined."

"There is no other way. What I'm doing will not only keep this country as it should be, but it will increase our personal wealth more than you can imagine."

That's when I knew it was hopeless. There was nothing I could do to talk him out of it. I had honestly tried my best to convince him.

"Go to bed, Ambrose. I have work to do tonight. No time for sleeping."

"Henry took an envelope from his pocket and placed it on his desk. He unlocked a drawer and took out some other papers and picked up the envelope, he put them in the grate and lit them on fire. He kept shuffling through the papers and adding them to the fire.

When he turned and saw that I was still standing there. He almost shouted at me. 'Leave me. Get out. Go to bed.'

"He took me by the arm and marched me to the door, opening it and pushing me through. 'And tell Wilson to hurry with those cigars.' I stood in the hallway and I heard the click as he locked the door."

# CHAPTER 76

Tears were streaming down Ambrose's cheeks.

"He had so spectacularly confused the Nazi propaganda with anti-Communism and he believed it would be the fall of all aristocracy, and that was more important to him than anything else. But he was wrong and if I couldn't talk him out of it—" Ambrose sat down, his head bowed.

"Ambrose—" Sir Samuel began, but Ambrose stood up again and interrupted him.

"But he was proud of it. Proud! He didn't care about anyone but himself. He was going to crush the happiness of his children, tear the whole family apart. We'd all be ruined because of his self-importance and his greed. Don't you see? He might even have done irreparable damage to England. I had his cigarette case that he'd left on the table. I had seen what was inside, but I didn't understand why he had it until that moment and then I knew what I had to do. After we spoke, I used his Nazi poison to soak one cigar and I waited." Ambrose looked at Sir Samuel with desperate eyes. He had said too much and he couldn't go back. He sat down. Lilian kept pushing.

"So you came back downstairs, waited for him to leave the library, and you switched the fresh cigars with the one that you poisoned."

"I couldn't let him do it. It would've meant our ruin. The end of any possible happiness his children might have. I couldn't let him." Ambrose's voice was faint, almost a whisper.

Lilian had to hear him say it. She had to make him confess to the details. "Do you admit that you left him a poisoned cigar knowing that he would smoke it after the sun rose?"

"I knew he had no cigarettes in the library. He gave his empty case to Wilson, I knew he'd have to go wandering for a cigarette later if he stayed up. I hid and waited, and when he left the library to go to the smoking room, he left the door open. I removed all the new cigars, and yes, I left the single poisoned one there for him, knowing he'd smoke it in the morning."

"What did you do with the cigars?" Richard asked, glancing at Ngaio across the room. She looked back at him with wide eyes.

"I distributed them into the other cigar boxes around the house," Ambrose replied. "In the drawing room, the study, the smoking room. Then I went to my room and couldn't sleep a wink. I tortured myself, knowing he'd smoke that cigar in the morning. I changed my mind a thousand times, almost going back downstairs and getting rid of that cigar."

Ambrose covered his face for a moment, then dropped his hands and sat up straight. He seemed calmer since he had confessed.

"But if Henry had been allowed to go through with his plans, he would not only have ruined the name of Heathcote, and harmed our family irreparably, he might even have caused damage to England. He was trying to help the Nazis! His metal processing plants, his businesses that could transport anything anywhere, maybe dangerous things. Who could know the result? So I stayed in my room, and let fate take its course. I took the chance that he would, like he did every morning, smoke his cigar. Letting that Nazi poison take his life seemed somehow . . . fitting."

"And was it you who found Margery Allingham in the library looking at his papers?" Lilian asked.

"I thought he had burned everything he thought of as evidence, but when I saw her in the library, I realized he must've forgotten something. I needed to erase all proof of his plans. Get rid of anything that would ruin the family, otherwise the whole undertaking would have been a waste." Ambrose looked at Margery. "I'm so sorry."

It was obvious that Sir Henry's children were shocked but also moved. Charles rose and came to Ambrose's side.

"Charles." Ambrose had tears in his eyes. "I'm sorry."

Charles couldn't speak. But he clamped his hand on Ambrose's shoulder and looked at him with conflicted emotions. Then Philippa and Kate joined them, and they put their arms around him. Ambrose wept. Then he pushed them away gently and stood up slowly.

Lilian looked directly at Ambrose.

"Ambrose Heathcote, you are under arrest for the murder of Sir Henry Heathcote," Lilian Wyles began. Richard Davidson moved toward Ambrose.

"Just a moment, Chief Inspectors." Sir Samuel rose and stood next to Ambrose. "I think it makes sense for my people to take over now. Rana, call our offices and let them know we'll be on our way."

"But, sir—" Lilian began.

"Excellent job, Chief Inspectors," Sir Samuel nodded to both of them. "But this is a case for the Special Branch."

"Yes, sir," Richard said. Lilian was dumbstruck.

"Ambrose," Sir Samuel continued. "You and I will go upstairs and pack your things. My driver will take us to London."

Ambrose stood and looked at his family. Charles stepped forward. "Sir Samuel," he said. "Please let me know what we can do."

"Of course, Charles," he said. "I'll have Rana call you in the morning. Don't worry about your uncle. I'll make sure he's comfortable tonight."

Charles turned to face the group.

"I would like to say," he began, "that for many reasons, but most especially for my Uncle Ambrose, I would ask that all the details of this weekend be kept confidential. We have a lot of work to do, preparing for the funeral, press announcements, business arrangements."

"It must be kept confidential," said the home secretary. "National security is at stake."

"It's all quite overwhelming at the moment." Charles stopped and looked at his family. "The last thing we need is a scandal and a flock of reporters buzzing around Hursley House."

"You have my word that Scotland Yard and my office will be discreet," Sir Samuel confirmed.

"We'll all help, Charles," Philippa said, and she and Kate clasped hands and came to be by his side. "Thank you, Sir Samuel. We're counting on you."

"Davidson, I think you should accompany us upstairs," said Sir Samuel. "And then gather your things, you'll travel with us tonight."

"Yes, sir." Richard looked at Lilian. His face showed his surprise, but he was not displeased. He reached in his pocket and handed Lilian the keys to his automobile. She nodded.

Richard and Sir Samuel Hoare walked on each side of Ambrose Heathcote as they left the room.

"Thank you, all," Lilian said. "For your help and your honesty. And my sincere apologies for any distress we may have caused." Lilian wasn't usually one to open a door for reproval in a case, but then she'd never been on a case like this before.

The family members nodded to her, still in shock, and slowly left the room, following the others upstairs.

# CHAPTER 77

Lilian looked at the four writers—Agatha Christie, Dorothy L. Sayers, Ngaio Marsh, and Margery Allingham.

"And thank you, all of you," Lilian said, finally letting a smile break out on her face. "I don't know if we could've done it without your help."

"Did you know it was Ambrose?" Agatha asked.

"I suspected, but I wasn't sure," Lilian admitted. "There was no solid evidence, I knew I'd have to get him to confess."

"But how did you know?" Ngaio asked. "He was the last one on my list."

"I noticed how defensive he was about Sir Henry," Lilian said. "Everyone else admitted his flaws and their contentions with him. We all knew, saw and heard, the trouble he made with everyone in his family. But Ambrose never let down his guard. He behaved as if it didn't exist when everyone else admitted that it did."

"To paraphrase the bard, methinks he protested too much." Ngaio gave a wry smile.

"Precisely," Lilian agreed. "And then Sofia refuted the time he said he went to bed. That extra hour was all I needed."

"He's the most mild-mannered gentleman," said Margery. "I can't believe he was the one who bashed me on the head!"

"If it came out that his brother was connected with such despicable politics, it would have been all for naught," Lilian remarked.

"He killed him to save the family name, and he couldn't let anything else be found that was damning."

"To commit murder, to kill his own brother," Dorothy shook her head. "He must've been desperate."

"Desperation is often part of the equation of murder," said Lilian. "But it never justifies the sum, even if it might be true that Ambrose has done the world a service. Who knows what damage to England Sir Henry Heathcote might've done? But of course, we'll never know."

"What will happen to Ambrose?" Margery asked.

"That's up to the home secretary now," Lilian said. But she wondered if his case would ever go to trial.

"*The evil that men do lives after them; The good is oft interred with their bones.*" Ngaio quoted Shakespeare.

"When Marc Antony said that," Dorothy added, "it sounded like he was referring to Caesar, but he was really talking about Brutus."

They all let that thought absorb into their hearts and minds for a moment.

"Chief Inspector Wyles, you have my admiration and congratulations," said Agatha Christie. "We all tried our best to figure out who the murderer was, but you beat us all."

The other Queens of Crime nodded in agreement.

"But of course," Detective Chief Inspector Lilian Wyles said. She smiled at them. "I'm the detective."

★　★　★

Not too early the next morning, Lilian sat at the kitchen table below stairs at Hursley House, a steaming cup of tea in front of her, Elspeth Anderson sitting across from her. They had finished late the night before and Elspeth had arranged for her to sleep in an empty servant's room for the night. Lilian felt refreshed and energized after the deep night's sleep and her third cup of tea. Richard had left the night before with Sir Samuel, and she was to drive his car back to London. Lilian was glad to have a quiet morning with

302 ⟿ Rosanne Limoncelli

Elspeth. She had a new appreciation of the friendship that was budding between them.

"Do you think you'll stay on?" Lilian asked.

"It's too soon to even think about making a change," the housekeeper said. "I couldn't leave the family until everything is settled, there's so much to do and they're feeling so lost."

"They are lucky to have you taking care of them. It's going to be a rough time.

"Not to mention what will happen if war is announced." Elspeth shook her head. "If it's anything like the Great War, all our lives will change again."

Lilian thought that there were so many things that could be even worse than the last war. But she put those thoughts aside for the moment. They had just solved a difficult case and it was Sunday. She would go home and spend the day with her parents, whom she loved and appreciated.

"And you, Lilian? What does your future hold?"

"Back to London, Elspeth. The CID never sleeps. Always work to do. Do good and do well, that's what my father always says." She smiled at her new friend. "You should come visit once things are settled here. We have a spare room. You can make it a little vacation. Stay as long as you like."

"Oh, that would be lovely," Elspeth said. "I love a good visit to London. I'll take you up on that offer one day. In the meantime, I think I'll send you a postcard now and then, if I may. We can be 'pen-friends'" Elsbeth chuckled.

"Won't that be lovely," Lilian said and finished her tea. "Although I think people say pen pal these days."

"Oh, I like that, pen pal." Elspeth laughed.

Lilian thought her laugh was charming and cheerful. How nice it will be to have a friend from outside the dark business of policing crime. Elspeth could be a bright spot in her life. She stood to say goodbye and gave her new friend a quick hug.

# CHAPTER 78

All four writers were up early, bags packed, coffee or tea gulped down, toast spread with butter and marmalade, or dipped in soft-boiled egg, and consumed. They had said their goodbyes to the family and stood in front of Hursley House waiting for Agatha's and Margery's automobiles to be brought from the garage.

"I appreciate the ride back to town," Ngaio said to Margery.

"Not at all," Margery replied. "I appreciate the company."

Agatha was glad that Dorothy was riding with her. In some ways she wanted to talk it all through, out loud with her, but then she also thought she might just want to think about it in silence. She knew that Dorothy would be fine with either scenario.

"I have to admit," Dorothy began, looking at the other three, "I'm quite sure I'll never write another murder story."

"What? Really?" Agatha hadn't expected this news.

"Yes," Dorothy continued. "Seeing a real murder case play out, the dead body itself, the impact on the family. Marge in danger." She reached out and touched Margery's shoulder and gave her a concerned smile. "I'm enjoying writing for the theater and radio, very different kinds of stories. Yes, I know my mind at last, I'm finished with murder mysteries."

"It's always good to know your own mind," Agatha looked at Dorothy with admiration. "How many years can it take person to do that?"

"Some people never know their own minds for the whole length of their lives," Ngaio agreed.

"I can't deny this weekend hasn't had an impact on me as well," Margery said. "I've never been one for politics, and my puzzles have always been more about the human condition, at least, that's how I felt them to be. But with the state of the world as it is, these concerns can't be ignored. I can't see how I'd write another story that didn't incorporate the bigger picture of how such political questions have an impact on us all."

They all thought about that for a moment. Agatha was thinking that her own view of politics was more about how she and the other women she knew fit into the world. Sir Henry Heathcote's control over his daughters had vexed her and it wouldn't leave her mind. Her main character, Hercule Poirot, was nothing like Sir Henry Heathcote, but she couldn't help feeling annoyed with male characters in general. She had been thinking about retiring Poirot for a while; he was wearing on her. And now, as new puzzle pieces floated around her brain, and the seeds of new stories, she found herself thinking about her little old lady, Miss Jane Marple, who had appeared in one novel and a collection of short stories. Why shouldn't she be the main detective in her future novels?

"I really admired that Detective Chief Inspector Lilian Wyles," Agatha said out loud. "She showed complete confidence in her work. She gave and got respect. How delightful to witness that. And they did seem to work well together, she and DCI Davidson."

"Yes, they did, didn't they? And such nice people, all round. For coppers." Ngaio laughed. She thought about her budding relationship with Richard Davidson and her own DCI Roderick Alleyn, and how maybe Scotland Yard detectives didn't always have to be the lone wolves as they were so often written in novels. Maybe it was time for Roderick Alleyn to settle down. This might be an interesting discussion with Margery as they made the drive back to London. Margery had mentioned she was toying with a committed romance for her Albert Campion too.

"Yes, Ngaio, they were nice people," Margery laughed. "We couldn't help but notice you seemed to make a friend this weekend. Richard Davidson is lovely, isn't he?" She poked Ngaio's shoulder and the women laughed.

"Yes, he is lovely," Ngaio admitted and couldn't stop herself from smiling.

Bernard and Wilson came up the drive, one in Agatha's automobile, one in Margery's. They helped the women load their bags in the boots, accepted tips graciously, and left them to themselves.

The four Queens of Crime stood together shaking hands, kissing cheeks, and saying their goodbyes.

Before they got into their automobiles, Margery stopped and looked at them. "Hang on," she said. "We never talked about dividing up any clues from this case."

"But none of us knew it was Ambrose," Agatha said. "Or even got close."

"I leave it all to you three," said Dorothy. "I'm serious, I'm done with murder mysteries. Lord Peter is happily married to Harriet Vane and what better place to leave them?"

"I think we should just let it all take us where it will take us," Ngaio said. "I'm not worried about seeming similar to each other. That's never been a problem before. We're too different."

"You're right," Margery said. "We always use whatever happens in our lives, what we see in the world. We can't help but weave our experiences into the stories we write, and it doesn't matter if there's some crossover, our styles are too different."

"Very well said," Agatha replied. "We write the way we write, and even if we each told the story of this weekend with every detail, each version would be completely unique. And isn't that why we write? We are who we really are when we write, and we do it in our own inimitable way. Everything in life is fodder for fiction—it would be a waste otherwise."

They all nodded in agreement, said their final goodbyes, and got into their automobiles. They rolled down the long drive, by the trim lawn, past the clumps of shady trees, and the green hedgerows, and their tires kicked up a cloud of dust behind them as they drove on the road back to their lives.

THE END

# ACKNOWLEDGMENTS

THANKS: To John and Valentino, who always embrace me with encouragement; to my entire extended family, who made reading a big part of my life; to my brilliant writer friends for their years of help and encouragement, Ariana, Marlie, Zeeva, Marcia, Julia, Linda, Shannon, Estefania, Spencer, and Patrick; to Ronni, Margaret, and Cristy, who helped me survive high school; to the wonderful PANO Network; to all of my students, past, present, and future, who fill my life with inspiration; to my whole New York University community that continues to prove anything is possible; to parents, teachers, and librarians everywhere who help make sure the world is full of readers; to my wonderful agent, Murray Weiss; and to my amazing editor, Sara J. Henry.

And to Agatha Christie, Dorothy L. Sayers, Ngaio Marsh, and Margery Allingham!